Praise for *Tricks Every Boy Can Do*

"Read this once, and you'll read it a second time. Then you'll put it on the shelf and keep it along with the rest of your favorite books. This is an absolutely authentic portrait of an era and a portrayal of characters whose entangled lives become as hauntingly real as the people you know."

—James P. Blaylock, award-winning
Author of *The Rainy Season*

TRICKS EVERY BOY CAN DO

By

Paul Buchanan

Harvard Square Editions
New York
2016

Tricks Every Boy Can Do, by Paul Buchanan

Copyright © 2016 Paul Buchanan
Cover Design by Katelyn Seitz

ISBN 978-1-941861-15-8
Printed in the United States of America

Published in the United States by
Harvard Square Editions
www.harvardsquareeditions.org

For Melody

PROLOGUE

1966

MR. POPINGA SITS on the edge of his desk in front of a half-furled map of South America and beams at his fifth-grade class. The clock on the wall above his head reads two-forty, and he is about to read his students the daily Brainbender, which he clips from the crossword, bridge, and horoscope page of *The Richland Ledger*. He uses these puzzles to keep the class busy for the last fifteen or twenty minutes of the day when he has run out of material early—which is, to say, every day.

His sluggish charges, unable to shake off the end-of-the-school-day torpor, play along. Each day he reads the puzzle, and they good-naturedly pantomime bafflement. They look up at the perforated ceiling tiles with furrowed brows. They theatrically scratch their heads. They do this even if the riddle's answer is obvious—even if their parents subscribe to *The Ledger* and have already posed the question over breakfast. Even Lance Kruger, bespectacled Class Genius, plays along—though he could no doubt unbend the most devious

Brainbender any *Ledger* editor could devise. This innocent arrangement saves both teacher and student from having to rise from their afternoon stupor. All they can manage at this hour is to suppress their yawning and watch the minute hand creep towards the twelve. Outside, in the late spring light, rows of banana-seat stingrays wait in the bike racks, their sissy bars gleaming. At home, troll dolls and Superballs wait on bedside dressers.

Mr. Popinga holds the clipped strip of newsprint, tiny as a Chinese fortune, and peers at the class over his reading glasses. "Ready?" he asks.

They are ready. They nod. Their faces are set in a lazy approximation of expectancy.

And he reads:

> *Two boys share the same parents, and they are born on the same date in the same year—yet they are not twins. How can this be?*

And there, from the second-to-last row, a girl's hand rockets up. She raises her arm so fast, the motion pulls her butt clear off her chair. She is that odd redhead with the spay of freckles across her cheeks—the one the other kids tease because of her odd, old-womanly way of phrasing things. She is eighteen months younger than anyone else in the room, yet somehow—with her precise gestures and her earnest precociousness—she seems their elder by a decade or more.

She waves her hand in the air with uncharacteristic abandon. *Oh! Me! Me! Call on me!* Her heart is beating double time, and she squirms in her seat because this is not really a Brainbender at all. This is the story of how she came to be.

Mr. Popinga shifts his weight from one buttock to the other and points at her with his newspaper clipping.

The girl clears her throat and feels the edgy distrust of twenty-eight fifth graders bear down on her. There will be consequences. If she answers the Brainbender correctly, Mr. Popinga, in a huff, will pass out another mimeographed long-division worksheet to eat up the extra time. This is his way of enforcing their little end-of-the-school-day social contract.

This redheaded girl knows the cost of answering, but she cannot hold back. The impulse is irresistible. This feels to her, in some deep-rooted sense she can't quite understand, like a defining moment. After all, this is a question about who she is. This is a riddle about where she came from.

"They are two brothers from a set of triplets," she says clearly and loudly.

She is correct, of course. From the generous groans around her, she knows she has slipped a few rungs in the classroom pecking order. She glances over at Lance Kruger, unable to stop herself, but he is scowling, and she realizes, at that very moment, that he will never marry her. But that epiphany stings her less than she would have guessed. Answering this riddle feels vital to her because the question is the prologue to the story of her interchangeable father and uncle, identical twins—who were, more accurately, the two survivors from a set of triplets.

CHAPTER ONE
TRICKS EVERY BOY CAN DO
1932

BUCKY, THE LINE FOREMAN, tapped Rose on the shoulder just as she was twisting the wrapper on the last of the Sunkist oranges for the crate she was packing—another full box, another stamp, another nickel.

"Phone call!" Bucky shouted over the din of packinghouse machinery. He held one fist to his ear and another near his chin, as if he were speaking into a telephone. It was barely one in the afternoon, and Rose could already smell Bushmills on his breath. "It's the school," he shouted.

Rose sighed. She tugged off her work gloves finger by finger and stuffed them in the pocket of her smock. Frankie again. What had he done this time? She turned from her slot to find plump little Gladys DeMello already there, eager to take Rose's spot at the belt. Rose had just rotated to the last slot, the one with the biggest oranges, the quickest crates to fill. Of *course* she'd be called away now! Rose stepped aside before Gladys could push her way into her slot.

Rose made her way along the belt line, back through the empty break room with its coffee urn and radio, and out to the hallway where the wall phone for the sorters and packers stood. She couldn't remember a week going by since school started a month ago without at least one call from the boys' school—Frankie in a fight, Frankie using salty language, Frankie stuffing the classroom hamster down his coveralls. It wasn't that he was a bad kid; he was just rambunctious—the kind of boy you couldn't rein in.

The earpiece dangled from the wall phone, slowly twisting on its cord. Before she picked it up, she smoothed down her hair and took a deep breath. The phone was sticky and smelled like the cull bin out back. "Hello," she said brightly into the mouthpiece. She turned to the wall and pressed a hand over her open ear to muffle the rumble of the big fans up in the roof space. "Rose Farrell speaking."

"Mrs. Farrell," the nasally woman's voice on the other end said—and then there was the usual flustered backpedaling from the formal married title, which didn't apply in Rose's case. "I'm sorry, *Rose* Farrell. Is this Rose Farrell?"

"Speaking," Rose said again, refusing to let her upbeat tone slip.

"This is Miss Thermos, you know, from Mr. Pasco's office at the school?"

Rose blinked twice but kept the smile on her face. Rose knew Miss Thermos: a perky young blonde who chewed on pencils and wore those unnaturally pointy bras everyone seemed to love. "Yes?" Rose said. "How may I help you?"

"Well, it's your son," Miss Thermos said. "He broke a window at the school. A *big* window."

Rose's smile tugged down at the corners under the gravity of this information, but she refused to let it disappear completely. "Are you sure it was Frankie?" Rose said. Her son, she suspected, had become the default defendant when anything at school was broken or stolen or set on fire or—in one case—coated in Vaseline. "Did anyone *see* him do it?" Rose heard papers shuffling on the other end of the line.

"Not *Frankie*," Miss Thermos said. "The other one." Again the sound of papers being stirred about.

"Well, certainly you don't mean Alvie!" Rose told her, almost laughing at the notion.

"Yes—that's right—*Alvie*."

Rose's smile vanished. "*Alvie* broke a window?" Rose asked, incredulous. "You can't be serious. It must have been some kind of accident."

"No accident, Ma'am. He threw a softball clean through it."

"*Alvie*?" Rose said. "Alvie *Farrell*?"

"Mr. Pasco wants you to come down to the school right away."

"*Alvie*," Rose said again. "You're sure it was Alvie. You know they look alike."

"He's right here in the office. He says he's Alvie."

"It's *Frankie*," Rose said. "He's pretending to be his brother again. Can you just put him on the phone a minute?"

"He won't stop crying."

Rose stared silently at the phone numbers and messages penciled on the wall in a dingy, ragged oval around the phone. "He's crying?"

"Yes, Ma'am. Can't seem to stop."

Rose pressed a hand over her heart. "I'll be right there," she said, and hung the earpiece back on its hook.

ROSE PULLED OUT of the parking lot and turned onto Road 19, letting the clutch out a little too fast and nearly stalling. The ranks of orange trees swept past her as she picked up speed and shifted gears. She'd miss the rest of her shift, no doubt.

How many crates was that? She tried to do the math in her head, but the numbers got all jumbled. She couldn't afford to lose *any* money—that was the truth of the matter. Over the years she'd had to sell off most of the furniture she'd been allowed to take with her when her father disowned her. The Blaisdell grandfather clock had been the first thing to go, and then the mahogany credenza and the biggest of bookcases from the parlor, the one with the hand-tooled trim—along with all the books it held.

Rose still had her looks, though. She was, after all, barely thirty, and she could still fit into the drop-waisted skirts from her school days. But the hard-scrabble life of packing oranges and raising boys and keeping up a house—not to mention appearances—had begun to wear on her. She was beginning to feel invisible to the younger men who worked the Woolworth counters or stood behind her in the teller line at the bank. Her eyes were often rimmed red these days, and her hair seemed to grow less vibrant and more unruly each time she washed it.

Rose passed a band of orange pickers, their truck wedged in the narrow corridor between the rows of trees, all their ladders turned to the shade. She'd already missed packing ten crates by now, she guessed—a loss of fifty cents. And what made it worse was that this all had to be some kind of mistake. It was probably Frankie who had gotten himself in trouble. It was always Frankie. And now, no doubt insisting he was Alvie, he had everyone at the school muddled again—and he was probably reveling in every confounding minute of it. If that were the case, Rose would probably be gone a few hours trying to untangle the mess for everyone. And then she'd likely take the rest of the day off, going home with a headache, and would have to beg for a Saturday shift to make up for the lost money.

Rose tightened her grip on the steering wheel and downshifted as she passed the line of lofty eucalyptus trees and joined the traffic on the outskirts of Richland, her small Southern California town. Her two boys were identical. Both were thin and knobby, with close-cropped, cowlicked hair that was red as a Butterfinger wrapper. But, looks aside, they were as different as oranges and avocadoes.

Growing up, Alvie sometimes seemed nearly absent from the house, perched on a corner of the leather sofa with a trance-like stare; whereas Frankie was everywhere at once, all boisterous scramble and noise. Alvie hid behind his mother's skirts while Frankie yanked her this way and that by her fingers, throwing his whole angry weight into dragging her wherever he wanted to go.

That Alvie was such a kind, thoughtful, boy—sweet and clumsy as a new foal. For her birthday last February (which Frankie chose to ignore) he had put on a magic show in the parlor, all decked out in one of her old capes and a top hat fashioned from a Quaker oatmeal container that kept toppling from his head. Alvie's show had been the expected nine-year-old fare—the card trick where he made her three of clubs rise to the top of the deck, the rope trick where the knot was made to vanish, the gauzy scrap of silk tugged up his sleeve by a rubber band pinned inside the armpit of his shirt. Tricks all, no doubt, taken from that grubby magic book he kept checking out from the library. After each of his tricks, Rose pretended breathless astonishment—while Frankie, who studied Alvie's every move, blurted out how the feat had obviously been accomplished. "It's in the *other* hand! I can see it between your fingers!" Poor Alvie. His eyes fixed on Rose, seemed to be trying to will his brother to vanish.

But, with his final trick, Alvie astonished them both. He took a large, empty flour sack from beneath the coffee table, along with a single Valencia orange and a grease pencil. He gave Rose the orange for inspection, and she pretended to scrutinize every inch of its dimpled peel for hidden doors or spring-wound mechanisms before she handed it back to him. Alvie then pointed dramatically at the globe on its stand in the corner. "I want you to name a city," Alvie announced, affecting a deep and stentorian stage voice. "Anywhere in the world."

"London," Rose said immediately. She'd been re-reading *Oliver Twist*, and that answer just sprang to mind. Alvie, tongue peeking adorably from the corner of his mouth, carefully printed LONDON on the orange in neat uppercase letters with his grease pencil.

He turned the orange so Rose could read it, and, when she nodded, he dropped it into the flour sack. For a few long seconds he fumbled with the bag, and then tipped it upside down. No orange fell out. He turned the sack inside out. It was empty. Rose must have looked shocked, because a smile spread over Alvie's face—a smile crowded with adult teeth that seemed too numerous and large for his tiny mouth.

"And now if you will go outside and look in the glove box of the car," Alvie said, waving theatrically in the direction of the front door.

Rose just sat there.

"Go look in the car, Ma," Alvie told her in a whisper—as if there were really an audience present, and not just her and Frankie.

Frankie, of course, was the first one up and headed for the door at a gallop. Rose got up from her seat, and Alvie, holding her hand, led her out to the front porch, looking up at her with sly sidelong glances. He stopped on the porch, and Rose went down the front steps to her car, where Frankie had already yanked open the driver's side door and was scrambling inside. Rose got to the car just as Frankie, kneeling in the driver's seat, pushed the button for the glove box. The tiny door dropped open. An orange tumbled out onto the passenger seat.

Frankie picked it up and looked at it, and then handed it to Rose, who stood in the car's open doorway. The writing was a little smeared now, but Rose saw the word LONDON written in Alvie's distinct and careful printing. The fine hairs on her neck stood on end. She looked over her shoulder at Alvie, who grinned down at her from the porch steps.

How had he done it?

All the rest of that night, Frankie wouldn't give Alvie a moment's rest. He *had* to know how the trick was done. He begged and pleaded all through dinner and then all through *Buck Rogers in the 25th Century*, a radio show during which he usually demanded complete silence. He made Alvie wild promises—free use of his BB gun, any ten baseball cards from his extensive collection, his desserts for the rest of the school year—if only Alvie would explain how the trick was done. But Alvie just sat in his usual spot on the edge of the sofa, grinning slyly and licking the icing from one of the cupcakes Rose had made for her own birthday. No amount of coaxing or cajoling would make this magician reveal his trick.

"Ma," Frankie whined at Rose, when it was finally time for bed, and the boys were brushing their teeth in the bathroom. "Make him tell. It isn't fair that he won't tell."

Alvie regarded Rose apprehensively in the mirror over the sink, toothbrush prodding out one cheek, flecks of baking soda on his chin. Rose wondered if this was the first time in his life Alvie had ever had the upper hand with his brother. She smiled down at him, wanting so much that he would enjoy this moment. Who knew when it might come again?

"It's a secret," she told Frankie, resting a hand on both their shoulders and looking at their identical faces in the mirror. "A good magician never tells." Alvie smiled and started again to brush his teeth. Frankie just shook his head, disgusted at the injustice.

But an hour later, when Rose herself was getting ready for bed, she opened the hamper in her bedroom closet and found an orange riding atop her laundry. ROME it said. She picked it up and smiled. Now that she thought about it, it was so obvious. But that was always the way with magic tricks, wasn't it?

In the kitchen, she scrubbed the letters off the orange with a dishrag and then went looking for any others that might be lying about, so she could clean them and replace them in the bin before Frankie stumbled onto one and figured out the trick. She found TOKYO under her blue hat on the entry table and MADRID in the sugar tin. Who knew how many more he'd forgotten to reclaim in the flush of excitement after the trick had gone so well? An hour later Rose gave up her search and went to bed. But she found another orange, weeks later— deflated, the words NEW YORK barely discernable on its puckered skin—in the back of the linen closet. And then, months after that, she'd found a green mossy globe on the tool-shed shelf.

How could that sweet little boy have done anything to merit a call to the principal's office?

TO GET TO Mr. Pasco's office, Rose had to cross the playground and then pass through the school's broad, uncovered courtyard. Usually, looking around her at the broad, blank windows of all those classrooms, she felt an obscure sense of shame—but not today. Today she strode towards the office door with a sense of motherly purpose, barely taking notice of the large window—shattered into a delicate cobweb of glass on the brink of collapse—in one corner of the quad.

When Rose pulled open the office door, Miss Thermos looked up from a fat novel that lay open on her desk. She closed the book and smiled professionally at Rose. Across from her a boy sat crumpled in a large chair next to a trophy case, weeping miserably.

It was definitely Alvie. Rose knew instantly. Not that there was any definable physical difference between the boys—at the age of ten, their features and physique were still identical—it was more in the way Alvie's spirit inhabited his frame. His limbs seemed to sag on him a little, as if his body were a few sizes too big for him. His pigeon-toed walk made it look like he was working hard not to slip out of his own feet. There was an awkwardness in the way he moved and sat and cocked his head at you—the way his shirt tails always came untucked at the back of his dungarees. There was just something klutzily endearing about his every posture and expression, and Rose saw it now as she closed the office door behind her.

When she squatted in front of him, Alvie slumped limply into her arms, his face glossy with tears and snot. He wouldn't look at her. "What happened, sweetheart?" she asked him, holding his body at arm's lenght so she could see his face. His head toppled this way and that like a rag doll's—anything to keep from looking her in the eye. She pulled him in and hugged him.

He gasped, clung to her neck, his whole body shuddering and gasping for air. "I didn't do it," he sobbed damply into her ear. "It just happened. I was looking at the window and it just *broke*."

IN MR. PASCO'S office, the story emerged: Alvie—who, because of his exemplary marks and citizenship, had been appointed this month's Equipment Monitor—alone remained on the playground after everyone filed back to class after the bell. He was responsible for gathering up all the balls and chalk and jump ropes and dragging the bin to the shed in the courtyard. That's when the cafeteria's kitchen window was shattered. The boom of it brought everyone, including Mr. Pasco, to his window—and there stood Alvie, alone in the quad, gazing blank faced at the broken window. Next to him sat the bin of playground equipment, which he had not yet put into the shed. No one else was anywhere in sight.

Once the furor died down, and Mr. Pasco got everyone back on track in the classrooms, he took Alvie, who seemed numb with shock, back to his office. Inside the cafeteria kitchen—amid all the broken glass—Mr. Lumpkin, the janitor, found one of the playground softballs where it had come to rest on the slotted drain cover in the center of the tile floor. The yellowing ball now rested on top of Mr. Pasco's desk blotter like Exhibit A in the case against Alvie.

Rose looked over at her son, who was again racked with sobs. He was slumped so far forward in his seat she wanted to reach out a hand to catch him in case he toppled. "Where was Frankie?" Rose asked Mr. Pasco.

"All the other children were back in their classrooms," Mr. Pasco said. He pinched the bridge of his nose and blinked, as if warding off a migraine.

"But *Frankie*," Rose said. "Where exactly was he?"

Mr. Pasco nodded dismissively. It was clear the same suspicion had crossed his mind. "I checked his alibi personally," Mr. Pasco said. "He was at Miss Decker's desk getting help with his spelling list. He didn't have anything to do with it."

Rose sat back in her chair. "You're sure?" she said. She felt a stab of wariness. "He was at the *teacher's desk*?"

Mr. Pasco nodded. "Positive," he said. "I had Miss Decker in here not twenty minutes ago."

"And he—Frankie—was asking for help with his work?" It seemed as uncharacteristic of Frankie as hurling a ball through a window was of Alvie.

It was eventually settled: Alvie received a three-day suspension, and there was talk of the school district billing Rose for the replacement window, though both she and Mr. Pasco knew such a demand would be fruitless. There was no way she could afford to pay—nor had she ever managed to pay for anything Frankie had broken in his long career of school-property destruction. Finally; Rose led Alvie by the hand back out through the school's courtyard, feeling eyes from every glinting window following their progress.

Alvie shuffled and tripped along beside her, wilting with shame.

AT HOME, ALVIE retreated immediately to the bedroom he shared with Frankie, and he stayed there the rest of the afternoon with the curtains drawn and the lights out. Rose brought him a slice of apple pie and a glass of milk, but she found them untouched on the desk an hour later when she looked in on him again. He was still lying in the bottom bunk, face to the wall, on top of his bedspread.

A little after three, Frankie bounded up the back steps and burst into the kitchen, glazed in sweat. He doffed his newsboy cap and tossed it on the counter, then took a bottle of milk from the icebox and drained a glass of it sitting at the kitchen table. Rose watched him for any hint of discomfort or guilt, but he just sat swinging his legs and humming one of those tunes he'd picked up from the radio.

After a moment, she slid a slice of pie and a clean fork in front of him. "What do you know about that window at school?" she asked him. She leaned back against the draining board and eyed him keenly. "It seems so unlike your brother. Don't you think?"

"I'll say," Frankie agreed. He wiped the milk from his lips with the back of his wrist. "He throws like a girl." He seemed pleased with his answer. He burped softly, pushed his empty glass away and pulled the pie closer. "Of course, who knows *which* window he was aiming at," he said. He took the fork and used it to pick apart the slice of pie as if suspicious of what she'd put in it.

"So you think he did it on purpose?" Rose said, trying her best to look skeptical and knowing.

"How else could it have happened?" Frankie said smugly. He cut off the pointy end of the pie slice with the fork and stuffed it in his mouth.

There was something taunting in his tone. *You'll never figure it out*, he seemed to be saying. *I have committed the perfect crime.* Rose crossed her arms and scowled down at him.

Frankie looked back at her unblinking. "You know, he's not the angel everyone thinks he is," he said around the apple filling in his mouth.

ALVIE SAT SILENTLY through dinner that night and asked to be excused when he'd choked down only a few bites of meatloaf. He slunk down the hallway towards his room, slope-shouldered, whereas Frankie just sat there humming and looking down at his nearly empty plate, smiling inwardly.

Rose dabbed her lips with her napkin and spread it on her lap again. She didn't have much of an appetite tonight, either. There was a knot in her stomach she just couldn't make disappear. She studied Frankie as he nudged a carrot slice around his plate with a fork.

He had always been a handful, that one. When Rose used to take them with her to the cemetery on Saturday mornings to tend Baby Doris's grave, she'd sometimes have to yank him away by the arm just as he was about to take a wiz on a gravestone. He'd pelted the cocker spaniel with olives from the backyard tree until the thing finally took a chunk out of his finger and had to be taken back to the pound. He'd made that noise with his armpit all through the Brenner girl's high school graduation, no matter how many times Rose cuffed him on the head and threatened to take him out to the car.

"*Frankie?*" Rose said.

Frankie stopped humming and looked up suddenly, like he'd forgotten she was there.

"You had something to do with this window business, didn't you?"

A practiced look of angelic innocence spread over Frankie's face—and then he looked offended at her question and a little saddened by her unjust suspicion. It was a nuanced performance, Rose had to admit—but it was a performance nonetheless. "I have no idea what you're talking about," Frankie said in an unsullied singsong soprano.

Rose leaned forward. She bore down on him with all her will—glared at him with every last ounce of parental authority and threat—but Frankie met Rose's gaze unflinchingly. *He* was never one to avert his eyes in shame. It was Rose who looked away first, and then Frankie went back to corralling his vegetables and humming.

Rose sighed. Where had she gone wrong with the boy? She'd tried everything over the years: reasoned with him, ignored him, dragged him to church. But Frankie was immune to reasoning. He saw being disregarded as a challenge. And no church in town proved willing to embrace a single mother and her two bastard sons—especially when one of them was Frankie. Rose pressed her hands on the edge of the table and took a breath.

"Frankie, I'm not going to get mad," she said. "And I'm not going to punish you."

Frankie looked up at her. She'd got his attention; he stopped humming again and regarded her with wary curiosity.

"I promise nothing will happen to you," Rose told him. "I just have to know how you did it."

Frankie looked at her quizzically, weighing her words. A guarantee of immunity? In their ten years of family history, they'd never wandered into this territory before. Rose was a yank-them-and-spank-them kind of mother. Punishment was swift and inevitable. Frankie looked at her uncertainly. "I have no idea what you're talking about," he said, but it was a formal plea—something purely for the record. There was no mimicry of wide-eyed innocence this time.

"You have my word, Frankie," Rose said. "Have I ever broken a promise to you?"

Frankie set his fork down beside his plate and seemed to mull this over.

"Tell me how you did it, and we'll never speak of it again," Rose said. "I won't even tell your brother."

Frankie finally began to look a little anxious. He glanced at the kitchen door and then back at Rose. He twisted one of the buttons on his shirtfront. "Serious?" he said.

Rose nodded back at him gravely.

"No punishment?" Frankie asked.

Rose shook her head.

Frankie pushed his plate away and studied Rose, biting his lower lip.

"Tell me," she said. "I've got to know."

Frankie looked from one of her eyes to the other and back again, as if searching them for something. He folded his hands on the tabletop. "Potato cannon," he said at last.

Rose took a sharp breath. She bit the inside of her cheek a moment before she spoke. "A potato cannon?" she said, keeping her voice even.

"I made it out in the tool shed," he said.

Was that the thing Rose had found under the kitchen steps last week when she was bringing in the wash? For months the boys had been pestering her to get them a pet—not a dog this time, something smaller. Rose knew what was behind this: Jimmy Sullivan, an older boy a few doors down, walked around the neighborhood with a tame mouse in his shirt pocket. He'd taught the mouse to scramble up on his shoulder and take a peanut from his lips. He'd taught it to roll on its back like a dog and offer up its belly for scratching. When Rose found the column of tin cans all lashed together with duct tape, she'd assumed the boys were building some kind of trap to catch a mouse of their own. She'd peered down the dark tube and found it empty. It looked harmless—not just to the boys but to any creature that might wander into it—so she'd put it back under the steps and forgotten about it. Let them have their fun. *But a cannon?* She cringed to think that she'd actually had it in her hands and slid it back into its hiding place.

"How did you fit a softball in that thing?" she asked.

Frankie nodded, like this was a question he'd seen coming. "I rolled the softball into the kitchen after lunch," he said. "The cannon had a potato in it."

Rose took another sharp breath. Of course! The ball had been there all along! She imagined Mr. Lumpkin, Frankie's unwitting accomplice, coming upon the planted softball, broom in hand, and plucking it from among the shards of glass. "Nobody would notice a stray potato in a kitchen," Rose said aloud. "They'd only see the softball."

Frankie nodded. "I hid the cannon in the bushes under the window and used a really long fuse. I lit it when the bell rang."

It all made sense. It was the perfect illusion. "And then you waited at the teacher's desk, so she'd be sure to know where you were when it happened," Rose said.

Frankie nodded, and then sat quietly watching her, waiting to see what would happen.

Rose nodded. She mentally smoothed down the last pieces of the jigsaw she'd assembled in her head. She took the napkin from her lap and folded it, her fingers trembling only slightly. She positioned it on the table, next to her plate, and flattened it down with her palm. Then she slowly scooted back her chair. She stood, shook crumbs from the front of her dress and strode to the other side of the table. She reached out and took Frankie's right earlobe in a grip so fierce it made him yelp. She dragged him from his seat, toppling his chair and sending his fork skittering across the floor. Rose tugged him into the parlor where she set to spanking him over her knee until her right hand felt like it was on fire, and her arm felt like rubber.

CHAPTER TWO
BABY DORIS
1935

THE GHOST OF BABY DORIS haunted the Farrell's Craftsman bungalow on Grove Street. Alvie was certain of it. Her presence—or, perhaps more accurately, her *absence*—seemed to lurk everywhere: a tingling void in the shape of a growing girl. She was there, creaking the floorboards at all hours, upsetting vases, borrowing tubes of Cutex lipstick from their mother's bureau, and bending teaspoons in the kitchen drawers.

Alvie might push open the front door and glimpse her, sprawled, belly down, on the parlor floor surrounded by a scattering of crayons and an unfurled roll of butcher paper. Her legs, bent up at the knee, would sway a beat while she considered him there, her freckled face propped on one pale hand. And then—with a quick upward puff of breath that stirred her red bangs—she would vanish, along with her paper and art supplies, leaving only the scent of Bazooka bubblegum. Or, months later, Alvie might pass the kitchen doorway and glimpse her standing on tiptoe to fill a cup with water from the faucet—but, when he backed up, his heart pounding, and leaned in through the doorway, the kitchen would be empty, the tap drizzling into an empty sink.

It seemed to Alvie that Baby Doris, their missing triplet, was growing along with Frankie and him, keeping up with them in some parallel, half-existence. While the brothers progressed from picture books to New Fun Comics, from kick-the-can to stickball, Baby Doris passed through her own girlish phases and preoccupations. Invisible feminine gestures seemed to inscribe themselves on the air around him—the tugging up of knee socks, the quick tuck of hair behind both ears, the swish of pleated skirts.

For weeks she might be fascinated with the garden. Wands of lavender would be plucked and strewn in odd places. Pebbles, brushed clean of soil, were found arranged on the kitchen steps. Then, for a month, she might move indoors. Alvie would find his mother's collection of tiny ceramic bells subtly rearranged on the entry table; a favored teapot might go missing and would turn up in a cupboard that had already been searched twice. And then she might hole up moodily for weeks in their mother's back bedroom—where she had, in fact, spent most of her few days of life. Passing in the hall, Alvie might hear a soft rustle and sigh behind his mother's closed door when no one was home, and he would know Baby Doris was there, tossing and turning on the big bed in a turbulent unfathomable feminine sullenness.

And now, with Frankie and Alvie both nearly thirteen, Baby Doris's presence began to take on a womanly yaw. Their mother's gold chains and clip-on earrings would show up in the hearth or fallen into the gap between the radio and wall, or the air might faintly fill with the scent of a ghostly menarche. It was as if she were leaving both boys behind, as Alvie had seen other sisters do, in her journey toward some phantasmal womanhood.

Alvie never spoke of Baby Doris to the others—the mere mention of her name could still bring a mist to Rose's eyes—

but he watched and listened for her. Sometimes he spoke aloud to her when no one else could hear and then waited through long stretches of breathless silence for an answer that never came; sometimes he set out a few cinnamon Necco Wafers or a Cracker Jack ring or a handful of jacks and a tiny rubber ball—anything he thought she might find and enjoy. In a few days, they'd disappear.

The knowledge that Doris's ghost paced these floors weighed on Alvie. How must she feel, seeing them all corporeally present, assembling a jigsaw or listening to Al Jolson on *The Lifebuoy Program*, or quarreling at the kitchen table over Spam and noodles, while she was a mere wisp of a phantom among them? Bodiless. Invisible. Excluded.

And so Alvie arranged the séance for a Wednesday night, when his mother worked her double shift at the packing house and would be gone past midnight. Lydia Bublik, a girl who lived across the street and three doors down, the house with the Modal A truck in the driveway, would act as medium. Lydia—who was in the same grade as the boys, though almost two years younger—insisted she had inherited certain clairvoyant gifts from a gypsy grandmother. She cut a fearsome figure with her hands on her hips and her chin jutting pugnaciously, her voice booming across the playground and ringing back off the classroom walls. She was cockier than anyone tended to guess, based on her petite, doe-eyed cuteness and her slanted home-cut brunette bangs.

To be fair, there *was* some evidence of Lydia's occult powers—she had a knack for guessing the weight of produce, could draw perfectly straight lines without the aid of a ruler, and had the unerring ability to tell Alvie and Frankie apart, even from a distance. It was also schoolyard lore that she had once pronounced a curse on a playground foe who was immediately spattered from above with gullshit. At any rate, Alvie was desperate to communicate with Baby Doris, and Lydia seemed his best prospect for doing so.

After dinner that Wednesday, Alvie waited by the window, keeping watch through the curtain gap for any sign of Lydia. Behind him, Frankie lay inert on the sofa, listening to *The Columbia Orchestra Showcase* on the radio, his distended belly taut with gas. "God, Alvie," he moaned. "I swear I'm going to explode."

With Rose working late one night a week, she'd leave a chicken casserole in the icebox that the boys could heat in the oven. The casseroles did indeed contain a few shreds of chicken but were mostly packed with victory-garden broccoli and cauliflower, which Frankie discovered produced in him a potent flatulence, with which he could torment his brother for hours. Now Frankie lay on the parlor sofa groaning with self-inflicted over-inflation. He ran both hands over his taut belly. "God, Alvie, this is the worst it's ever been," he groaned. "I swear I'm going to pull a Hindenburg in about a minute."

Alvie, at the window, swallowed down his irritation. Only Frankie would be so tasteless, so callous, so immune to the feelings of others.

"The humanity," Frankie moaned from the sofa. "Oh, the humanity."

Alvie bit his lip to keep from responding. To scold Frankie would be just the opening he needed to start up some kind of squabble—one Alvie was certain to lose.

From his post at the window, Alvie finally saw Lydia approach the house, slipping across the neighbors' front garden, ducking under the post rail fence and then crouching in the shadow of his mother's rosemary bush. She glanced behind her and then slipped across the Farrell's driveway and up onto their front porch. She tapped out the elaborately prearranged secret knock on the front door. Only then did Alvie move from his spot behind the curtain.

When Alvie pulled the door open, Lydia stood on the porch in all her bright-eyed bossiness. She wore a gauzy purple scarf draped over her head like a veil, and it was eerily backlit by the streetlamp at the road's edge.

"Good evening," she said, affecting a Bela Legosi. "It ez good to find you here." Lydia swept through the doorway and stood in the hall, looking around herself as though she hadn't been in the house a hundred times before. "I feel a strong a-presence here," Lydia announced, her accent slipping in the direction of Chico Marx. "A very strong a-presence."

Lydia's words brushed goose bumps along Alvie's forearms and stirred the small hairs at the back of his neck. He pushed the door shut and turned the deadbolt, feeling a chill of foreboding. What if this girl really *did* have supernatural powers? Was contacting the dead really such a brilliant idea? Surely dabbling in the supernatural might have consequences Alvie couldn't possibly foresee. His hand still on the doorknob, he looked around the front hallway as if he had just arrived in it himself for the first time. He considered the suddenly peculiar slants and edges of architecture, the cluttered entry table, the broad parlor archway, the dusty globe of the ceiling lamp.

Frankie appeared in the parlor doorway, running both hands over his bloated belly with a sly slant of a smile. The *wah-wah-wah* of a muted trumpet burbled from the Philco behind him. He leaned against the archway and cocked his head at Lydia, who was now fluttering her fingertips across both temples and tipping her head this way and that, apparently tuning in otherworldly voices. "What the hell is she doing?" Frankie asked Alvie. "She looks like she's draining pool water from her ears."

Alvie didn't answer. He should have planned this better. He could have found a time when he and Lydia would be alone in the house. Frankie was not one to indulge anyone else's fancies.

Lydia flickered her fingertips up around her head like she was playing invisible castanets and blinked up at the corners of the ceiling. She tugged the purple scarf from her head and waved it before her with a clumsy flourish and then wandered, trancelike, past Frankie into the parlor.

Frankie watched her with an expression equal parts disgust and amusement. He rubbed the back of his neck and then shook his head at Alvie, as if to indicate that he was as much a nutcase as this girl with her crystal-ball histrionics.

In the parlor, Lydia nudged picture frames. She brushed her fingertips across the spines of books, as though their titles were in Braille. She ran her hand across the mantle and up over the hump of the clock—as if each object she touched confided its secrets to her. She raised her chin haughtily and paused in front of the radio cabinet, stroking the back of one hand across the fabric-covered speakers. "Your sister likes this room," she finally announced dreamily but with no attempt at a foreign accent. "She likes it here by the fireplace. She likes it when you play the radio, Frankie."

Alvie stood in the center of the parlor, his heart aglow in his chest. So Baby Doris listened to the radio with them! He was certain now that he had sometimes caught her translucent voice singing along with Phil Spitalny and his All-Girl Orchestra or giggling at a Jack Benny one-liner, while the rest of them sat, leaden with animal existence, oblivious.

Lydia turned quickly and swept past Frankie, back into the front hall. She made her slow way down the hallway, running one hand along the wall and swirling the purple scarf before her with the other. Alvie followed her with eager trepidation, and Frankie, hands burrowed deep in his pockets, brought up the rear.

Lydia paused by the kitchen doorway. She peered into the dark room, but didn't enter. She blinked rapidly and took a deep shuddering breath. Alvie stood behind her on tiptoe to see past her into the empty, suddenly eerie, kitchen. His and Frankie's chairs were still drawn out on either side of the table. Two dirty plates stood on the draining board next to the sink, waiting for their mother to clear them away. The moonlight, beaming through the scalloped curtains, cast odd curvilinear shadows across everything. For a long moment they stood looking in. It occurred to Alvie that he was holding his breath. All was still and silent, and then the Frigidaire heaved suddenly, switched on by its thermostat, and Alvie flinched and then tried to cover it with a polite cough into his fist.

"She likes the pantry," Lydia said at last. "She likes to stand by it and watch while you all eat. She listens to what you say."

Lydia at last turned away from the kitchen and paused with the back of one hand pressed to her forehead like a fainting damsel in a silent movie. She floated down the hallway towards the bedrooms.

Alvie followed her, a lump of dread in his belly as they approached the part of the house where Baby Doris was found, cold and still in her bassinette, before she had lived a week. The barrier between him and the world of spirits seemed tissue-thin right now—as flimsy and translucent as the scarf Lydia waved before her as she paused in the doorway of his mother's bedroom. Alvie went to Lydia's side and stood looking into the darkened room.

Lydia sighed. Her whole body seemed to sag with calmness. She stepped through the doorway aglow with serenity.

Before he followed her, Alvie reached around the doorjamb and flipped the switch that turned on his mother's 40-watt bedside lamp. He swallowed, entered the room uncertainly, and stood beside Lydia. He looked around breathlessly, almost pressing himself against her in his trepidation. Moonlight breathed a soft penumbra of silver light around the drawn blind. The giant four-poster bed loomed in the same spot it had occupied since the boys had been born. Its columns slashed broad shadows up the far wall. A ghostly breeze seemed to stir in its canopy. He wondered now if his baby sister's whole short life had been spent right here in the cramped space between this door and the window opposite, if the colors and smells and creaks of this small space had been the full extent of her physical experience. The bedroom was filled with their mother's scent—part orange peel, part sweat, part coffee, part perfume. Alvie sometimes came into this room alone just to sit on the edge of the great bed and breathe the air and look around in awe at the sacred and womanly furnishings. Maybe Baby Doris did the same.

Frankie stood silent and watchful in the doorway, lit low-key by the lamp at the far end of the hall, his hands still dug in his pockets.

Lydia made a slow circuit around the huge bed. She ran her hand over the counterpane and up one of the tapered mahogany posts. She turned and studied her dim reflection in the oval mirror above the vanity. She lifted a silver backed hairbrush and set it down again. Faint music seeped down the hallway from the parlor radio.

"I feel vibrations in this room," Lydia said. She swirled the gauzy scarf in the air before her. "I feel very *strong* vibrations here," she said.

"I'm feeling some strong vibrations myself," Frankie said from just inside the doorway. Both Lydia and Alvie turned and looked at him. Frankie hadn't said much since Lydia arrived, and both of them had more or less written him out of the scene.

"You feel it?" Lydia asked warily.

Frankie nodded gravely. "*Very* strong vibrations," he said.

And suddenly the room reeked pungently of rotten eggs.

"Oh, god," Lydia sputtered. She waved the scarf in front of her frantically.

Frankie backed into the doorway and grinned at them, wholly pleased with himself. He raised both palms in front of him in a practiced posture of innocence. "Wasn't me," he said.

"Oh, god," Lydia said again. "Get me out of here." Swirling the scarf in front of her, she propellered her way between the boys and fled down the hallway to the front parlor.

Alvie paused a moment. He wanted to glare at Frankie, perhaps shake his head at him, heavy with disappointment, the way their mother often did, but the air was too vile for theatrics, and he couldn't trust himself to hold his breath much longer. He pushed past Frankie and jogged down the hallway to open the front door and all the parlor windows.

LYDIA SLID THE BLANK SHEET of newsprint across the mahogany coffee table to Alvie, who knelt across from her, wedged between the broad table and the sofa. "We're going to need twenty-eight pieces," she told him. Now that her trance was over, and they were all back in the parlor, she'd reverted to her customary bossy tone. Her abandoned purple scarf lay puddled at the base of the floor lamp near the doorway.

Behind Lydia, the voice reading the news on the radio left off, and, after a hiss, an orchestra began sawing its way through "The Star-Spangled Banner." One by one the West Coast stations were signing off for the night, and Frankie, squatting by the dial, was having trouble finding a big band broadcast.

"Try to make the papers all the same size," Lydia told Alvie. She twisted around and looked behind her. "*Frankie*," she said, "make yourself useful. Go find an ashtray and a pencil."

Frankie, apparently bored enough to be obedient, switched off the radio and trudged down the hallway towards the kitchen.

Alvie did the math in his head. He folded and refolded the sheet of paper Lydia had given him until it was a tidy rectangle about the size of a box of matches. He unfolded it to find thirty-two creased rectangles, which was four more than he needed. He wetted the edges with his tongue and carefully tore the paper into even strips along the sharp edge of the coffee table. He tore each strip into smaller rectangles and made a neat stack of them.

Frankie wandered back into the room, plinking a glass ashtray with a yellow pencil, as if it were a drum.

"What took you so long?" Lydia asked him.

He gave his belly a pat with the hand that held the pencil. "I felt a big one coming on," Frankie said. "So I fired it out the kitchen door." He smirked and set the ashtray and pencil on the coffee table in front of Lydia. "You might not want to leave the house any time soon," he said. He went back and squatted in front of the radio.

"Could you maybe give that thing a rest?" Lydia said. "We're ready to go here, and we'll need your help."

Again, to Alvie's surprise, Frankie did as he was told. He switched the radio off again and came and sat on the floor opposite Alvie. He propped both elbows on the coffee table and rested his chin in his hands, looking bored.

Lydia took the pencil and wrote the letters of the alphabet, one girlish upper case letter on each rectangle of paper. "These are so she can spell out words," Lydia explained. In a moment she'd arranged the letters, in alphabetical order, in a rough oval around the coffee table's glossy surface. She chose two more scraps of paper. She wrote *YES* on one and *NO* on the other. These she placed, widely spaced, inside the oval. "These are so we can ask questions," she said. "It'll be a lot faster than having her spell everything."

"She was a *baby*," Frankie pointed out. "How the hell is she going to spell anything?"

Alvie looked down at the alphabet of paper arranged on the table facing Lydia. Damn that Frankie. Nothing was sacred with him. This was the boy who, in one of the many Sunday schools they'd briefly attended, once rearranged the Flannelgraph nativity scene so the camel was humping the donkey. He was clearly planning to sit here passing gas and heckling until Lydia took a swing at him or stomped out of the house in one of her rages. It made Alvie want to cry in frustration.

To Alvie's relief, Lydia chose to ignore Frankie's comment and looked squarely into Alvie's eyes. "Now we make contact," she said. "Ready?" She turned the ashtray lip-side down and set it in the center of the oval between the *YES* and *NO*. She looked from Alvie to Frankie and back again and then raised two fingers, as if she were holding an invisible cigarette. "Just two fingers each," she told the boys. "Barely touching. Don't push it. Wait for it to move on its own."

Alvie leaned forward and placed two trembling fingers on the cool glass bottom, but Frankie just sat there looking doubtfully at Lydia, his arms crossed. "What about you?" he asked her.

"I'm the medium, *moron*," she said. "I ask the questions. I don't touch the ashtray."

Frankie looked her over a few seconds more with grudging admiration, evidently trying to come up with a rejoinder—but he soon gave up, shrugged, and set two fingers on the glass like his brother.

Lydia tucked her hair behind her ears and rested both palms on the table's edge. She looked down, as if gathering her thoughts, and took a deep breath. She angled her face at the ceiling and squeezed her eyes shut. "Is anyone here?" she asked, her voice achieving a surprisingly resonant contralto. She opened her eyes and looked down at the table.

Alvie felt the ashtray pull across the table beneath his fingers. The sudden movement shot electric goose bumps up his arm. He yanked his hand away. Frankie lifted his hand from the glass too. Alvie stared down at the ashtray, his mouth agape, his fingers suddenly numb. "It moved," he managed to say. "Did you see that? It moved!"

"That wasn't you?" Frankie said skeptically, squinting across the table at Alvie, his hand still hovering over the ashtray. "You're full of it," he said. "It *had* to be you."

"It was *supposed* to move," Lydia reminded them, but the cocksure tone had vanished from her voice. She seemed nearly as shaken as Alvie. They sat around the table, staring speechlessly at the ragged alphabet and the inverted ashtray. For a few seconds the only sound was the mantle clock's oblivious ticking.

"Come on, you guys," Lydia finally said with unsteady bravado. "Put your fingers back, and don't let go this time."

"*You* do it," Alvie said, a squeak of panic in his voice.

"I'm the medium," Lydia reminded him. "I'm not supposed to touch it."

"Can't *I* be the medium?" Alvie begged.

"No," Lydia said, bossiness rounding out her voice again. "It doesn't work that way."

Alvie looked across the table now at Frankie whose fingers were back on the ashtray. He regarded Alvie with cool disdain. "It's an *ashtray*," he told Alvie. "What's it going to do to you?"

Alvie stalled a moment longer, rubbing his damp hands on his trousers. He took a fortifying breath and set his fingers on the glass again, feeling a little sick. The ashtray seemed unnaturally cold to the touch.

Lydia again closed her eyes. "Is anyone there?" she repeated, but there was an undertone of uncertainty in her voice this time. The clock ticked. Attic timbers creaked.

For a few seconds nothing happened, but then Alvie watched the ashtray beneath his fingers drift across the table and nudge the scrap of paper marked *YES*. As soon as it touched the paper, he pulled his hand clear.

"She's here," Lydia said.

Even Frankie, on his side of the table, looked impressed. He picked up the ashtray and inspected it, like it was one of Alvie's magic tricks, and then he narrowed his eyes at Lydia. "How did you do that?"

"I *didn't* do it," Lydia informed him. "I wasn't even touching the ashtray. I'm way over here." She pressed both hands against her flat chest in a pleading, feminine gesture of innocence and then leaned closer. "You *know* who did it," she said, her voice a dry whisper.

Frankie sighed loudly through his nose and handed the ashtray to Lydia. Nothing annoyed him more than the possibility of being duped. He leaned forward, elbows propped on the coffee table, and studied Lydia's every move, as she set the ashtray down in the middle of the table, adjusted the position of a few of the paper scraps, and then gestured for the boys to rest their fingertips on the ashtray again.

Frankie squinted distrustfully at Alvie. "One more time, brother," he said. He waited until Alvie had put his fingers on the ashtray, and then he placed his own, spread wide to straddle his brother's.

Lydia grasped the edge of the table with both hands. She closed her eyes, and turned her face to the ceiling. "Are you dead?" she asked. Her voice accomplished an odd, involuntary quiver as she pronounced the word *dead*. She opened her eyes and looked down at the table.

To Alvie's great relief, the ashtray remained inert. But then he felt a small uncertain trembling under his fingertips, and it began to creep, reluctantly, towards the YES card. The ashtray's progress was painfully slow this time, but it was straight. Each centimeter it moved doubled Alvie's dread. This slow progress was somehow even more unnerving than when it had lurched under his touch. When it crossed half the distance to the *Yes*, Lydia slid the paper closer. The ashtray finally grazed it and stopped dead, its energy apparently spent.

The boys let go, and Lydia slid the ashtray back to its place. Though she was clearly trying to act blasé, she seemed taken aback—farther from her cocky playground persona than Alvie had ever seen her. She moved the YES card back to its original position.

Alvie opened and closed both hands. They felt drained of blood. He wished he had never suggested this venture. He wished the radio was still on and that Lydia was still across the street in her own parlor waiting for her parents to get home from choir practice. He wished he would hear his mother's footsteps on the porch outside right now—the chiming of her keyring and the deadbolt drawn back—and that she would step into the hallway smelling of smoke and citrus, and pronounce an abrupt end to this unnerving experiment.

Frankie leaned back, propped by both elbows on the sofa behind him. He looked Alvie and Lydia over appraisingly, as if one of them—probably both—were pulling something. Then he dropped down to the floor on one elbow and looked under the table, as though he thought he might glimpse a magnet or some other apparatus, before his brother could whisk it out of sight. Frankie sat up straight again and scrutinized the slips of paper arranged on the table. He looked at Lydia and then reached over and slid the *YES* and *NO* cards so they were in swapped positions.

Alvie shook his head. It was just like Frankie to be so untrusting, to assume that everyone was like him—and that nothing, therefore, was ever simple or honest or above board.

Frankie pushed himself up from the table and stood. "Swap places with me," he told Alvie.

Lydia looked up at him annoyed. "Why?"

"Just tell him to do it," he said. "Humor me."

Lydia sighed, and Alvie scooted to the end of the table and around. Frankie stepped over Lydia and sat down across from Alvie again. "Okay then," Frankie said. "Let's see what she has to say now." He rose up on his knees and set two fingers on top of the ashtray. With his free hand he waved for Alvie to do the same. Alvie swallowed, took a deep breath and set two mottled fingers on the cool glass.

Lydia held the corners of the coffee table and looked up at the ceiling. She kept her eyes open this time. "Do you have a message for us?" she called into the air.

There was no hesitation. The ashtray slid the opposite way across the table and bumped the *YES* card aside.

Alvie jerked his hand away and pressed himself back against the sofa, both arms pulled up against his chest. His breath was ragged. He wanted to run somewhere, but this was the only lit room in the house.

Frankie rubbed his jaw and looked down at the ashtray. "Ain't that a sweet load of clams," he said. All three leaned back now and regarded each other, weighing their collective will to continue. A dog barked somewhere out in the night. A passing car's headlights whisked across the curtains. A choir of crickets in the front garden maintained its tremulous music.

Alvie was the first to speak. "Maybe we should stop," he said hopefully, looking from Lydia to Frankie and back again. "I think we've done enough for one night."

Lydia swallowed. She propped her chin on both fists on the tabletop and mulled the proposal over. "You wanted to talk to her," she said, looking at the table and not at Alvie. "She's your sister."

"I *did*," Alvie said, and before he could stop himself he added, "But I didn't think you could really…"

Lydia straightened up, affronted. The tiniest thing could set her off. "Well, it turns out I really *can*," she said hotly. "And now you want to weenie out on me?"

Alvie looked at her scolding face. All her hesitancy had evaporated again. Here was the familiar schoolyard swagger. One ill chosen half-sentence, and he had destroyed any hope of calling this séance off. His lips moved, but he could think of nothing to say. He felt cornered—pressed between the table and sofa, between Lydia's scalding anger and Frankie's frosty skepticism.

"Come on Alvie-boy," Frankie said. "What are you afraid of?"

Everything, Alvie could have answered—and it would have been close to the truth. He was riddled with phobias. He was frightened of cats, the ocean, new shirts, cash registers, browning lettuce. Even cursive handwriting made him uneasy. The papery thumping of a moth trapped between the window glass and the screen could send his pulse racing and make him retreat to another room. But what could he say? He was most afraid of looking afraid. So, still pressing back against the sofa, he reached out two trembling fingers so they hovered over the center of the table.

"Atta boy," Frankie said.

Lydia slid the ashtray back to the center of the table, and gave Alvie a fortifying nod. She tipped her face to the ceiling again. "Do you want something from us?"

The ashtray, in a wobbling trajectory, slowly arched around the YES card without grazing it, and tipped the *B* askew.

"*B?*" Lydia said. She skated the ashtray back to the center. "It was a *yes* or *no* question."

"Maybe she thought it was multiple-choice," Frankie suggested unhelpfully.

Lydia glared at him and then turned to Alvie. "Let's try something different," she said. She took the *YES* and *NO* cards and set them on the floor beside her. "Okay," she said. "Get ready."

Both boys put their fingers on the ashtray.

Lydia kept her eyes on the ashtray instead of looking at the ceiling. "What is your name, spirit?" she said loudly.

The ashtray lurched and paused, lurched and paused, but scrawled an erratic path to the torn slip of paper marked with a *D*. Lydia stared at Alvie with a smile of supreme vindication. Alvie dropped his eyes to the table. He watched Lydia's hand set the ashtray back in the center of the oval.

Frankie immediately put his fingers back. "The plot thickens," he said.

Alvie chewed at the corner of his thumb a few seconds and then, without enthusiasm, placed his fingers on the ashtray. In his mind he begged Doris to stop what she was doing and leave them all alone. She hadn't spoken all these years. Was there really any urgent reason to break that comfortable silence now? But Alvie's mental pleading was ignored; the ashtray drifted in a broad curve against the smooth grain of the wood and came to touch the corner of the *O*. No one spoke. No one moved. Even the chorus of crickets outside the window fell silent in deference to what was happening in this room. It was Baby Doris. It was really her. She was making her presence irrefutable.

Lydia nodded with the air of someone who had known all along. She slid the ashtray back into position, and this time it drifted in one direction but then reversed itself and drifted over to nudge aside the letter *G*.

"*Dog*?" Alvie said. "That can't be right."

Lydia picked up the ashtray. She gave it a scolding look, like it was being willfully disobedient—a sniffing spaniel refusing to return when called. She set it back in the center, and, when Alvie added his fingers to Frankie's, the ashtray immediately made for the letter *S*.

"*Dogs*?" Alvie said.

Lydia picked up the ashtray again, clearly growing peevish. "I don't know what she's doing," she said crossly. "Did you guys ever have dogs?"

Frankie shrugged. "Just the one that bit me," he said. "He got put down. Maybe *he's* trying to contact us. He's probably pissed about it."

"Maybe *Doris* has got a dog," Alvie offered. "A ghost dog." He gestured at the front window. "Maybe that one Mrs. Brenner ran over."

Lydia ignored them both; she placed the ashtray back inside the circle of letters. "Try it again," she said. "Maybe it's just the beginning of a sentence. We need more."

This time when the boys touched the ashtray it scooted directly to the *H*. When it finally spelled out *dogshit*, Lydia and Alvie sat back from the table and glared at Frankie.

Frankie looked back at them stone faced. He held his palms up again in that formal pose of innocence. "Wasn't me," he said, a self-satisfied grin breaking over his face.

A LITTLE AFTER midnight, Alvie, in his lower bunk, heard the front door open and the jingle of his mother's keys as she dropped them back in her purse. A few minutes later he listened to her footsteps move along the hallway and the click of her closing bedroom door. It was only then that he finally let go of whatever he'd been holding onto since the séance began. He took a couple of deep breaths in the darkness and felt his shoulders slacken. Maybe he could finally sleep. He rolled over and faced the wall.

"You awake?" Frankie said from above.

"Yeah," Alvie said, making his voice sound more stern than he felt.

"I've got to tell you something."

"What?"

"I made it spell out that word," Frankie said. "But I only did it after the *D* and the *O*."

Alvie propped himself up on his elbows. "What do you mean?" he said, unable to stop himself.

"Swear to God, Alvie: I didn't start screwing around until after the *D* and the *O*." Frankie's voice in the darkness sounded as flat and hard as a tabletop. His words had no animus—none of the usual bluster that rounded them out and filled them with life. Alvie couldn't fathom what that meant.

"I didn't make it do the first ones," Frankie said. "I promise."

Alvie lay back down on his back, wide-eyed now, staring up at the springs of his brother's bunk. How could he have doubted it? His sister had spoken.

"That Lydia's full of crap," Frankie whispered down to him. "But I swear to God, it really *was* Doris."

CHAPTER THREE
THE DUCHESS OF WINDSOR
1937

IF IT HAD BEEN just Frankie, Rose would have been suspicious. But that Sunday night Alvie said *he* didn't feel well, either. He had the same headache and sore throat, and he just sort of wilted at the table all through dinner, sagging in his kitchen chair like a tomato vine past its season. Neither of the boys managed to choke down more than a few bites of the corned beef on their plates, when most nights they'd have scarfed it down, along with mashed potatoes and corn. But tonight they stirred their food listlessly; stared, frowning, into the distance; and answered Rose's questions in croaky monosyllables.

After she'd packed the leftovers away in the refrigerator and washed all the dishes, Rose came out to the parlor to find Frankie curled at one end of the couch, nested there among the pillows and her crocheted Afghan. The radio was on, but it had drifted from the station he'd tuned it to, so the music was cloaked in static. Rose crossed to the radio and switched it off, and, when Frankie made no objection, she knew something was definitely wrong.

She gently sat down next to him. His head was wreathed in the Afghan, so he looked like a Russian peasant woman from that Greta Garbo movie. His face was flushed, and he seemed barely able to move. She could feel the heat radiate from his lanky thirteen-year-old body, even before she reached over to set a hand on his forehead.

She made him sit up, which he did reluctantly but without complaint, and then she pulled the Afghan down and turned his head to face her squarely. His face looked jowly, and he winced when she pressed the swollen area at the base of his jaw. She made him open his mouth and then tilted his head to catch the light from the floor lamp. She squinted at the angry swollen glands in his throat. "It's just the mumps," she told him, her voice more assuring than she felt. "You go on to bed. I'll call Doctor Wilkins in the morning."

She had to more or less lead Frankie down the hall to the back bedroom, one arm around his shoulder, but he made the trip unresistingly. Alvie was already flopped on the lower bunk, on top of the covers, still dressed in his street clothes, inert as a pile of laundry. While Frankie dragged himself up onto the top bunk, Rose felt Alvie's forehead and found it even hotter than his brother's. "I'll get some aspirins, and we'll see if you can swallow them down," she said. "I'll call the doctor first thing."

"I'M SURE IT will just run its course," Doctor Wilkins told her on Friday morning after he'd made his examination and scrubbed his hands at the kitchen sink. He and Rose stood together in the entryway with the front door still closed. "Have they complained of any pain in…?" The doctor paused, glanced at Rose and then back down at the black satchel he held in front of himself with both hands. "Any pain in their testicles?"

Rose felt a sudden, unfamiliar flush of intimacy. Here she and Dr. Wilkins were: two adults, a woman and a man, talking privately of grown-up things—why did this happen to her so rarely? "Why, no," she said haltingly, flustered by her own foolishness. "No, they haven't. Complained about anything. In that. *Region*."

The doctor nodded—had his eyes always been that lovely shade of hazel?—and set his satchel on the entry table. He pulled the prescription tablet from the inner pocket of his tweed sport coat. "I'll give you something to try on them," he said. "At least it will bring the fever down. And I'll stop by again tonight when I leave the office."

Rose watched his hands as he scribbled on the prescription pad with his Parker fountain pen. His fingers looked strong and gentle, the nails immaculate and evenly trimmed. His scuffed gold wedding band was deep-bedded on the hand that held the paper tablet. For one wild instant Rose had the impulse to reach out and run a fingertip over the even mounds of his knuckles, and the notion startled her so much that she lost track of the conversation they'd been having. "When should I bring them by?" she blurted, wanting only to fill the sudden awkward void with words.

Dr. Wilkins glanced up from his prescription pad at her and smiled quizzically. He held her gaze a good second or two longer than felt comfortable. "No need to bring them in," the doctor said, still smiling. "I'll swing by here on my way home from the office. We don't want them infecting anyone else."

A rush of flustered laughter overtook Rose then—an embarrassed habit she thought she'd shed in her teens. "Right. Right," she said. "I'm sorry. I haven't had my coffee yet."

Dr. Wilkins tore a sheet off his pad and handed it to Rose, who stared down at it in her hand, one long, brainless beat, like it were some wondrous and impenetrable missive delivered by an archangel. "I'll come by around seven," the doctor said, and Rose found herself looking at his neatly trimmed silver hair, and not at his gentle eyes because—well, she didn't *know* exactly why.

He picked up his satchel and his hat from the entry table. He opened the front door and then ducked his head in an awkward bow. "See you this evening, Mrs. Farrell," he said and stepped outside, pulling the door shut behind him.

Rose stood staring blankly at the door, feeling deflated. She listened to his car start up and pull away. Had he called her *Mrs.* Farrell?

ROSE ARRIVED LATE for her shift. She'd run down to the Rexall to fill the boys' prescription and dosed them with it. She'd left cold sandwiches in the icebox if they got hungry. She'd told them to call Old Mrs. Brenner if anything came up, and then she'd rushed out to the packinghouse. The rest of the morning she spent packing frantically, trying to catch up with where she'd have been if she'd arrived at work on time. When the lunch break arrived, her overworked hands felt permanently cupped in the shape of an orange, and her shoulders were knotted.

At the break table, Rose sat quietly eating her sandwich while the rest of them passed around the new issue of *Life* and aired their opinions on The Romance of the Century. Tina kept clucking her tongue and shaking her head—but she was one of the two Catholics on the shift, and that was only to be expected. Harriet was of the opinion that any man who would give up the throne for a divorced woman ought to have his head examined; if she'd done it to two men already, what was to keep her from doing it again, even if he *was* the King of England? Francine Steele, whose husband was a henpecked

meat inspector, announced imperiously—and with no evident
irony—that any man who'd let an abrasive and vulgar woman
like that domineer him had no business running a country in
the first place.

Rose looked down at the photo on the open magazine
spread. Most days she did her share of talking at lunch, but
today she quietly chewed her sandwich and sipped tea from the
lid of her thermos bottle. She, personally, thought the whole
situation was romantic. What could be more passionate than a
man who would sacrifice untold power and fortune to marry
the woman he loved? And it cheered her to think it was
happening to a woman in her forties.

Rose glanced down again at the halftone of Wallis
Simpson and Prince Edward on their wedding day. The couple
stood together: he dapper and aloof in his morning coat; she
dressed in a fetching white jacket and skirt. While the former
king peered diffidently at the horizon, his new wife looked
directly at the camera, smiling. Wallis Simpson was slim and
clearly happy, her long ordeal behind her. She looked trim and
smart, much younger than her years.

Rose took a final, petite bite of her sandwich and wrapped
the rest up again in its wax paper.

Really, Rose had kept *her* figure, too.

AFTER HER SHIFT, Rose made a special trip to the butcher
shop, feeling a little guilty to leave her sick sons waiting for her
at home. She asked for a whole fryer this time, instead of just
drumsticks and thighs, and then chewed at her lower lip,
counting out coins, while Mr. Franklin wrapped it up for her.

At home she quickly checked on the boys—Alvie was
sleeping on his bunk, and Frankie was out in the parlor, lying
on the hard floor with a pillow under his head, listening to the

radio. Rose slipped back to her room and changed into her teal dress. Glancing at the bedside clock, she fussed a bit with her hair in the dresser mirror. But looking at her reflection she felt suddenly like a foolish old woman, and she changed into a gray housedress and then rushed to the kitchen to get the chicken in the oven.

At seven twenty, Dr. Wilkins still hadn't arrived. Rose checked on the boys. She'd made them change into clean pajamas and comb their sweat-slick hair, so both looked more or less presentable, lying on their respective bunks. In fact they seemed noticeably improved, which sent an odd sense of alarm through her. Back in the kitchen she checked on the chicken, which she was keeping warm in the oven. Its perfectly browned skin now looked dried out and puckered.

When the doorbell finally rang, Rose ripped open the oven and set the roasting pan on the trivet she'd already set in the center of the table. The doorbell rang again, and she rushed into the hallway and paused a second, catching her breath, before she opened it. "Why, of course!" she said brightly. "Dr. Wilkins! We were just sitting down to dinner. Have you eaten?"

In her dream, she and Wallis Simpson, who was still wearing that white jacket and skirt from her wedding, were walking along Laguna Beach, south, towards the pier. They were chatting and eating vanilla cones. The melting ice cream kept dripping on the new bride's clothes, but the woman took no notice—and for some reason Rose couldn't bring herself to point it out to her. And then they passed the place where the swarthy Italian man sold donkey rides, and Simpson seemed fascinated with the donkey's red straw hat and how it had holes cut in it for the ears. "Oh, they're all that way," Rose told her. "It's one size fits all." And then suddenly they were at baby Doris's grave, and they were absorbed in some elaborate ceremony that involved the donning of gold chains, the laying down of wreaths, and ranks of costumed liverymen standing at attention. And then Rose woke up and lay a moment blinking up at the canopy over her bed, wondering what had brought all *that* on.

She got up and checked on the boys. Alvie was still asleep on his lower bunk, all twisted in the sweaty sheets. But Frankie was awake, curled in a ball, breathing raggedly. She put a hand on his hot forehead, and he opened his eyes and looked at her blearily. "It's like I got kicked in the nards," he moaned.

"IT'S SORT OF an emergency," she said into the phone. "Could I just speak with the doctor?"

"Please hold, ma'am," the nurse said.

Rose heard muffled speaking, a clunking sound and then silence until, a full minute or two later, the doctor's voice arrived on the phone.

"Doctor Wilkins speaking," that reedy voice announced, and it sent something strumming through Rose.

"Yes," she said. "This is Rose. Rose Farrell. I'm calling because you asked the other day if the boys had been feeling pain." She stopped talking suddenly, and then felt like a fool because she'd given no thought to what she would say once she got him on the phone. "Pain," she repeated. "You know, *pain*. Down *there*." She caught herself pointing down at the hallway floor, though she was talking to the doctor on the phone, which made her feel just that much more foolish.

She could hear the doctor's breathing, but a few long seconds went by, and he said nothing.

"I could bring him in," she offered. "Or should I bring them both?"

"Yes," he said. "You'd better come on in. I won't be able to get out there for a few hours. Tell them to let you wait in my office at the back. Don't just sit in the waiting room with everyone else."

"Thank you," she said, feeling an inexcusable swell of happy expectation at being invited into the doctor's own private sanctum. "Thank you. I'll see you in a little bit."

"THERE'S NO RECOGNIZED treatment," the doctor told her, after he'd left Frankie in the examination room. He now sat behind the big oak desk in his office. "We generally just let it run its course. Just take him home and try to keep him comfortable. Keep giving him asprin." The doctor looked past Rose at Alvie who sat on the leather sofa against the back wall, under the row of framed diplomas. "There *is* something else," he said. "Maybe it would be best to talk about it in private."

Rose felt a sudden warm flush of suspense. "Yes," she said. "Yes of course." She looked back at Alvie who was glumly flipping through a wilted issue of *Boys' Life* one of the nurses had fetched him from the waiting room. "Alvie," she said. "Alvie, sweetheart. Get two bits from my purse and run down to the Rexall."

Alvie looked up at her doubtfully and closed the magazine.

"Get a bottle of Bayer," she told him. "And get something for yourself, too, if there's money left over."

Alvie gave her a sour look, and then he just sat there.

"Go *on*," she said. "*Scoot.*"

Alvie dragged himself slump-shouldered across the sofa to where her purse sat tucked at the opposite end. He took out her coin purse and made a big production of trying to find a quarter.

"*Al*vie," Rose said. "*Get a move on.*"

Alvie finally slipped a quarter into the pocket of those baggy overalls he insisted on wearing everywhere and dropped her coin purse back in her handbag. He trudged to the door, glanced back, and finally made his reluctant exit.

When the door clicked shut behind him, Dr. Wilkins paused a few silent seconds as if trying to render difficult thoughts into words. "He'll be fine," he said finally, and for a confused second Rose thought he was talking about Alvie. "The swelling is beginning to go down," the doctor went on in a kind of mumble. "And we're treating him with antibiotics. I'll give you a prescription. He'll be back to normal in a few days. But there are complications."

Rose's heart began to hammer. "What?" she said. "What's the matter?"

"Well in my medical opinion, he'll almost certainly be unable to…." The doctor's voice trailed off like he was hunting about for a layman's term with which to describe some horrible, disfiguring medical condition. "He won't be able to have children."

Rose pressed a hand to her chest. She tried, while the doctor kept mumbling, to sort out in her head the scope of this news—Frankie would be fine, but she'd have no grandchildren from him. Was that dire news, like an amputated limb? Or just an inconvenience, like a small scar somewhere no one could see? The doctor was still talking, but it required an effort on Rose's part to catch up to his words again.

"…up to you if and when you want to give him the news," he was saying, "but really it shouldn't be treated as something debilitating. He'll be able to function normally in every other way."

The doctor stopped talking, so Rose tried to think of something to say. "I understand," she said, though her thoughts were swimming in every direction. "I understand."

THE ROAST WAS in the oven, and both boys were sound asleep back in their room—neither of them had had much luck sleeping the night before—so Rose had a rare hour to herself. She'd slip out for just a few minutes. She wrapped a couple of slices of coffee cake in wax paper, filled a thermos with freshly-percolated coffee, and headed next doors to Mrs. Brenner's. The old widow was out on the porch as usual, wrapped in a plaid blanket, though it had to be more than seventy degrees in the shade. The front lawn was looking rangy, and Rose made a mental note to send the boys over to mow it once they were feeling themselves again.

"Why, hello, Mrs. Brenner," Rose sang out from the sidewalk. "I've brought us some coffee and cake. May I come up for a visit?"

The old woman raised a spindly hand and, without speaking, waved for Rose to join her. Rose set the cake plate and thermos on the flat porch rail and pushed the empty Adirondack chair closer to the one the old woman was sitting in. "Shall I go in the kitchen and get us some cups?" Rose said.

In the kitchen, Rose got two glass cups from the cupboard and rinsed them out—Old Mrs. Brenner, god bless her, was not the best of housekeepers—and then she got down a second plate, and rummaged around in the silverware drawer for two matching forks.

Back out on the porch, Rose poured Mrs. Brenner a cup and set it on the flat plank arm of her chair. The old woman liked her coffee black, so that's the way Rose drank it, too, when she visited, not wanting to be difficult. Rose took a petite sip of coffee, which was still piping hot from the thermos.

"Was Sylvia here today?" Rose asked. "Did you have a nice visit?"

The old woman shook her head and made a sound with her lips like air escaping from a tire. She was always peevish after her daughter's visits.

Rose smiled down at her coffee cup. "I'm sure it's a treat to have your daughter visit," Rose said.

"She's a beast," the old woman pronounced, glowering out at the trees on Grove Street.

"Oh, dear," Rose said, suppressing a chuckle. "I know you don't mean that."

"She'd slip me arsenic if she thought she could get away with it," the old woman said. She sniffed at her coffee cup as if wary of poison even now. She finally turned to look at Rose. "How are your two?"

"The boys?" Rose said. "Why, they're fine. Growing like weeds. Eating me out of house and home." She looked down at the cup she was holding. "Had a brush with the mumps, but really they're just fine."

"Oh, *mumps*," Mrs Brenner said, as if that small fact had solved a considerable mystery. "I kept seeing the doctor's car in the drive at all hours. Didn't know what that meant."

Rose felt again the odd compulsion she'd been struggling with the last couple of days: the wish to talk out loud about Dr. Wilkins. It was a peculiar impulse: whoever she was talking to or whatever the discussion was about, she found herself bending the conversation in directions that would allow her to mention the doctor's name—though she always caught herself in time to stop. It was as if saying his name out loud might relieve a kind of pressure building up in her. And now here it was: she could speak of him. "He's really been such a dear," Rose said. "Such a thoughtful man."

"I prefer Young Doctor Evans," the old woman snapped. "He's the one I always ask to see."

"Yes, he's a fine doctor, too," Rose said. "But not nearly so seasoned. Not nearly so distinguished." Now that Dr. Wilkins was finally the legitimate topic of conversation, Rose had an equally irrational urge to shoo the conversation away from him before Old Mrs. Brenner could malign him. "Your son-in-law," Rose said, apropos of nothing. "Did I see him working on a road crew down on Glass Street the other day?"

THAT NIGHT WHEN the boys were asleep, Rose looked at her reflection in the dark kitchen window while the sink filled with hot water from the faucet. She watched her face soften and then fade as the rising steam fogged the glass. Rose washed the plates first, which had piled up inexcusably over the last couple of days. She slid each squeaky rinsed dish into the wire draining rack before she dried them and stacked them in the cupboard. She sighed and wiped her hands on the dishtowel. There was something calming about the heat and the water, the quiet house, and the dark window at the end of the day. God help her, it was sometimes the only minute she had to herself—her only chance to collect her thoughts and mull things over.

She soaped up the mugs and drinking glasses next and thought of Dr. Wilkins sipping coffee in this very kitchen earlier that evening. Oh, that poor, awkward man! He had this way of suddenly looking down any time Rose caught his eye. And then there was that charming ungainliness to the way he'd hold his hat, moving it from hand to hand, as he was about to leave—like he was fretting about the exact moment he should put it on his head.

The poor man was just too reserved, too standoffish—but as a fault, Rose found it charming. She wouldn't have it any other way. Dr. Wilkins was an old-fashioned gentleman. He had that stiff-backed Laurel Place sense of decorum and correctness—but he wore it so well, she had to admit. It wasn't at all off-putting. She thought of the *Life* photo of the Duke of Windsor, standing stiffly, hands linked behind his back, looking downright dyspeptic on what must have been the happiest day of his life.

Rose frowned at the clean-rinsed glasses and coffee mugs lined up, upended, in the dish rack beside the sink. She had no recollection of having put them there. Where was her mind these days? She dried them one by one and arranged them, meticulously, on the cupboard shelf, and then she got to work on the silverware.

It wasn't easy being a woman in this day and age. Certain things were the man's job—she *knew* that. But over the years Rose had taken on so many manly duties: she knew how to use a tire gauge, how to file her income taxes, how to fix the kitchen drawers when they slipped off their runners. Just last summer she'd taken the old Bakelite-trimmed toaster apart with a screwdriver right there at the kitchen table, figuring out the function of each little gizmo as she did. She'd finally found the tiny thingamajig lever that had been clotted with crumbs. She'd scraped it clean with a hat pin, and now the toaster worked just as well as it had the day she'd brought it home. She'd even gone out in the dead of night last September and dug her own post holes for the new back fence and then told Mrs. Gruber in the house behind that she'd had a man in to do it.

But it was true: the universe seemed designed for couples, for typical families. Every form the boys brought home from school had spaces Rose had to draw a line through. Every recipe in *Lady's Companion* was devised to feed four. Every radio show had its affable, witless dad who forgot anniversaries and invited the boss to dinner at inopportune times. Being a single mother was like being left-handed, and this was a world where even scissors refused to work for you.

To Rose's mild surprise, the utensils now lay glistening silver in the dish rack, lined up like sardines in a can. Rose dried them with the now-damp towel and sorted them into the wooden tray in the silverware drawer.

She thought then of Wallis Simpson and her ambitious, assertive ways, her headstrong willingness to take matters into her own hands. Why did those adjectives sound so shrill when they were applied to a woman? She thought of Amelia Earhart, Eleanor Roosevelt, Katharine Hepburn, Dorothy Parker.

She pushed the silverware drawer shut with a thunk and watched her reflection emerge again on the foggy kitchen window.

WHEN ROSE CAME out of the packinghouse restroom Friday afternoon, the break room was empty: the coffee urn abandoned, the radio switched off. The tabletop still had damp arcs from being sponged down. The newspapers and magazines were now neatly stacked on the corner table. The *Life* magazine they'd all been looking through a few days before sat face-up on top of the stack. Rose went to it, reached down and flipped through the pages at arm's length until she saw the photo she kept thinking about: The Duchess of Windsor, standing next to her new husband, stared directly up at Rose. Here was a woman who shaped her *own* destiny, even when it involved a sitting monarch. Here was a woman of the future.

Rose closed the magazine and looked down at the limp and finger-smudged cover. She glanced at the doorway, rolled the magazine into a tube, and slipped it into her cardigan.

THAT EVENING THE boys were both in the backyard whacking at toadstools with a golf club when Dr. Wilkins checked in on his way home. Rose had to go out and shoo them both inside. They bounded up the back steps, a patina of healthy sweat on their faces, to gape at the kitchen table while the doctor shone a tiny light into their mouths.

And then he was gone, without even touching the cup of coffee Rose had poured for him.

He'd check in one last time in the morning when he went in for his half-day at the office, he had promised. But both boys seemed fine now, he thought. Ready for school on Monday.

LATE THAT NIGHT Rose lay sleeplessly on her bed, staring up at the canopy. Her mind was a wakeful jumble of ideas, a tangled junk drawer of sharp odds and ends. For a while she thought of Frankie, who was already back to his usual rambunctious self. (After dinner she'd caught him at the bathroom sink brushing his newly sprouted armpit hair with Alvie's toothbrush.) How could she tell a boy who was so juvenile himself that he'd have no children of his own? He was thirteen years old; what would the news even mean to him? How could he possibly understand without either blithely shrugging it off or blowing it all out of proportion? It was just too early to tell him. She'd have to wait until he was old enough to really take it in. Face it: this was the sort of thing a father should sit his son down to talk about in that direct and hard-edged way men spoke.

She rolled on her other side and looked at the alarm clock. It was a few minutes after two. There on the bedside table lay the stolen issue of *Life*. For a few seconds, Rose considered switching on the bedside lamp and flipping through it yet another time—but what would it reveal to her at this hour that she hadn't already gleaned from it all the other times she'd leafed through?

She rolled on her back again and imagined the photograph of the Duke and Duchess. Though she knew the photo in the magazine was black and white, she seemed, curiously, to recall it now in color—the emerald English grass underfoot, the tawny castle wall behind them, the royal blue cravat knotted beneath the former monarch's chin. It was as though she'd been there herself and was remembering how it had looked at that moment, the wind astir in everyone's hair.

SATURDAY MORNING ROSE was watching from the front window when Dr. Wilkin's roadster finally pulled up at the curb in front of the house, facing the wrong direction. The door opened, and the doctor, wearing a gray sport coat and yellow tie, stepped out. He turned and ducked his head into the car again and straightened up with his black leather satchel in hand.

Rose stepped into the hallway, so she wouldn't be seen gawking out the window. When the knock came, she counted to ten in her head before she pulled the door open.

"THEY BOTH LOOK fine," Dr. Wilkins told her in the kitchen after he'd scrubbed his hands at the sink. "One hundred percent, I'd say." Was it her imagination, or had his voice struck a minor chord of reluctance? "I don't see any reason to come by here again." He glanced at Rose then. Regretting, perhaps, that he'd have to stop these daily visits.

Looking at the doctor's mild and handsome face, Rose formed the words in her mind: Do you *need* a reason?

She stood there, heart racing, drinking in the doctor's every ungainly gesture. She pulled back her shoulders, stood taller. She willed herself powerful and womanly—a duchess who could, this moment, grasp her own destiny in a clenched fist. Rose could feel the texture of the words on her tongue, like bitter grape seeds: *Do you need a reason to visit?* She'd either have to spit them out this moment or swallow them down.

But the doctor had already turned toward the kitchen door; and now Rose was following him to the entryway, her ears roaring; and he was opening the door; and he was saying something; and he was pressing his hat on his silvering hair. And now Rose was holding the door's edge, watching the doctor walk across the lawn to his waiting roadster; and she was watching the car pull away from the curb; and now it was heading down Grove Street toward some remote and marvelous world of love and warmth and human fellowship, which Rose would never visit.

CHAPTER FOUR
AN ACCIDENTAL GATHERING OF MEN
1938

THE LAST SATURDAY MORNING in October, Alvie looked out from the Palace Theater projection room, his cheek warmed by the great lens of the projector. The Oswald Rabbit cartoon was running to a half-full house—a rabble of kids, mostly boys. The cartoon ended with a big musical number, and Alvie flipped the projectors to the Universal Newsreel, though he never saw the point of screening it for the Saturday matinee crowd. The kids in attendance only used it as an opportunity to administer Indian burns and launch Milk Duds at the girls in the front rows.

While he rewound the cartoon, Alvie glanced out at the clips of Hitler and Roosevelt, the scene of Eleanor visiting a hospital, the segment about a yoga master. Alvie put the cartoon in its can and put it up on the rack. He took down the first reel of *Flash Gordon's Trip to Mars*. The serial was Alvie's favorite part of his Saturday morning job. He loved the convoluted plots and cliffhanger endings—Dr. Zarkov's ship plummeting through the nitron beam or Flash Gordon in the disintegration room with Ming the Merciless poised to throw the switch. Alvie loaded the projector and then watched the tail end of the newsreel for the blip at the top right corner of the screen. When it flashed, Alvie flipped projectors.

Alvie had started at The Palace as an usher when school let out for summer—and he still ushered three nights a week now that his junior year classes had started up at Richland High. But when Ronnie Edwards went off to USC in the fall, Mr. Suggs chose Alvie to replace him as the Saturday matinee projectionist. The Palace didn't pay much, but it felt good to bring a paycheck home to his mother since money was so tight, and Alvie loved that he got to see the movies free.

Alvie had just racked the newsreel, when he heard a gentle tapping at the projection room door. Hardly anyone worked in The Palace on Saturday mornings—just a couple of junior ushers and Mrs. Goldmacher out front. None of them would leave their posts. When Alvie pulled the door open, he took a step backwards.

There, at the top of the narrow staircase, stood Sandra Celey, the midweek ticket girl. Alvie's thoughts scattered like pigeons from a pit bull.

Instead of the maroon box-office uniform Alvie was used to seeing her in, today Sandra wore a plaid skirt and a short-sleeved white blouse embroidered with ivory stitching. She clutched a patent leather pocketbook in front of her with both hands and offered a shy smile.

Alvie had been lovesick over Sandra since his first week as usher. He'd pumped the other ushers for information about her. She was a sophomore at Immaculate Heart. Her family lived on the Plaza Circle above her father's barbershop. She was sometimes seen at Watson's soda counter with Bridget McClusky or in the listening booths at the High Street Music Shop. She had two older sisters, both homely, who worked the notions counter at Nortons.

On the nights Alvie ushered, Sandra sat in the brightly lit ticket booth in the center of the Palace's grand front entrance.

From the front corner of the lobby, Alvie could see her, in profile, as she tore tickets and counted change. Watching her work, he sometimes wondered how any man could stand in her line, watch her lips speak through the circle cut in the glass, take the ticket from her tapered fingers, and enter The Palace without his knees buckling. And here she was, on a Saturday morning, standing, unaccountably, in front of him.

"Come in," Alvie managed to say. "What can I do for you?" As Sandra slipped past him, Alvie smelled Lux soap and Doublemint gum. He had never been this close to her.

"I've always wanted to see in here," she said. "But not with *Hap* around."

Alvie nodded; Hap Hanson, the Palace's evening projectionist, was unsuitable company for a girl from Immaculate Heart. He had the chiseled looks of a Nordic skier sent over from central casting and a knack for maneuvering girls against the wall and chatting them up, one arm propped beside their heads. It seemed like every week some new blonde entered the lobby, ticket in hand. She'd loiter there, checking her reflection in the glass poster cases, until Mr. Suggs' back was turned—and then she'd slip down the back hallway to the projection room stairs.

Sandra looked around the room, then went over to the folding table, where Hap's *True Detective* magazines and his deck of Bicycle playing cards lay where he had abandoned them last night. Sandra put a hand on the back of one of the steel folding chairs. "Okay if I sit?" she asked. "Just to watch how it's done?"

Alvie found himself unable to speak, so he nodded, with enthusiasm.

Sandra sat and then leaned forward on the table, hugging her pocket book. The tiny gold cross she wore on a serpentine chain slipped from her blouse and dangled over the tabletop.

Alvie swallowed and turned to the clattering Bell and Howell projector. "This is the projector," he announced—like an idiot—and immediately wanted to bang his head on its steel housing.

But Sandra studied the massive machine with an expression of rapt fascination—as though it had never occurred to her that she might find a projector in the projection room.

"And here's the other one," Alvie heard himself say. He couldn't help but wince.

It occurred to him that he had yet to load the second *Flash Gordon* reel, and he was relieved that he actually had something to do. His fingers were clumsy and seemed drained of blood, but he managed to thread the film through the projector's sprockets, feeling Sandra's eyes on his back like a sunburn. When he was done, he went to the porthole and looked out gravely, as if checking for something important. On the screen, Ming the Merciless monitored Flash Gordon's movements on his Televisor. Alvie took a deep breath, wiggled his fingers to get the blood flowing again, and then turned back to Sandra. She sat smiling at him. He could do this, he told himself. He could talk to her. He just needed to relax.

Except for Dawn Clancy, Alvie's hatchet-faced lab partner in biology, he rarely spoke to the girls at school. They were enigmas in their buttoned wrap skirts and their middy slacks. And those shoulder pads that were suddenly in style only made them that much more frightening. If a girl so much as asked Alvie a harmless question—*Are you in line? Is this seat taken?*—it emptied his head of thoughts and made him itchy.

Alvie went over and sat in the folding chair across the table from Sandra. Her gold chain was draped over her collarbone now, and the sight of it stirred in Alvie a confusing mix of desire and reverence. He opened and closed his hands under the table. How had they become so sweaty? He squeezed his knees with both hands. He needed to loosen up, he knew. He took another breath and for some reason thought of Erroll Flynn—his sly Robin Hood smile, his Captain Blood swagger.

"I wish they let girls be ushers," Sandra was saying. "It must be fun."

"But *you* get to sit on a stool," Alvie told her, in what he hoped might be a swashbuckling tone. "I'm on my feet all night."

"But *you* get to see all the movies," Sandra said. "I never do." Her face was wonderfully animated, her voice playfully contentious. "And everyone talks about them on the way out," she went on. "So they're ruined if I ever *do* get to see them."

Alvie smiled. "But *you* get to see all the money," he said. "Ushers never do."

Sandra giggled, and the chime of her laughter filled Alvie with an unexpected swell of buoyancy. Sandra seemed to bubble over with words then. She told him about how she hunted for Canadian coins in the till and how she always arranged the bills so the presidents were looking up at her. She told him about the man who gave her a five and then went to Mr. Sugg's claiming she'd short-changed him on a ten.

As she spoke, Alvie let his eyes fall to the lovely hollow at the base of her throat. He took in her plump unpierced earlobes. He studied the pearly threadwork on her blouse's collar. But even while he was sitting so close, some part of Alvie felt detached—like he was watching the scene from the back of the house. He was surprised to find himself so miscast as leading man—and even more astonished by how well he seemed to be playing the role.

"You don't work Monday night, do you?" Sandra asked him.

Alvie thought he caught a quickened glint in her eye. "No," he said, a little on guard now. "I work the same nights as you."

Sandra let go of her pocket book and lined her fingers up on the table's edge, as though about to run through some piano scales. "So," she said, "are you going to the dance?"

Alvie's breath caught. "Dance?" he said. He coughed into his fist suddenly and for no reason.

"The Halloween Cotillion," Sandra said, still looking down at her fingers. "At the Bon Tom Ballroom."

"No," Alvie said. "I mean yes. I mean—could I take you?" He had flubbed his lines, but it had come out okay.

Sandra looked up at Alvie then and sagged a little in her chair, as if she'd been holding her breath. "Of course you can take me," she told him. "Pick me up at six? On the Circle by the barber shop?"

Alvie nodded and was trying to formulate a fitting response when it dawned on him that he was hearing a rising chorus of jeers and catcalls. And then came the *thwack, thwack, thwack* of the loose end of film slapping the projector housing as the played-out first reel spun.

Alvie leapt up and darted to the porthole. The Palace's great screen showed a vast rectangle of blinding light, and the kids below, stomping and hammering their armrests, started up some kind of feral chant. Alvie clumsily flipped the projectors and fired up the second reel of the serial, but when he turned back, feeling like an idiot, Sandra had already slipped out the door.

AFTER WORK, ALVIE loitered around the lobby a few minutes, just in case Sandra was still around, and then he strolled down Glass Street to Benny's for a grilled cheese sandwich to go. The sun had burned off the morning haze, but the air was autumn crisp. As he walked, he felt poised and happy—nearly euphoric. He held his head high and felt, every inch, a matinee idol.

The brunette girl was working the counter at Benny's—the pretty one with the mole above one eyebrow, who clattered her nails on the counter when the register gave her trouble. She was much too old for Alvie—twenty-two if she was a day—still, any time Alvie was required to speak to her, his tongue swelled in his mouth like a dampened sponge. But today was different. Alvie chose the stool nearest her cash register. He smiled easily and looked her in the eye when he gave her his order. He even found himself shooting the breeze while they waited on the cook. He made a joke about the new menus as she wrapped his sandwich in wax paper. When he paid, he left the fifteen cents of change on the counter and, with a debonair nod, told her she should keep it.

To his utter astonishment, the girl gave him a sly wink.

Alvie stood blinking at her a few blank, brainless seconds—and then she said, "Thanks, Frankie. You're a sweetheart."

Alvie blushed and beat it for the door.

When he got to the corner, he slowed his pace and caught his breath. *Frankie?* How did she even know who Frankie was?

Just like that, his mood had changed. The heady soap bubble of confidence he'd felt after Sandra's surprise visit was burst with a single word: *Frankie.* Alvie fell into a shuffling gait, eyes on the pavement.

The number 16 bus would get him home in five minutes, but Alvie decided to walk. He wanted time to think. He walked past Sears and the Heritage House, taking bites of his sandwich, which seemed flavorless as newsprint. When he reached the bowling alley he'd finished only half of it, and he had no appetite for the rest. He folded it in the wax paper and dropped it in a wastepaper bin.

He stopped at the corner of Olive Street, where a few strangers stood waiting for the light to change. Two men discussed some new golf course out by the marine base. A third man joined them at the curb's edge and tugged down the sleeves of his overcoat. A delivery boy, maybe twenty, coasted up on a bicycle and leaned at the curb balancing with one foot. A package wrapped in brown paper and tied up with twine rode in the steel rack between his handlebars.

There all of them waited, an accidental gathering of men, with Alvie standing at their back. They were, Alvie felt sure, like the men in movies. They spoke their minds and followed their hearts. These were men who could lean close and kiss without asking permission.

The light changed, and the four strangers crossed, but Alvie stayed rooted where he stood and watched them move away.

Before they reached the far curb, he turned away and found his reflection in window of the shoe repair shop on the corner. The harsh noon sunlight made him hollow eyed. His slope-shouldered posture gave him a shapeless, tentative look—like something not yet fully formed. Alvie pulled his hands from his pockets and stood straighter. He drew his shoulders back and tilted his face up to the sun a little—and, just like that, he was Frankie.

HIS MOTHER SAT at the kitchen table, peeling a sack of Granny Smith apples with a paring knife. She hadn't heard Alvie come in, and he paused, unseen, in the kitchen doorway. Rose's elbows rested on the tabletop, and her hands worked with mindless efficiency. She seemed off in some distant realm. Alvie watched the apple turn in her hands, dangling a coil of green skin.

"I'm home," Alvie said from the doorway.

At the sound of his voice, Rose started. She looked at him one befuddled beat, and then quickly recast her face so it was a picture of joyful astonishment. "*There* you are," she said, as though she had spent the morning ransacking the house for him. "How was work?"

Alvie smiled back at her. "It was good," Alvie told her. "The usual swarm of brats." His fingers were still greasy from the grilled cheese, so he went to the sink to wash up. He studied his hands under the running water. They seemed small, as if they didn't belong to him. Behind him, his mother began humming "Has Anybody Seen My Gal?—as if she felt pressed to furnish evidence of the great pleasure she derived from being a mother. Alvie soaped his hands.

In the last couple of years this house had grown impossibly small—like the walls were creeping in. Alvie knew it wasn't the house, of course; it was the three of them. There just wasn't enough room for two grown boys and their mother. Knees bumped under the kitchen table. Alvie and Frankie had to slide sideways to pass each other in the cramped hallway. The boys' belongings, collected over the years in their bedroom, sometimes seemed poised to avalanche on them at the slightest peep.

And there was no privacy. Even the latch on the bathroom door had been broken the better part of a year. When all of them were home at night, the stale closeness could make Alvie claustrophobic, and he would have to slip out to the front porch to sit on the steps and breathe.

To be fair, Frankie didn't spend a lot of time at home since school started up. Weekends, he'd usually stay out past midnight, prowling who-knew-what unsavory corner of town. And then he'd come home smelling of Swisher cigars and Old Crow, and he'd clamber into the upper bunk without a word to Alvie. In the morning, at breakfast, he'd spin some elaborate yarn for their mother—he'd been riding with Billy Odin when his pickup threw a rod or he'd found the Stallards' German shepherd out by the gasworks and had to chase it down. And Rose, with what seemed a Herculean gullibility, would take Frankie at his word.

And then there was Rose, herself. As her sons branched out into the world, she seemed to shrink closer and closer to home. She no longer picked up double shifts at the packinghouse and now drove straight home each night from work. Those gabby, gossipy phone calls she used to get after dinner dwindled over the years and gradually stopped. These days she seemed to want her boys home as much as possible, making Alvie feel guilty about his three nights of ushering— even though *she* was the one who encouraged him to find a summer job. She seemed to expect Alvie to do his homework at the kitchen table, so he'd be in the same room with her as she made dinner. When she went grocery shopping these days, she'd want Alvie to come along—as if even navigating the aisles at Chaffee's was too much for her to tackle on her own.

And then there was Baby Doris, if she even existed. In the bright light of day, Alvie felt like a fool that he had ever convinced himself she was haunting the house. But at night her presence seemed palpable in the groan of a floorboard or the sudden scent of blueberries. Nickels appeared on the nightstand when he woke in the morning. Cancelled postage stamps dropped from his book bag when he pulled out his reader. He once found a stick figure, sketched with a dainty finger, in windowsill dust. Really, who could say how many souls crowded this house?

Alvie dried his hands on a dishtowel. "I think I'm going out tonight," he ventured. He turned to check his mother's reaction.

Rose pouted her lips in what seemed an attempt at girlish disappointment, but it only served to accentuate the vertical lines that were deepening around her mouth. She plucked another apple from the brown paper bag on the table.

"I was thinking I'd go back to The Palace for the feature," Alvie said, leaning back against the sink. "See what it's like sitting down."

"You've seen that movie every night this week," Rose told him, her tone a little scolding.

Alvie crossed his arms. "I've seen it *three* times," he said. "Don't exaggerate." Was it just Alvie, or had the two of them taken to bickering like an old married couple on some radio comedy?

"*Still*," Rose said, but if she had a point to make, she let it go unsaid.

"It's a good one," Alvie told her. "I want to really pay attention to it for once."

To be honest, this week's feature wasn't even close to being good. It was some brainless romance, where Judy Garland kidnaps her widowed mother in an Airstream trailer, to keep her from marrying the wrong man.

Rose paused in her work. She looked wistfully behind Alvie at the kitchen window. She'd been doing that a lot lately: staring off at some invisible horizon, as if trying to get her bearings in some new landscape. "Would *I* like it?" she asked.

Alvie flinched. "The movie?" he said.

Rose turned her gaze on him. "Yeah," she said. "Maybe I could come along."

Alvie turned back to the sink and washed his hands a second time, trying to think of a reason to keep Rose at home. He stared out the window at the blisters of paint on Mrs. Brenner's drainpipe. "It's about mobsters," he said finally. His mother couldn't abide gangster movies.

"I thought it was called *Listen, Darling*," Rose said.

Alvie regarded his dim reflection in the window as he spoke. "The *gangster's* name is Darling," he said, making the lie up as he spoke it. "Blackie Darling. Boss of the Chicago mob." He shut off the faucet and dried his hands on the same dishtowel. When he finally turned to look at Rose, she had already started into peeling another apple.

ALVIE FIDGETED IN the back row of The Palace through the newsreel and the Robert Benchley short. He endured the first reel of *Listen, Darling*, and when the blip finally flashed, and the feature started into its second reel, he slipped back to the lobby and down the back hallway, past Mr. Suggs' office. He climbed the narrow staircase and rapped on the projection room door.

Hap, when he opened the door, seemed let down to find Alvie there. He mustered a half-hearted smile. "Boy Scout," he said. "What are you doing here on a Saturday night?"

"SANDRA *CELEY*," Alvie told Frankie a third time.

"Don't know her."

The two boys had finished cutting the front and back lawns for Rose, taking turns with the push mower. All that was left was to rake up the trimmings and wash up for Sunday dinner. They sat on the porch steps glowing with sweat, drained lemonade glasses on the steps beside them. The scent of Rose's meatloaf wafted out from the kitchen.

"She lives right on The Circle," Alvie said. "You know the girl I mean."

"That fat one who sings the National Anthem at assemblies?"

"That's Cindy *Sutton*," Alvie told him. "Sandra doesn't go to our school. And she isn't fat."

Frankie shrugged. "If she doesn't go to Richland, I sure as hell don't know her." He picked up his glass, tilted it up and shook an ice cube into his mouth.

"You *know* her," Alvie said. "She's the barber's daughter. She's the weeknight ticket girl."

Frankie crunched the ice and squinted out at the street, and then he suddenly turned to look at Alvie. He swallowed the ice. "Wait," Frankie said. "The girl in the booth? The one who sells the tickets?"

"*Yeah*," Alvie said. "*Her.*" Alvie leaned back on the porch steps and watched the look of stupefaction on his brother's face.

"Black hair?" Frankie said. "Funny little pillbox hat?"

Alvie grinned. "Yeah," Alvie said. "*Her.*"

Frankie stared at him a long moment, then he picked up his glass again and shook the remaining ice. "You sure?"

"What do you mean, am I sure?" Alvie said. "Am I sure of what?"

"That *she* asked *you* to take her to a dance."

Normally Frankie's emphasis on the words *she* and *you*, would have felt insulting, but the plain look of envy on Frankie's face took away the sting.

"And *she* made the first move," Alvie said, doing his best to rub it in.

Frankie frowned down at his lemonade glass and shook it. He seemed to be having trouble comprehending the situation in some fundamental way. He shook his head, as if to clear it, and then looked up at Alvie. "How are you getting her to the dance?" Frankie asked. "Please tell me you're not taking the bus."

Alvie's grinned. This would be the kicker. "Hap Hanson's roadster," he said. He watched Frankie's befuddled face as the news sank in.

"That black convertible?" Frankie said. "The Delux? Not possible. He gets lathered if anyone even *looks* at it."

"I promised to fill in for him a couple of nights next month, so he can go to Yosemite," Alvie said. "He's leaving the key on top of the tire. I just have to have it back before he gets off work."

Frankie tilted his head to one side and gave Alvie a long appraising look, like he was sizing up a new rival. He shook his head disgustedly and held his glass over the porch rail to spill the last ice cubes into the rosemary bush. He stood and gazed out at the street. "Wars are breaking out all over," he mused. "We're in the middle of a goddamn depression. Society is crumbling around us. And *you've* got a date with the ticket girl." He took his empty glass and went to the front door.

ALVIE SWITCHED ON a couple of lamps in the parlor while his mother cleared away the dishes. Frankie was sitting cross-legged on the oval braided rug in front of the cathedral radio waiting for the set to warm up. When Rose came in from the kitchen, she perched on the opposite end of the settee from Alvie. She had started a new jigsaw—a photo of a snow-blanketed Vermont village—and it was spread out on the coffee table. The white church spire floated inside the puzzle's frame like an island. She bent over the coffee table, puzzle lid in hand, hunting among the strewn, knobby pieces.

At the first squeal of a radio signal, Frankie leaned forward and twisted the dial, looking for a station. He found *The Charlie McCarthy Show*, and leaned back, propped on both arms to listen. Frankie wasn't a big Edgar Bergen fan—*A ventriloquist on the radio? What the hell is the point?*—so Alvie knew he'd drift away from the show before long. Like every other aspect of his life, Frankie never saw anything through to the end. It was all shortcuts and whims.

While Frankie listened and Rose pressed puzzle pieces into place, Alvie thought about tomorrow's date with Sandra. From his post at the back of The Palace he'd learned how to light a woman's cigarette; how to pour champagne with a twist of the bottle; how to take off his jacket and sling it rakishly over his shoulder, hooked on a finger. Perhaps he was actually better suited for the world of the Bon Tom Ballroom than for the locker-lined halls of Richland High.

Frankie snorted at some Charlie McCarthy quip on the radio, but Alvie hadn't been paying attention. The orchestra started up, and Nelson Eddy began crooning "The Song of the Vagabonds."

> *Come all you Beggars of Paris town,*
> *You lousy rabble of low degree…*

Frankie made a sour face and reached for the dial. With a few twists, he found a station playing yet another big band rendition of "Stardust," so he lay back on the rug with his hands behind his head.

They were sure to play "Stardust" at the dance, Alvie guessed. He seemed to hear that tune every time he passed an open window. He closed his eyes and felt his hand on Sandra's trim waist, her heart beating so near his own.

"*Shhhh*," Rose hissed suddenly. Alvie looked over at her. She sat straight-backed on the sofa, staring straight ahead. Alvie followed her gaze to the radio. The music had stopped without Alvie having realized, and they were now listening to some sort of news broadcast: something about disturbances on the planet Mars and a crater in rural New Jersey.

After a few seconds, the music was interrupted again: a remote broadcast from a farm somewhere called Grover's Mill. A crowd had gathered to see a vessel that had fallen from the sky. The radio signal was crowded with shouting voices and shrieking sirens.

"It's a joke," Frankie said. "It's got to be a joke."

Alvie looked at Rose. She was fretfully pleating the Afghan in her lap and frowning at the front window. The announcer interrupted again.

"Listen!" Frankie said. "That's Orson Welles, isn't it?" He jabbed a finger at the radio's fabric-covered speaker. "You hear that voice? It's him."

"Just shush a minute," Rose said. Her face had taken on a grim and resolute cast—a tightening at the edges of her mouth, a subtle crease between the eyebrows.

Now, according to the radio announcer, the New Jersey countryside was littered with smoldering corpses, and the military had been called in. Alvie's scalp tightened. There was no need for panic, the radio announcer assured them. But now the Secretary of the Interior cut in. Meteorites were raining down all across the country.

Alvie stood and crossed wordlessly to the front window. He tugged the curtain aside and looked out on the dark street. The only light was the waxing quarter moon, tangled like a kite in the leafless sycamores. "Maybe we should turn off the lights," he said.

"What?" Frankie said. "Are you serious?"

Alvie turned away from the window and found Rose staring blankly back at him with a stunned and ashen face. "So it looks like no one's home," Alvie explained to her.

Frankie snorted a laugh, but Rose nodded gravely. She reached over and turned off the lamp on the end table, so Alvie went to the floor lamp and tugged the chain. He went over to check the dead bolt on the front door and then switched off the hall light as well. When he got back to the parlor, it was lit eerily by the amber glow of the radio dial. Alvie floated over to the settee and sat numbly.

More reports poured in from around the country. More explosions were spotted on Mars. And now the radio links dropped off one by one.

The headlights of a passing car swept across the front curtains, and Alvie felt Rose flinch beside him. Frankie sat on the rug, backlit by the glow of the radio dial, watching him with an amused and steely smile.

Alvie wanted to stampede through the house, barricading windows with bookcases and box springs. But Frankie's smile pinned him where he sat. His heart beating wildly, he thought of Sandra Celey—would he ever see that lovely face again?

And then the program went into intermission. Frankie had been right, of course. It was just some Mercury Theater show, not even some kind of hoax. It should have been obvious. But it had *sounded* so real.

Rose sheepishly switched the table lamp back on. In its sudden light, Alvie's great rush of relief turned to mortification when he saw Frankie grinning in his direction.

WHEN THE MANTLE clock in the parlor chimed midnight, Alvie still lay wide-eyed on his bottom bunk. A train whistle sounded over by the switchyard, and the sound of it set a couple of dogs to barking. Frankie was snoring and muttering on the upper bunk, but at least he was asleep. He'd been taunting Alvie all night. When Mr. Granger pulled into his driveway across the street, fan belt squealing, Frankie had flown into a mock panic. "Oh my god!" he'd shrieked at Alvie. "They're here! We're all going to die!"

"Fuck you," Alvie had said, but not loud enough for Frankie to hear.

Now, with Frankie asleep, Alvie rolled on his side and pressed his forehead to the wall. Frankie would mock him for weeks—that much was certain—and Alvie deserved it. But what truly bothered Alvie was that he *had* believed—*really* believed—and he hadn't *acted*. He'd wanted to arm himself with kitchen knives and to nail boards over the windows. He wanted to call the neighbors to organize some kind of militia. But, instead, he'd let Frankie pin him to the sofa with nothing but a look. What kind of man would he ever be?

IN THE FRONT hall the next morning, Alvie cracked the door open to look outside. He'd just wanted to check the weather to see if he should bring a jacket, but Frankie was there behind him looking over his shoulder. "Is it safe?" Frankie asked.

It didn't matter that hundreds of people all over the country had believed the broadcast. It made no difference that *The Ledger* had run a front-page story about the local panic. All that mattered was that he had made a mistake. That's all Frankie ever needed.

Alvie took off walking fast while Frankie was locking the front door. Frankie jogged after him.

"They could be anywhere," Frankie said when he'd caught up. "We should travel in pairs."

They passed a broad sycamore trunk, and Alvie wanted nothing more than to shove Frankie's face into it. "I'm not the only one who thought it was real," Alvie told him.

"Yeah, the world is full of scrubs," Frankie observed. He gestured around at all the bungalows that looked out on Grove Street. "That's why this is the right planet for you."

"Well," Alvie said, "when you're home tonight, listening to the radio and being oh so smart—I'll be at the Bon Tom with Sandra Celey. So you can bite me."

The words seemed to have the effect Alvie had hoped for. Frankie walked beside him finally silenced, he looked ahead down the sidewalk then spat in the direction of an old Model A parked at the curb. "Yeah," Frankie said finally, "you've got the girl, but you won't have any idea what to do with her. You won't even get to first base."

"Fuck you," Alvie said. "She's not like the girls you know. She's not some counter waitress."

Frankie looked at him. He seemed astonished and bemused by Alvie's words. "Counter waitress?" he said.

Alvie stopped walking and turned to face his brother. He opened and closed his fists. "Sandra is a nice girl," he said. "She goes to Sacred Heart."

Frankie snorted a lusty, knowing laugh. "Yeah," he said. "Those catholic girls don't let you do anything."

Alvie swung hard but Frankie stepped back, and he managed only a glancing blow, up around Frankie's shoulder—the graze of a collarbone in the groove between two knuckles. Frankie took another step back to keep his balance and then regarded Alvie with cool, detached reckoning.

Alvie raised both his fists, bracing for Frankie's reprisal. He was beyond the point of caring. What did a black eye or a split lip or even a broken nose matter? He only wanted to land a single hard punch—just to hurt Frankie this once. He'd take a beating if he could only inflict a bruise, and he stood his ground, waiting for Frankie to come at him.

Frankie didn't speak. He nodded slightly— as if he were trying to commit the moment to memory—and then he tugged down the hem of his shirt. He turned and strode, rolling his shoulders, towards the corner where the bus was now waiting at the curb.

ALVIE DIDN'T EXACTLY *avoid* Frankie at school that day, but he kept his head down—he ate his lunch in the side yard, where the Mexican kids tended to congregate, and he didn't go to his locker, since it was right above Frankie's. He walked the long way to English class, past the home-ec kitchens, and made it to the final bell without any kind of public showdown with his brother.

Frankie missed the afternoon bus home, which was not unusual, so Alvie sat alone near the front, looking out the window. He'd been steeling himself all day for a confrontation, and now he felt let down that it hadn't arrived. He had to remind himself about Sandra and how happy he should be feeling.

At home, Alvie couldn't find his suit in the cluttered closet he shared with Frankie. He looked in the hall closet and then the wardrobe in his mother's room, but he couldn't find it anywhere. He stood in front of his closet again, taking stock of the clothes available. He finally pulled a v-necked tennis sweater over his white shirt and knotted up the striped tie Rose had bought him for the county spelling bee. In Rose's dresser mirror, he tugged the wrinkles from the sweater and scrutinized himself. It wasn't Cary Grant, or even Tyrone Power, but it would have to do.

A little after four, he slipped down the front steps, and made his way on foot to the florist on Petrie Street. He picked out an affordable bunch of daisies and slid his coins one by one across the moist counter. In that dark and perfumed moment his mood began to brighten.

He wasn't even thinking about Frankie by the time he got to the parking lot behind the South Street shops, a comfortable twenty minutes ahead of schedule. He walked each row of cars twice—but Hap's black Ford wasn't where he usually parked it. Alvie strode briskly, careful not to work up a sweat, the two blocks to The Palace.

Old Mrs. Goldmacher was working the ticket booth, and Alvie nodded to her as he passed. He slipped through the lobby, down the hall, and back to the stairs. He knocked on the projection room door, and, when there was no answer, he rapped again, louder.

Hap pulled the door open a scant foot, releasing a cloud of cigarette smoke. He leaned out, holding the door firmly against his back. The collar of his shirt was twisted. Was there a hint of lavender among all that smoke?

"You look pretty good, kid," Hap said grinning. "Don't forget to fill her up." His voice dropped in volume. "And be back on time; I'm going to need her." Hap ducked back inside, but Alvie slapped the door with his free hand.

"Wait," he said. "*Wait.*"

Hap leaned out again, a little less genial.

"*Where's* the car?" Alvie asked.

"Parking lot," Hap said impatiently. "Where it always is."

"I didn't see it," Alvie told him.

"Look. Again," Hap said and shut the door in Alvie's face.

ALVIE PACED THE parking lot again in the mellow afternoon light, panic beginning to grip him. Every spot was occupied. In fact, two women in a black Dodge crept along the rows behind Alvie, hoping to take his space.

Alvie headed down the side streets inspecting the cars parked along the curb. At one point he thought he'd found it, and he was feeling around under the fender for the key when he realized the car wasn't even a Ford, it was a Studebaker. Before long, he was jogging the streets in ever-widening circles, constantly checking his watch as the minute hand crept towards twelve.

At a few minutes before six, Alvie abandoned the search and headed over to the Plaza. He'd explain the whole thing to Sandra, and the two of them could look for Hap's car together. Who knew? If they ended up a couple, it would be the story they'd tell about their first date. *It was all the way over by the depot! It took us hours to find it!*

But when Alvie got to the Plaza Circle a little out of breath, he stopped dead at the corner. Hap's car was parked at the curb in front of the barbershop. It made no sense, but he felt buoyed by a surge of relief.

Alvie stood waiting for a break in traffic so he could cut across the circle's park to Sandra's. He glanced at his watch. He'd be there almost to the minute—a little sweaty, admittedly, but right on time. There was a break in the circling traffic, but the moment Alvie stepped down into the street, Hap's car pulled away from the curb.

Alvie stood bewildered as the roadster arched around the circle toward where he stood on the road's edge. He shielded his eyes from the slant of sunlight and squinted at the windshield. It was definitely Hap's car—it had the Four Aces label on the corner of the windshield.

As the roadster approached, he held the bunch of daisies aloft, like he might be hailing a taxi. But then the car pulled even, and he saw its two passengers: *himself*, dressed in his gray suit, and Sandra, looking nervous and expectant. Neither pivoted to catch Alvie, stranded a few feet from the curb, holding up his flowery torch.

The roadster sped past, listing a little from the turn, and then veered down Reasner Avenue and out of sight.

FOR THE NEXT four hours, as night came on and the stars came out, Alvie paced the Plaza park, kicking at benches, slamming his fist into the trunks of palm trees. He peeled the tennis sweater off over his head, loosened his tie, and rolled up his sleeves. He twice splashed his face with murky water from the fountain pond, where the flotsam of daisies now bobbed.

After ten o'clock, each pair of headlights that raked across the Plaza had him racing to the edge of the park to investigate. When Hap's car finally appeared, pulling up outside the barbershop, Alvie sprinted at it, in a blind fury.

Sandra Celey got out of the car sobbing. She left the car door swinging wide and rushed through the door next to the barber shop and up the stairs, clutching her cardigan around her shoulders.

Alvie sprinted towards the car, his brother's pale face framed, wide-eyed, in its side window. Frankie gunned the engine and tried to wrench it into gear, but Alvie headed him off before he could release the clutch. Alvie stood, arms spread wide, sputtering senseless profanities. He blinked into the blinding headlamps. He wanted to dive between them and tackle the whole car by the grille.

For a few long seconds the Ford's engine gunned. And then the car lurched forward and swerved away—but not far enough. Alvie dodged sideways, but the open passenger door swung wide. The blow sucked the air from his chest and flattened him against the road. The shock of it was so great he didn't even feel the rear wheel when it rolled across his ankle.

Alvie lay on his back, emptied of thought. Propped on one elbow, he watched the car's red taillights sweep around the corner. He lay his head back on the road and looked up at the stars. He could feel his heartbeat inside his skull. When he managed to breathe, he tried to push himself to his feet, but something crumpled under him.

Alvie looked down and saw—as if on a distant screen—his own left foot slanting at a squeamish angle. He lay back down and rolled onto his stomach, his cheek against the gritty asphalt, and squeezed his eyes shut. On some level he understood—in that brief lull before pain rang him like a fire alarm—that his life's first reel had just spooled out.

CHAPTER FIVE
RIGHT HAND RIFFS
1945

FRANKIE GRIPPED the handrail and looked out the window as his train shuddered to a stop. A few knots of people waited on the platform, some with luggage at their feet. None were people he knew. The train's doors hissed open, and Frankie stepped down into Richland for the first time in nearly two years. His field uniform had him prickling with heat, so he set his duffle in the shade of the station's broad shingled awning and pulled off his jacket. He'd sweated through his shirt, and the breeze stirred up by the train as it pulled away from the platform gave him a welcome chill. He shook the last cigarette from a pack of Lucky Strikes, lit it, and looked around the station platform. He didn't recognize the young guy who was manning the newsstand—old Joey Bumps must have retired—and he didn't know the black kid over at the shoeshine stand. A bus rumbled to life on the far side of the station, and pulled away.

Frankie actually *heard* Alvie before he saw him—that clumping sound he made trudging across the platform boards, dragging and dropping his bad foot. Frankie turned towards the sound, and there was Rose, brandishing a hankie and blazing her smiling, tearful way towards him, arms already spread to pull him into a hug. Alvie hobbled a few yards behind her. A young woman clung to his arm and seemed to be whispering instructions as they made their halting way.

Frankie dropped his barely lit cigarette and ground it out with his toe. He held his arms out and Rose plowed into him. While they hugged, Frankie looked over Rose's plump shoulder at Alvie and the young woman on his arm. They were still making their slow approach. The girl wore a gray skirt and white blouse with a light blue collar. She seemed to be talking intently to Alvie, as if coaching him how to use his legs. Was she some kind of nurse? She was a shade or two short of attractive, Frankie thought. Her eyebrows were set a little too high, which gave her an imperious look, and her brown hair was tied back in a ponytail so severe it made her look quarrelsome. Her figure, on the other hand, was as lean and lithe as a Rita Hayworth pinup.

While Rose still clung to Frankie's neck, Alvie came and stood listlessly behind her, as if waiting his turn for something necessary but unpleasant—like when their mother used to dose them with cod liver oil. Only when Rose, still sobbing, finally released Frankie and stepped aside did Alvie raise his eyes from the platform and look his brother in the eye. Frankie opened his arms magnanimously, but Alvie held out a hand, so Frankie took it with both hands and shook it. He let his eyes wander over to the girl who stood now to one side with her arms firmly crossed under her breasts.

Alvie cleared his throat. "Frankie, you remember Lydia."

"No, I don't believe I've had the pleasure." Frankie gave her a nod and held out his hand to her. He beamed at her with every ounce of his considerable charm.

The girl barely glanced in Frankie's direction. Rather than shake his hand, she took Alvie's arm again, as if worried he would drift off on some current. "Of *course* we've been introduced," she said frostily.

Something in the young woman's surly tone teased loose a thread of memory. "Lydia?" Frankie said, squinting at her. "You mean Lydia from down the street?" *Lydia, the holder of séances? Little flat-chested Lydia?*

"Of course," Alvie said.

"I thought you moved away," Frankie told her. He allowed himself another comprehensive head-to-toe appraisal.

"I *did*," Lydia snapped. "I'm back."

"Lydia works at the fruit co-op," Rose explained merrily. "She and your brother are practically engaged." She dabbed her eyes with her hankie. One son back from the war and the other with a girl on his arm—it all seemed too much for her. "Oh, Frankie, you look so thin," she told him, and then she was overcome by a new wave of sobbing.

"Well, let's get him a home-cooked meal," Alvie said. His words seemed designed to cultivate a more upbeat mood, but the tone of his voice undermined the effect.

"Oh, goodness yes," Rose said. She tucked her hankie into the sleeve of her cardigan and pressed a hand to her heart as she took a deep, steadying breath. "It's already in the oven," she said. "Let's get you home." Given a purpose, Rose seemed braced and eager to get them all back to Grove Street. She turned and blazed a trail across the platform towards the station's double door. Frankie hefted his duffle bag over his shoulder and followed her.

Lydia, still clinging to Alvie's arm as if he needed help to walk, fell in beside Frankie. "You might have recognized me if you'd bothered looking at my *face*," she whispered in a voice only Frankie would hear. "Still a jackass, apparently."

Frankie glanced over at Lydia's scowling profile and then looked ahead to the depot's big double door, which Rose— grinning through her tears—held open for them.

THEY'D BROUGHT LYDIA'S car to the station, a Chrysler Airflow, but not a new one. Lydia drove, and Alvie rode shotgun. Frankie sat in the back seat with Rose. In the gap between them she rested her hand on his. Frankie watched the shabby, familiar buildings pass his open window. The same storefronts and the same old slogans painted on the high brickwork. BANK OF ITALY. DID YOU MACLEAN YOUR TEETH TODAY? I'D WALK A MILE FOR A CAMEL. He wished he'd picked up another pack of cigarettes in the station concourse.

Nothing much had changed in Richland while Frankie was away—and yet everything seemed different. The downtown streets were narrower, the shop windows more gloomy. From the patched awnings to the patched sidewalks, everything had taken on a seedy, threadbare look—a town too lived in. Every now and then Frankie glimpsed a familiar face, but it was gone again more quickly than he could match it to a name.

When they came up on the Plaza circle, the silence among them thickened—this was, after all, the scene of Frankie's great crime, the spot where he had accidentally maimed his brother—all for a single squeeze of Sandra Celey's fully-clothed breast. Sid's barbershop was still there, and as they passed it Frankie thought he glimpsed a stooped and wizened version of Mr. Celey, leaning on a broom just inside the glass door. How distant—even innocent—that whole episode seemed now! It felt a world away. The car peeled off the circle and turned down Glass Street.

THE CRAFTSMAN BUNGALOWS on Grove Street also seemed miniaturized—the lawns and hedges ragged-looking in the unflattering noon sun. They passed the house where Lydia once lived, then did a quick U-turn and pulled up at the curb. The others paused in their seats while Frankie studied the old house through the window he was cranking up. He tried to get a fix on the emotions he had expected to feel at this moment, but all those feelings fled him. On his bunk in the airfield barracks, he'd struggled to remember the place, each cupboard and porch rail, and it had all shimmered in his mind like a mirage. But here it was in all its shabby truthfulness: scabbed paint on the siding, loose shingles askew on the roof.

Rose walked Frankie up the front path, holding his hand and looking around as though she expected neighbors to rush outside or lean out of windows, cheering, like that Norman Rockwell cover for the *Saturday Evening Post*. Then Frankie, feeling more puzzled than pleased, climbed the steps to the porch and pushed the front door open. The smell of chicken and rosemary wafted through the open doorway—his mother's trusty special-occasion recipe—and Frankie stepped inside, feeling, for all the world, that he'd just come home from Richland High, and not from twenty-five hundred miles across the Pacific.

DURING THAT FIRST long, deep sleep on the parlor sofa, which had been made up as a temporary bed, Frankie heard the others rustling through the house like poltergeists, but he couldn't rouse himself, couldn't swim up to the surface of wakefulness. He felt dragged down by inertia and seemed to wake again and again and again without waking. When he finally managed to stir his limbs it was bright outside the drawn parlor curtains, and the house was empty. Frankie took a long shower, shaved, helped himself to some civilian clothes from

Alvie's closet, raided the icebox and then went back to the parlor, which now seemed to have taken on his smell.

In his time away, Frankie had thought of his mother and brother on occasion—had even jotted a half dozen bland and newsy letters—but what he truly hungered for in his long pointless hours on that remote Hawaiian airfield was his record collection. What Frankie craved while in uniform was Billie Holiday, Duke Ellington, Art Tatum.

So now he sat on the parlor floor flipping through his orange crate of records, which he'd found on the floor of the hall closet. Each cover conjured tunes—music he had tried to play through in his head while he lay on his bunk in the dark.

He shook a Benny Goodman record carefully from its sleeve and cued it up. He turned the phonograph up as loud as it would go. He stood at the window looking out over the bright street, letting the bass notes vibrate up through the soles of his feet, feeling, finally, like he might be home. After that, he played record after record: a wonderful, aural gluttony.

OVER A COLEMAN Hawkins song, Frankie heard a car rumble up outside. Through the front window he saw Lydia's Chrysler at the curb. She was bent over, her head ducked in the passenger door. She wore a smart white blouse and a panel skirt the color of a Brillo Pad. When she straightened up, both her arms hugged bursting grocery sacks. She struggled blindly to kick the car door shut with both bags wedged under her chin and the strap of her purse swinging from her wrist.

Frankie went to the front door, but when Lydia saw him come out on the porch in Alvie's clothes—but with a crew cut and no limp—there was a quick catch in her step, and her expression hardened. Had she forgotten he was here? "Let me get those," Frankie said, breezing down the steps, a smile fixed on his lips.

Lydia twisted away from him, wresting the bags out of reach. "I've got them," she said.

"Let me get the door," Frankie offered. He jogged up the porch steps ahead of her. He held the door open, and, without a glance in his direction, she blew past him like a February draft and down the hall to the kitchen.

Frankie pulled the door shut and stood there in the empty foyer. "Exactly Like You" boomed from the parlor gramophone. He went in and turned the record down to half its volume. Frankie stood thinking through an entire drum solo, and then he headed down towards the kitchen. When he looked in, Lydia was closing the icebox. If she saw him there, she did not acknowledge the fact. She went back to the bags on the table and lifted out some green grapes and a wrapped head of lettuce. These she placed on the draining board next to the sink.

"Can I help?" Frankie asked from the doorway.

Lydia dipped into the grocery bags again and came up with a bag of sugar. Rather than answer his question she set the sugar sack on the table and pressed both hands atop it. She looked past him through the hallway door. "How can you *listen* to that?" she said.

Frankie turned his attention to the music wafting in from the parlor. "You don't like it?" he said.

"No," she told him. "I don't. What is it supposed to be?" She lugged the sugar and a matching sack of flour over to the pantry and nudged the door open with her foot.

"It's Coleman Hawkins."

"No, I mean what *is* it?" she said, her voice muffled behind the pantry door.

Frankie stepped into the kitchen and stood next to the stove. "It's a saxaphone," he said.

She turned from the pantry empty handed and gave him a look like he was being willfully obtuse. "No, I mean what is it *playing*?" She brushed past him to the grocery bags on the table again, her back to him now.

"Playing?" he said. "Bebop." Lydia's blouse showed a tapered narrow waist where it was tucked into the zippered back of her skirt. Frankie imagined his brother's arm around that waist, and the thought produced in him an odd consternation.

"It's *aw*ful," Lydia said. "Fingernails on a blackboard." She turned from the table and swept past him to the sink.

"It grows on you," Frankie said. "You have to learn to love it."

She turned from the sink and regarded him pitilessly, her hands on that waist of hers. "Well, I've learned enough for today," she said. "Could you just turn the damn thing down?"

"Sure," Frankie said. "Yeah." He headed for the door.

"And while you're at it, maybe you could just stay in the parlor until dinner."

Frankie paused in the doorway. There was something in him that rendered him incapable of turning away from confrontation—and, in his mind, he acknowledged this flaw, even as he cleared his throat to speak. "Why the hell are you so pissed off?" he asked.

Lydia whose hands were back in the grocery bags, straightened up with a can of Seaside lima beans in each hand. The expression on her face made Frankie suspect they might be coming in his direction, so he took a reflexive step back through the kitchen doorway.

Lydia shook the can in her right hand. "I know all about you, Frankie Farrell," she told him. The muscles of her jaw seemed to ripple in the light from the window behind her. "Alvie told me everything," she said. "I know every goddamn thing about you, you self-absorbed bastard."

Her words came close to shocking Frankie silent. It took him a few beats to formulate even a lame rejoinder. "There are two sides to every story," he said.

"Why would I want to hear *your* side?" she yelled at him. "You are a lying, cheating son of a bitch." Fine flicks of spit rained down on the tabletop. "And I'll thank you to stay out of my kitchen."

Frankie, feeling more impressed than intimidated, backed into the hallway and retreated to the parlor, where Coleman Hawkins was flying high through "I'm in the Mood for Love." Frankie went to the gramophone, his heart inexplicably thudding, and turned it down. He went to the window and stood there looking out at Lydia's Chrysler .

So it was *her* kitchen now?

* * *

LONG PAST CLOSING, the six of them were still playing five-card draw at a table dragged over near the stove. The old piano player, in his roomy linen shirt and his red suspenders, still sat stooped over the keyboard. He plinked out this and that melody, running through a few newer songs halfheartedly— "Jealous Heart" and "G.I. Jive." He seemed to be waiting for the game to break up, so someone would drive him home.

As the only white man in the house, Frankie thought it would be prudent to lose four bucks or five bucks this first night. He would keep his mouth shut, laugh at the jokes, try not to press his luck. If he was invited back, he'd break even the second time, and after that all bets were off, so to speak. He'd play full-throttle. Easy pickings at this table.

Frankie tilted his head from side to side, feeling his neck crack. This was it, he thought. This was living. This was what he'd been waiting for since he got home two weeks ago: a night like this, after-hours in a bar, poker and music and a bottle of Four Roses no one was keeping track of. The only other thing he could possibly want was a woman waiting for him somewhere.

The old piano player sighed and stopped playing half way through "Sleep Lagoon." He closed the fallboard on the piano and turned on the bench to watch the card game, his elbows propped on his knees.

With the piano silent and just the one ceiling lamp on, The Barn felt creaky and cavernous, their table a small bleary island of light in a dark sea. Frankie yawned and scratched at his collarbone under his shirt. That was the thing with jazz joints: without the jazz, they were just joints—cheerless, yawning spaces, emptied of charm.

The betting finally crept back around to Frankie, and he tossed in two dimes to stay in the game, and then the man to his left bit down on his cigar and frowned at his cards all over again, as though they might have changed on him since he'd last looked. The betting went around this table at a snail's pace; nothing like the frenetic, quarrelsome barracks games Frankie was used to. The man finally slid a quarter into the puddle of silver at the center of the table and then withdrew a nickel, dragging it back across the scarred wood surface under one fingertip—so everyone could see the transaction was on the up-and-up. "Call," he said, finally.

The players all showed their cards, and the bald guy across from Frankie won with a measly two pair—sevens over threes. He swept in the pot, and then set about meticulously stacking the won coins with his stubby, nail-splintered fingers.

It was Frankie's deal again, so, with a careful show of clumsiness, he gathered the cards into a pile and tapped the edges straight on the tabletop. He shuffled then dealt ploddingly, like he was unaccustomed to the feel of a deck in his hands. He'd be back tomorrow night.

WHEN THE GAME broke up around three, Frankie offered the old piano player a ride home in Rose's car. The old man—his name, he told Frankie, was Willie Sloane—gave a stooped nod to the other players and followed Frankie across the patch of gravel in front of The Barn to Rose's old Chevy.

As Frankie drove, Willie perched primly in the passenger seat, arms folded, as though wary of getting his fingerprints on anything. Frankie glanced over at him a few times as they rumbled through the moonlit orange groves towards town, but the old man just stared straight ahead through the windshield.

The Chevy's wheels finally clattered across the railroad tracks behind a row of packinghouses and then grew mute on the well-paved streets of town. "You want to go get a beer, or something?" Frankie said in the new and blatant silence.

"Now where are the two of *us* going to get a beer?" Willie said.

Frankie ran through the options in his head—but of course the old man was right: there were only two bars likely to be open at this hour, and both were white. Frankie rolled through a stop sign and turned the corner in front of the bus station. A plump man in coveralls swept the station floor behind the lit glass doors. Otherwise, there wasn't a soul in sight. It was a backdrop Frankie loved: a dark town deserted in the wee hours, the streetlamps mustering moths, and all the windows black. "We could go over to my house if we're quiet," he said. "We could have a few Falstaffs out on the porch."

"Think I'll just go on home," Willie said, his voice flat and noncommittal. "Thanks just the same."

"Suit yourself."

Frankie had no idea where Willie lived, but he headed in the direction of the Shadel's neighborhoods and the streets out beyond them, where the colored boarding houses edged out into the country lanes and orange groves. He knew the old man would let him know if he missed a turn.

When they passed The Bulldog on the corner of Lennox, Frankie let up on the gas a little. It looked like it was still open, judging by the scattering of cars along the curb and down the side street, and he thought he might drop in for a quick one after he dropped the old man off.

"Left up at the church," Willie said.

Frankie nodded and made the wide turn where he was told to, his headlights sweeping across the wrought iron fence and gray stone face of the First Congregational. They were in among the rooming houses now with their sagging communal clotheslines and their cluttered verandas. Frankie glanced over at his passenger again. "The Lion," he said, and waited for the name to warm the icy silence. "That bridge you played in 'Honeysuckle Rose'? You got that straight from him, didn't you?" Frankie kept his eyes on the road, but he could feel the old man looking him over now.

"You play?" Willie finally asked.

Frankie shook his head ruefully. "Not a note," he said, "but I've been in enough jazz joints to wonder why you're stuck playing for the Union Pacific crowd. You could keep up with the best of them." Frankie could feel the man uncoil a little on the seat beside him.

"Old stride player like me is just a relic," Willie said. "Got to play clarinet or trumpet these days." He folded his long arms across his lean chest. "*Big band*," he said, and the words seemed to leave a bitter aftertaste on his tongue.

"Bet you've played all over," Frankie said, trying to nudge the conversation along.

The old man nodded. "Seen a lot of country."

"How long you staying in *these* parts?"

"For the foreseeable future."

"And how much future do you foresee?"

"Not much if you don't keep on your own side of the road."

Frankie looked out the windshield and glided the Chevy back over the center line. "That's why I like the wee hours," he said. "Not much competition for the road."

"Not much competition," Willie repeated. He rubbed the stubble on his chin and crossed his arms again. "Same reason you wanted to join the game tonight, I reckon."

Frankie didn't say anything. He slowed a bit for a stop sign, shifted gears and let out the clutch again.

"I know what you're thinking," Willie said. "You're thinking you'll come back to The Barn tomorrow and clean up with them boys."

Frankie kneaded Rose's steering wheel cover with both hands and looked down along the street. The roots of the old maples had rippled up the sidewalk slabs. "I was going to wait till Monday," he admitted. "Tomorrow felt a little soon."

Willie nodded. He unfolded his arms and put his hands on his knees again. "I figured you were better at poker than you were letting on," he said.

"What gave me away?"

"You might know cards," Willie said, "but you don't know squat about playing dumb—leastways at a table full of colored men who have to do it half the goddamn day to keep you folks happy."

Frankie, affronted, turned to look at him. "*We* folks?" he said, a strained note of petulance edging into his voice.

"You know what I mean."

"No," Frankie said. "I don't. Enlighten me."

Willie sighed. "It's just the way you walked into that place like you had some God-given right to be there," he said.

Frankie gripped the steering wheel tighter and swallowed down the urge to object.

"The way you lean back in your chair and look everyone over," Willie went on. "Like we're all there for your amusement. You don't think those boys all read you like a goddamn racing form?" The old man squeezed his bony knees with both hands. "You got that entitled-white-man strut about you, boy."

"*Entitled?*" Frankie said, no longer able to master his urge to argue. "What the hell are you talking about? Give me *one* example of how I act entitled."

"Well, for one thing," Willie said, "you won't stay on your own side of the goddamn road."

Frankie glanced out the windshield again and veered back to the correct side of the road.

"Take a left when you get to the end of the street," Willie told him. "*If* we make it that far. Drop me off at the last place you see before you head into the groves."

They drove a mile or so in silence, out past the reach of telephone poles and lampposts. They clattered across another set of railroad tracks, and then the road ran out of pavement and they were driving on the hardpan clay. The houses grew more widely spaced as they bounced along. The low-hanging branches of the roadside oak trees blanched in the headlights as they passed beneath. Backlit dust swirled behind them in the rearview mirror.

"Up there on the right," Willie said, flinging a lazy gesture at the windshield with one hand. Frankie braked and pulled onto the rutted drive of a white clapboard farmhouse. Frankie squinted through the windshield. Four cars were parked in a row under a lofty, voluminous eucalyptus tree. All the windows in the house were dark. Willie opened his door, got out, and turned to close it again.

"I just came to hear you play," Frankie told him, though the old man's face was invisible above the roof of the car. "I just came for the music."

Willie swung the door shut. He paused a moment on the other side of the glass, his belly framed in the passenger window. His red suspenders looked like a pair of parentheses against his white shirt. Then he turned and came around the front of the car to Frankie's side. His baggy tweed trousers bleached to white as he strode in front of the headlamps.

Frankie cranked the driver's side window all the way down, letting in the scent of eucalyptus and orange peel.

Willie bent, one hand on the sill, to talk to him over the quiet rumble of the engine and the louder throb of crickets. "Come on back to The Barn tomorrow night," he said. "Bring all the cash you can afford to lose." He straightened up, paused, and then bent back down again. "Better yet, come by *here* around seven," he said. "I could use a ride out there."

IN THE MORNING, Frankie woke to smell of bacon frying. He sat up on the sofa, yawned, and then shambled to the hallway. Rose had left early, so Alvie was alone in the kitchen with Lydia, who was busy at the stove, spatula in hand, bacon sputtering in the skillet. Alvie sat at the table, the morning's issue of *The Ledger* open before him. The two of them formed a tableau of married life—a repellent preview of coming attractions.

Frankie, in his pajama bottoms and an undershirt, watched them from the kitchen doorway. "If it isn't Blondie and Peckerwood," he said. Lydia shot Alvie a look, the meaning of which Frankie couldn't guess. He kneaded his shoulder muscles and yawned. "You know, bacon sounds good," he said. "Let me wash up a little."

When he came back a few minutes later, buttoning up one of the flannel shirts Rose had brought home for him from the second-hand store, he was surprised to find a plate of bacon and fried eggs set out for him at the table. It was a generosity he hadn't expected from Lydia. Lydia and Alvie, who had been talking quietly, fell silent when he entered the room. Something was in the air, Frankie could tell. He pulled out a chair and sat down in front of the waiting plate.

Without otherwise acknowledging his existence, Lydia got up, poured a cup of coffee from the percolator, and thumped it down in front of him. She sat down next to Alvie and scooted in her chair.

Frankie shook salt and pepper over the fried eggs on his plate, and sliced off a piece with the edge of his fork. He dipped the white in the yolk and then put it in his mouth as the other two watched silently. Frankie swallowed and took a sip of black coffee. "So," he said. "What's the story? You two are acting like there's a surprise inspection in the works."

Lydia looked at Alvie. There was something about the slight drop of her shoulder that told Frankie she had just squeezed his brother's knee under the table—a gesture of encouragement or perhaps a kind of prompt.

Alvie pushed his empty plate to one side, and then made a project of flattening down the refolded newspaper with his palm. When Alvie finally looked up, he glanced at Lydia before he looked at Frankie.

"We were wondering if you had given any thought to the future," Alvie said.

"The future?" Frankie asked. He took another sip of coffee.

"If you'd forged any plans," Alvie said. "You know. To look for a job. Maybe get your own place."

Frankie set down his coffee cup and looked at Lydia. This was clearly her doing—it was, after all, *her* kitchen. He turned to Alvie. "No plans are currently in the offing, sir," he said. "I thought I'd take a little time off."

Lydia's shoulder dipped again, and Alvie gave her another glance. Why couldn't she just talk to Frankie herself?

Frankie looked squarely at Alvie. "Is there a problem, brother?" he said. "I'm being made to feel a little unwelcome."

"It's not that," Alvie said, in that backpedaling way he had when he felt challenged. "It's not that at all. You just don't seem to making any effort to…." Alvie's sentence trailed off.

Frankie clipped off another piece of egg with the side of his fork and stuffed it in his mouth. He looked at Lydia as he chewed. He swallowed and took another sip of coffee. "If she has a problem with me," Frankie said, still looking at Lydia, "why doesn't she just say so?"

Alvie tapped the tabletop with a finger. He seemed desperate to get Frankie's attention focused back on him. "This has nothing to do with Lydia," he said. "It's just that this house is so small. And so much has changed while you were away."

"While I was away *fighting for my country*," Frankie said. Nothing seemed to irritate Alvie more than Frankie's allusions to combat—though, in truth, the remote island airfield where Frankie had been stationed might have been a KOA campground for all the military purpose it seemed to serve. "While I was *away at war*."

Lydia's shoulder dipped again. It was like a player's tell in a poker game—these two were so easy to read. And it was clear which of them held the better cards.

"Be that as it may be," Alvie said. "Things have changed. I've been offered a promotion at the appliance store, and Lydia and I are planning to get engaged."

Frankie nodded. "Well, if *you* two are going to tie the knot, why am *I* supposed to look for a new place?"

"Because we'll be living *here*," Alvie said. "Rose needs help. She's not a young woman—and she shouldn't still be working at that packinghouse."

Frankie pushed his plate away without touching the strips of bacon. "So I'm supposed to wander off somewhere so you two can play house?" he said. "You know I have as much right to this house as you do, Alvie." He looked at Lydia. "And a hell of a lot more than *some* people."

"You'll get your share of whatever's coming to you," Alvie said. "We'll buy the place from Rose." Alvie slumped a little in his chair, like he was relieved to have accomplished the assignment Lydia had given him. "You have to admit this is the best plan for everyone," he said. "You have to see that much."

Frankie looked again at Lydia. "Oh, I see plenty," he told her.

THAT EVENING WHEN Frankie saw the clapboard house up ahead, the sun had already dipped behind the roadside oak trees, and lean shadows were slung across the rutted lane. Frankie turned up the drive and saw Willie already sitting out on the steps of the rickety porch, his arms hugging his knees. The old man was watching a couple of lanky teen boys, both black, who were trying to knock something—A football? A hornet's nest?—out of the high branches of a eucalyptus by throwing rocks at it. Frankie had driven right past the two of them without noticing. He pulled into the shade of the tree where the row of cars had been parked last night.

Up on the porch, the old man rose to his feet and dusted off the seat of his trousers. He wore another billowy shirt and the same red suspenders. He called something back at the screen door, and then ambled across the dirt and weeds to Frankie's idling car. He pulled the door open, got in, and pulled it shut again.

"Running a little late," Frankie said.

"No shit," Willie said. He arranged himself dourly on the passenger seat. "How much you bring?"

"Money?" Frankie said. "Eighty bucks and some change." Frankie put the car in reverse, and backed towards the house, his arm slung over the back of his seat. "Every penny I got in the world." He put the car in first and rumbled across the sloped ground towards the road's edge. "But I prefer to think of my situation on the homeward journey," he prattled on, trying to brighten the old man's sour mood. "I'll be rich as Nebuchadnezzar, wandering among my hanging gardens with my many camels and wives."

"Give me twenty," Willie said, clearly not amused.

Frankie braked at the road's edge and looked over at the old man, who sat pressed back in his seat, staring out the windshield. "Twenty bucks?" Frankie said. "What for?"

By way of explanation, Willie held out a long empty hand.

His foot on the brake, Frankie tugged his wallet out of his back pocket. "You know in poker it's customary to go through the formality of *winning* before you take someone's money." He pulled out a ten and two fives and passed them over to Willie.

Willie folded the money and slipped it into the roomy pocket of his white shirt, under the red strap of his suspenders.

"That's it?" Frankie said. "You're just taking it?"

"*Drive*," Willie said. "We were supposed to be there ten minutes ago."

Frankie looked both ways down the empty road and honked his horn once, in hopes that the boys throwing stones up at the branches might cease their fire before they put a crack in Rose's windshield.

When they arrived at The Barn, Frankie took his place on the farthest stool, leaning back against the bar with his elbows up on the rail. He watched Willie make his rounds of the tables, patting backs and whispering in ears, shaking hands and making quips. The old man seemed to want to approach the piano by the most circuitous route, as if it were some kind of prey that was easily spooked.

When he finally scooted the piano bench up to the keyboard, Willie glanced over at Frankie once, meaningfully, and then started playing, "After You've Gone."

IT WASN'T EVEN one in the morning when Frankie ran out of money, betting a buck twenty-five on three treys. Lester, who had turned over a queen-high straight, raked in the pot, and went about sorting out the loose change. It hadn't been a nickel and dime game tonight, and the betting rolled around the table at breakneck speed.

Frankie leaned his chair back on two legs with his arms folded and looked around gamely at the other players—the same men, but one, who had been in the game last night. Willie had been half-watching the game from the next table and half-reading a ratty Zane Grey paperback. He was the only one who looked Frankie in the eye.

"All right," Frankie said. "Somebody explain."

No one at the table made a sound.

"I was sitting in a quilting circle last night," Frankie said. "And now I'm on some goddamn riverboat."

FRANKIE REACHED ACROSS and unlocked the passenger door. "What the hell was that?" he said as soon as Willie pulled the door open.

"What was what?" Willie seemed to be having trouble suppressing a smile as he clambered into the passenger seat and pulled the door shut behind him.

Frankie started up the Chevy and slipped it into gear. "Was it my imagination or were they playing as a team?" Frankie said. In the rear view mirror he could see the other players mulling about in front of the dark bar, apparently arguing about who would ride home with whom. "All I've got left in my wallet is my library card."

A long-toothed smile broke over the old man's face. "They were just having fun with you," he said. "I vouched for you tonight."

"Vouched?"

"I told them you were okay," Willie said. "I told them you were with me." The old man reached into his shirt pocket and held out Frankie's twenty dollars, scissored between two fingers. "This can keep your library card company," he said. "I didn't want you going home empty handed."

THE NEXT AFTERNOON Rose came home from the packinghouse with one of her headaches. She went straight back to her room, and no one saw her after that. Dinner was silent and tense, with Frankie and Alvie and Lydia taking turns staring sullenly at Rose's empty chair, as if wishing she were there to summon forth their better angels. If the three of them ever spoke civilly or laughed together—it was purely for Rose's sake, and, without her as their audience, there was no reason to perform.

After dinner, Frankie put his new record on the parlor phonograph, one by that new kid, Dizzy Gillespie. He turned the music up to the exact degree he judged loud enough to provoke Lydia but not to bother his afflicted mother back in her bedroom. Joylessly he slumped onto the sofa, which, since he lacked a room of his own, seemed to have become his sole property.

Frankie had just flipped the record to side B and sat back down on the sofa when Lydia strode into the parlor and dropped into one of the armchairs angled at either side of the window opposite Frankie. She crossed her legs, smoothed down her skirt, and set about studying her nails.

"So what are you two up to tonight?" Frankie asked her, shouting over the music.

Lydia glanced at him, then looked away. "Movie," she mouthed, making no effort to be heard. She changed her position in the chair, angling herself away from Frankie. She crossed her legs and held her upper knee with both hands, so that one shapely calf dangled off to one side. Her hair wasn't gathered into a ponytail tonight, so it fell loose and shapely around her shoulders. The lazy setting sun lit the curtains behind her. Frankie interlaced his fingers behind his head and let his elbows sprawl out against the back of the sofa. He watched Lydia, while she systematically refused to acknowledge his existence.

She looked, Frankie had to admit, pretty—in some highly restricted sense of that word. *Handsome*, was perhaps the correct term. She was attractive in that angular Katharine Hepburn way. Her features, while not actually beautiful, were animated by a kind of willful intelligence that had its allure. She now held her face angled slightly upward, and her high cheekbones threatened to pull the corners of her mouth up into a smile she seemed to intentionally, forcefully, suppress. "So, what's at The Palace tonight?" Frankie shouted.

Rather than answer, Lydia looked at the doorway, as if hoping to find Alvie there dressed and ready for their date, although there was no way he could have clumped down the hall unheard by both of them—even with the saxophone solo blaring from the record player.

The kid on trumpet lit into his solo, and Frankie closed his eyes to let the music wash over him. He breathed deeply and let the riffs take him by the elbow and lead him away from the room, the situation. When the solo finally passed off to the drummer, Frankie, feeling more composed, opened his eyes.

Lydia sat across from him, her legs still crossed, looking blankly back at the window, still holding her knee with both hands. As if sensing Frankie's eyes on her, she turned to scowl at him. "What?" she demanded. "What are you grinning at?"

"Your foot," Frankie told her.

Lydia frowned down at her crossed-over leg. The high-heeled shoe that dangled from her toes swayed in rhythm with the music. She'd been keeping time. She froze, blushed suddenly and glared down at her foot as if it had betrayed her.

This, Frankie knew, was his first small victory in this war Lydia had waged on him. "Bop grows on you," he said, enjoying Lydia's fluster. "It gets under your skin."

Lydia crossed her legs the other way, turning as far as her chair would let her, so she was facing the doorway and not Frankie. He could see her willing her body into stony stillness, despite the siren call of the music.

"I won't tell a soul," Frankie said, and he sat there grinning until Alvie clumped down the hall and in through the parlor doorway doing up his tie.

AFTER THEY'D LEFT, Frankie went to the front window and looked out on the drive. Rose's Chevy was still parked there; Lydia had driven her own car to the movies. Frankie went back and knocked softly on Rose's bedroom door. When she didn't answer, he pushed the door open a crack. Rose lay on top of the covers in the dark, still fully dressed, face down, deep in a fathomless sleep.

Frankie went over and gently pulled off one of her shoes and then the other and set them on her dresser, next to her purse and keys. He went to the window and quietly slid it shut against the cooling night air. Rose was lying on one half of the bed, as if she expected someone to lie down next to her. Frankie pulled the unoccupied half of the bedspread over her, and then paused a moment to look at her plump and aging face in the light that came through the doorway. He plucked her keys from the dresser and slipped back out to the hallway.

As he drove out towards the edge of town, Frankie imagined his mother sleeping now in that dark and empty house behind him. He thought of Alvie and Lydia, sharing a bucket of popcorn, their faces lit up silvery by the movie screen. He didn't belong in their world anymore.

But, honestly, when had he ever belonged there? He had never really been one of them. He had never been more than an interloper in the house on Grove Street. Even as a boy he had twisted away from every one of Rose's motherly ministrations—as if she were dabbing at a forehead smudge with a spit-moistened hankie. And even now, long after he should know better, he was still doing all he could to antagonize poor 4-F Alvie with Falstaffian allusions to combat, none of which were true.

Frankie drove along Road 19 past the citrus co-op and clattered over the railroad tracks onto the uneven hardpan. The Chevy bounced and groaned as he hurtled along, deeper into the moonlit groves. Ahead of him, his headlamps lit up the ranks of orange trees on either side of the narrow lane, and stars crowded the crease between.

Then, even a mile away, he could see light from The Barn seeping up into the black sky. Soon he could see all the cars parked haphazardly in the gravel lot and along both shoulders of the road. And then there was The Barn itself: lit up out here in the night like a house on fire.

Frankie pulled over in front of the last car on the road's shoulder, set the hand brake, and got out. He closed the door and walked back along the empty road towards the bar. He could hear sounds from inside now: a burst of laughter, a chorus of boos, and then Willie careening stride-style into, "Ain't Misbehaving."

Before he climbed the front steps, Frankie glanced back in the direction of town—a streak of light above the dark swath of orange groves. He turned back to The Barn. Cigarette smoke and the sound of Willie's right-hand riffs wafted out the half-open front door. He had only twenty bucks in his wallet tonight, but Frankie could afford a few drinks with that—maybe even a couple for Old Willie.

Something would turn up soon—he'd find a job, get back on his own two feet, maybe find girl to call on—but tonight he'd just stay and watch the poker game.

CHAPTER SIX
PARROTS IN PALM TREES
1946

IT ALL BEGAN, in Rose's view of things, that Sunday when she and Lydia were reorganizing the kitchen, and she couldn't, for some odd reason, bring to mind the word "orange." After casting about in her head for the correct term, her lips working fruitlessly, she said instead, "Those orange-colored fruits."

Lydia, drying her hands on a dishrag, looked at Rose with a wholly befuddled expression. "Huh?" she said.

"*Those*," Rose said, jabbing her finger good-humoredly at the bin of red-ball oranges Lydia had slid under the table so they could clean behind the ice box.

Lydia looked at the bin and then back at Rose. "You mean the *oranges*."

"Goodness," Rose said. She pressed a flustered hand against her breast bone and chuckled self-consciously. "Of course—the *oranges*."

Orange-colored fruit? Rose tried to gloss over this glitch in her thinking as if nothing had happened. She showed Lydia exactly where on the counter the orange bin should henceforth be positioned, but she sensed that Lydia had flagged her mistake as something more than a simple failure of word retrieval. The girl's ears looked pricked up, like that cocker spaniel they'd briefly owned—What was his name?—when he heard the postman mount the porch steps. Trying not to look at Lydia, Rose scrubbed down the kitchen counter until she was glazed with perspiration. The rest of that afternoon she felt something tiny and hard, like a swallowed pip, churning away in her stomach. *Oranges*, of course. *Oranges. Oranges. Oranges. Oranges.*

But had Rose been more honest with herself, or perhaps just a little more aware, she would have admitted that this was just another in a lengthening list of mildly disquieting mix-ups. Twice in the last month, she had turned down the wrong spoke of the plaza circle on her way home and found herself over by the railroad depot, with no idea how she'd arrived there. At the Woolworth cash register, she'd dipped into her coin purse for her carefully folded five-dollar bill and found only a jingle of nickels and dimes. She ransacked her mind but found not a shred of recollection where she'd spent the rest. And only yesterday she'd come *this close* to crimping the top crust on an empty pie, while the sliced apples simmered on the stovetop at her elbow in plain view. She had a lot on her mind, she told herself. There was just too much for one woman to juggle. Was it any wonder she got all muddled?

But then, a few mornings after the orange bin episode, Rose—running late as usual—scurried out to her Chevrolet on her way to work. Lydia followed her out on the porch and called to her as she was inserting the key in the driver side door of her Chevy.

"Shoes," Lydia said from the front steps, pointing down at her own feet.

Rose's looked down to find herself not only shoeless but without stockings. Her flustered cheeks burned. The sight of her bare toes made her lightheaded. She braced herself with one hand on the car's roof. How had she trod across all that prickly brown grass without noticing?

Lydia came to her, took her by the elbow, and led her back inside. Lydia sat her down on a chair in the parlor and then knelt at her feet looking up at her, searching her eyes for something. The girl's pretty young face was etched with concern.

"My mind's just somewhere else," Rose assured her, making herself beam serenely down at the girl. "I was in a rush. It's nothing to fuss about."

But Lydia, ever headstrong, kept Rose pinned to the chair. The girl insisted on calling the packinghouse to say that Rose wouldn't be coming in today, and then she phoned the doctor's office. Rose sat in the parlor, hands twisting in her lap, feeling the cold floorboards under her bare soles and trying not to let herself get worked up. All the while she could hear Lydia talking quickly, and in a hushed voice, into the hallway telephone.

And then Lydia was back in the parlor holding a pair of Rose's shoes, which—though Rose felt it would be ungracious to point out at such a moment—didn't come close to matching the smart periwinkle dress she was wearing. "Honestly, I'm fine," Rose insisted, but Lydia was already slipping the shoes on Rose's bare feet, like that pushy salesgirl at the Florsheim shop.

On their way downtown in Lydia's car, Rose chewed on her lower lip and rehearsed in her head what she would tell Dr. Wilkins the moment she got him alone: She had simply come out to the car to get something she'd left there—the case for her reading glasses. Of course, she hadn't planned to drive away without her shoes! Lydia, who would someday soon be her daughter in law, could be a bit forceful at times. Jumped to conclusions. Wouldn't always listen to reason. She was a headstrong girl, that one—but a fine match for Alvie, didn't he think?

But when the nurse leaned into the waiting room with her clipboard and called Rose's name, Lydia stood along with her and led her by the elbow to the door the nurse held open. What was the girl thinking? That Rose couldn't walk on her own? Was she expecting to waltz with Rose into the private inner sanctum of her doctor's office?

In the examining room, Lydia sank into the corner chair, looking anxious and expectant, while the nurse took Rose's blood pressure, a second and third time, and then left the two of them alone. Rose perched uncomplaining on the edge of the padded examination table—since there was now nowhere else to sit except Dr. Wilkins' own rolling stool. It was ill mannered and presumptuous of Lydia to have pushed her way in like this, but Dr. Wilkins, that wonderfully understanding man, was sure to ask the girl to leave.

But Lydia's trespass was quickly wiped away by the next. When the knock came on the examining room door, in walked young Dr. Evans, his hair thinning on top now and peppered with gray. He wore one of those absurd flowered ties that were the newest fad. Rose stood up when she recognized him. Were those bags under his eyes? Most women found Dr. Evans dashing—even Rose would admit that he was handsome in a vulgar sort of way. But today he looked sallow and run-down, his face inflated with middle age. Someone should take a look at *him*, Rose thought. She suppressed a small wicked smile. Dr. Evans greeted her with a bowing sort of nod, but Rose just shook her head at him.

"I'm sorry," Rose told him, gathering the collar of her dress together at her throat. "But I'd like to be seen by Doctor Wilkins. *He's* my regular physician."

Lydia gave a little gasp and clamped her fist to her mouth. She looked at the doctor, who patted Rose's shoulder as if she were a crying child brought to him with a scraped knee. "Doctor Wilkins is no longer with us," Dr. Evans said—a little too loudly and consolingly, Rose thought.

"Not *with* us?" Rose repeated, bewildered.

"Doctor Wilkins *died*," Lydia told her, setting her hand on Rose's other shoulder. "Remember?"

Rose felt the air go out of her. She sat down suddenly on the examination table. She peered at the doctor's pale blue eyes and thickening features, and flattened her palm over her staggering heart. "When did this happen?" was all she could think of to say. The news struck a surprising chord of melancholy and regret in Rose, though she wasn't quite sure why.

Dr. Evans nodded at her with a look of contrived, professional consolation. "A little over a year ago," he said soothingly.

"Why did no one inform me?" Rose demanded, but, instead of answering, Dr. Evans rudely shone a tiny flashlight into one of her eyes and then the other. Rose wanted to look away, but he held her chin firmly in his rubbery-clean hand, twisting her head this way and that as he stared, his face a little upturned, into her eyes.

Clearly, someone should have brought Rose this news. Dr. Wilkins had been their family physician for years—he'd delivered the boys, took out their tonsils, nursed them through the mumps and measles and scarlet fever, admitted Alvie to the hospital the awful night of the accident. Why, he was so much more than just a physician to Rose!

"Why wasn't I told?" she asked again.

Dr. Evans finally surrendered her chin, and Rose looked over at Lydia. The girl sat slumped on the chair, leaning with one elbow on the tiny sink. Her other hand covered her mouth. She seemed about to cry. Rose brushed aside the doctor and stood. She went to Lydia and, standing over her, stooped and held the poor girl in an awkward embrace.

Lydia seemed to float up into her arms. "Oh, Ma," the girl sobbed. "It's going to be all right."

Rose stroked the girl's hair. "Of course," she cooed into Lydia's ear. "Don't be silly. Of course everything's going to be all right."

ROSE LAY IN her roomy four-poster bed wondering what time it was. The sun had barely gone down as far as she could tell, and here she was, tucked into bed by her son and his soon-to-be fiancée, like she was their toddler. Had they even eaten dinner tonight? Rose couldn't remember. She ran her tongue across her teeth but that revealed nothing. Had the rest of them sat down at the table together and forgotten her?

This whole situation just wouldn't do. She couldn't have her own children fawning over her the way they had done since she'd got home from the hospital. *Observation,* Dr. Evans had called it, but for three days those flighty nurses had rarely bothered to observe anything about her, and then there was that other awful doctor with his icy hands and his countless queries about the President and the months of the year! Who wouldn't be confused by such a tedious and trivial catechism! Had that boy got his medical training on some radio quiz show?

And now, to add insult to injury, she was back in her own home, with her children being *too* observant, *too* attentive. One of the three of them—she was counting Lydia as one of her children now, and why shouldn't she?—was sure to follow her from the room every time she got up, like dogs expecting to be fed. (What *was* the name of that dog they'd had? A poodle, wasn't it? Or had that been her mother's dog?)

Her children smiled at her inanely any time she addressed them, whispered to each other as if she wouldn't notice, insisted on doing things for her that she was perfectly capable of doing on her own. It was bad enough that they kept her from going to work, but now Lydia was doing all the cooking and household chores when she got home from the newspaper. What was Rose supposed to do with her days?

And then Frankie had gone out and taken a job. He'd jumped on the first one to come along—taking in rolls of film at the camera shop and sealing them in little envelopes for Mr. Passic in the back. Until last Christmas this had been the job of Liz Jusino's boy, a lanky, spotty kid not even out of high school. Was *that* any kind of job for a war hero like Frankie? Rose could picture it perfectly, and the image made her stomach roil: her Frankie behind the counter with a pencil stub tucked behind one ear. She imagined the jingle of the bell above the door and the dank chemical smell of the place. She pictured the glass case full of old cameras and lenses, the green ILFORD sign above the cash register. She imagined Frankie licking his dull pencil point and jotting on the envelope and listening to his customers' pointless stories about twelfth birthday parties and trips to the beach and the sunburns they'd all got. Her Frankie who had nearly died for his country! It was enough to make a person ill.

Rose picked fretfully at the lint on her quilted counterpane and thought now of the sorting belts at the packinghouse running the last few days without her. The notion brought a selfless lump to her throat. During the depression years the sorters had mostly been women like herself—pressed bravely into service by families in need, women from homes dotted around the various neighborhoods of Richland, women she'd bump into at the green grocers or the butcher shop on the weekends. But in the years since the war broke out, these women had drifted away from the packinghouse, replaced by smaller, brown-skinned, Spanish-speaking women—around whom Rose was at first self-conscious. But in the last year or two, she had truly grown to love these women and their rustic smiling ways. She advised them about the proper handling of citrus fruit, instructed them helpfully with their English, stood up for them when the line boss came around, listened to the comforting din of their fast and incomprehensible language—a constant burble, like the sound of oranges tumbling into their bins. Lying in her bed now Rose imagined all those tiny women without her to speak up for them. What would they do now? Who would be there to help them? She shouldn't be lying here like an invalid; that much was certain. She was just a little tired. Who wouldn't slow down a step or two by the age of fifty-one?

And fifty-one, now that she thought about it, wasn't any age at all—why her grandma Ellie was still sharp as a paring knife on her ninetieth birthday! A few days rest and she'd show them all she was the same old Rose—still the same woman who had been both mother and father to two strapping boys and guarded them through a depression and a world war.

She pulled back the covers and sat up on her bed, swinging her feet down to the floor. She burrowed her feet into her waiting slippers and stood—but couldn't then recollect where she was headed. When she came out to the front parlor, cinching her bathrobe around her, she found Frankie sitting in the dark, smoking a cigarette.

"Ma?" he said. "You all right?" He didn't look shocked to see her there, which told Rose it couldn't be terribly late yet.

Frankie reached up and switched on the floor lamp beside the sofa, and the sudden light seemed to bulge uncomfortably inside Rose's head.

She sat down heavily on the end of the sofa and blinked there a moment getting her bearings. She wanted to ask where Alvie and Lydia were but worried that she may have already been told and that it had slipped her mind. "I thought I'd do some reading," she told Frankie.

"Sure, Ma," he said. "You want me to turn down the music?"

Only when he mentioned it did the music seem to arrive in Rose's ears. How had she missed that blaring trombone? There was, she had to admit, a weird, hitching delay in her thinking these days, like the sudden stuttering of a film running through a projector—and then the movie would gather up, catch in the sprockets again, and run at normal speed, leaving her wondering if it had ever really happened at all.

"Have you seen my book?"

Frankie shook his head. "No, Ma, what book is that?"

The title was on the tip of her tongue—some drivel she'd been reading about a farm and two sides of a family feuding over the acreage—but she couldn't bring the name to mind, so, rather than look foolish, she said brightly, "Oh, that's right: I lent it to one of the nurses at the hospital! I suppose I'll have to start a new one." She waved blithely at the small case of books behind the floor lamp on Frankie's side of the sofa. "Pick one for me, Frankie," she said.

Frankie looked jadedly at the bookcase and then back at her. He rubbed at the stubble on his chin. "Anything?" he said.

"Yes. Just pick one out." She gave his knee a pat, as if this would be a grand lark for both of them. "One that looks nice."

Frankie shrugged and, without shifting his position on the sofa, slipped a squat green book from the shelf. The book had no dust jacket. Frankie turned it over, tilted his head to see the title on the spine and then handed it to her.

"Why, thank you, Frankie," she said, accepting the book with a smile of gratitude that was ceremonial in its grandeur. She set the book on her lap and opened it. *The Grapes of Wrath*: hadn't she read this one before? Or was she thinking of that song they used to sing at school? Or was it at church? Rose stared at the first page while Frankie yawned, got up and went to turn his record over. While her son cued up his music, Rose chipped away at the book's first impenetrable paragraph—something about the earth and the rain and the sky—but its meaning seemed to stiff-arm her away. Her mind kept being deflected off the page to other things.

Frankie sat back down next to her and arranged himself for a long haul of music listening, so Rose made herself content with being beside him, turning the page every once in a while when she thought it might be time to do so. Writers today, she had noticed, couldn't tell an engaging story to save their lives—how could anyone be expected to concentrate on these meandering sentences that swam on the page like a school of minnow in the shallows?

While she stared at the open book, and Frankie smoked beside her with his eyes closed, Rose's mind flitted about and lighted on the blue dragonflies in the Newport Beach estuary. As a child, she used to chase them from bush to bush until she caught them by the tail, between her finger and thumb. She felt the small frantic tugs and scrambles of the insect trying to free itself. She felt her own small fingers creaky with a seawater glaze.

For someone who couldn't these days call to mind which knob operated which burner on the stove she'd cooked on for more than twenty years, Rose now found her thoughts often intruded upon by impossibly vibrant memories she hadn't entertained in years. She thought now, abruptly and without antecedent, of Miss Figman, the typing teacher at Freemont Academy, the all-girl school Rose had attended in her early teens. Rose pictured exactly the way the tiny woman paced the rows, hands linked behind her back, peering at the text that accumulated above each clacking typewriter's black roller. Rose remembered the flock of escaped and breeding parrots that some mornings roosted noisily outside the second-floor window in the campus palm trees, squawking loud enough to drown out even the assiduous, collective tatting of all those typewriters.

Rose took a quick breath and looked up from her book. She glanced at Frankie, who sat beside her serenely, engrossed in his music. A ribbon of smoke dangled down to the glowing tip of his cigarette. Rose pressed a hand over her thumping heart. Where had those images come from? Why had they lain in wait all these years only to pounce upon her now? There was a flustering *presentness* to the memories that ambushed her these days. They were so lucid, so *authentic*—much more vivid than the parlor she blinked around at now. The objects in her memories were somehow more solid than the real book now in her lap, their people somehow more plausible than the man smoking beside her. Departing them was like stepping from a moving car and tumbling into the ditch of the real world.

BUT MEMORIES WEREN'T the only things that leapt to Rose's mind and set it skittering in unpredictable directions. One Saturday evening, a few weeks later, geometry began to press upon her from every side. She was sitting at the dinner table with the others, when suddenly the right angularity of the window casements and the cupboard doors and the corners of the ceiling leapt out at her in a way that took her breath away. She had the presence of mind to cover her look of sudden shock by pressing her napkin to her lips and coughing delicately, as if a shred of Lydia's chicken casserole had gone down the wrong way.

But, later that same night, when they all retired to the parlor to listen to *The Burns and Allen Show*, the same thing happened again. The round knobs and dials of Frankie's radio seemed to glow at her in their perfect crystalline circularity. The next instant, the grid of glass panes in the front windows achieved a blinding and beautiful symmetry. One by one the things around her in the parlor seemed to disassemble before her eyes into independent shapes, floating and marvelous— platonic ideals freed fleetingly from their instantiation in everyday objects. Rose had the urge to elbow Alvie, who had nodded asleep, chin on his chest—but, upon reflection, decided she had better not. This geometric epiphany was meant for her alone. It would only worry the others if she were to point it out to them—and the sensation never visited her again after that evening.

But then there was the afternoon when smells got inexplicably cross-wired. A bottle of uncapped Coca Cola hissed forth the scent of baking bread. The roses Lydia set out in a vase on the entry table, upon inspection, smelled pungently of shoe polish. A peeled banana reeked of wet dog. This muddle of scents robbed Rose of her appetite for days when a buttered cob of corn suddenly filled her mouth with the flavor of tarnished pennies.

Rose's days became increasingly punctuated with visions of the past that swooped her up to dizzying hallucinatory heights and then, just as abruptly, plunged her back into the mundane present. She again saw every age-slackened muscle on the old man she'd seen bathing naked in a river when she'd wandered away from a family picnic at the age of nine. Again, she doused the backyard fire nine-year-old Frankie set with Alvie's magnifying glass. Again she saw Baby Doris in her basinet between her brothers, grasping at the air with her small red fists—saw even the slits of her eyes, with their tiny arcs of damp black lashes, that uncanny apple birthmark on her shoulder. Rose saw all these things again—lived them, breathed them—and then quit them just as she was getting her bearings.

ROSE WAS SITTING on the front porch swing one afternoon, waiting for someone to come home and drive her to the Woolworth for some yarn, when the memory of Grady Weems, partner in her father's law firm, stole upon her. Weems, a man her father's age, wore a preened walrus mustache that was, despite his head of dense coppery hair, flamboyantly white. That particular drowsy afternoon Mr. Weems and her father lounged out on the sun porch of the summer home in Newport Beach. The men sat in their shirtsleeves, across from one another at the white table, a scattered pinochle deck abandoned between them. Both men had taken off their straw boaters, and the two hats lay brim up on the porch rail, as if the men might be using them as ashtrays for the cigars they were smoking.

Rose, the spinster daughter in her late twenties, had been sent out by the men's wives with two tall glasses of lemonade. These she primly set on the table between them. When Rose glanced up, she saw that Mr. Weems' red hair, slick with summer perspiration, had retained the shape of the hat he'd doffed. The sight of him—he looked as if the top of his head could be lifted off like a cookie jar—took Rose by surprise and made her smile. At that precise moment a breeze drew back the veil of cigar smoke between them and strummed a wind chime somewhere overhead. Mr. Weems straightened suddenly and smiled back at her, and then glanced guiltily beyond her at her father who was leaning on the railing, looking out over the water. Then, eyes still on her father, Mr. Weems had reached out and brushed his fingertips across the back of Rose's hand, which still rested on the table top.

Rose retreated, without a word, to the house's dark entryway, and paused there a moment, her heart racing. His touch had been deliberate, that much she understood—but what could it possibly mean? Her face stinging, she trotted up the stairs to her bedroom unseen. She pulled the door closed, sat on the edge of her single bed and looked numbly at the bright curtains that billowed out from her windows. Down below she heard her father cough and mumble, and then she heard the chairs pushed back and the sound of the two men scuffling down the porch steps and away towards the beach. She lay back on her bed and closed her eyes, still feeling Mr. Weems' touch tingling on her skin.

And then Rose looked down to find another manly hand on her own. "Were you asleep?" Alvie asked, crouching before her.

"Asleep?" she said. She blinked and looked around. She was sitting on the porch swing now, and there was Lydia's car parked out in front of the house, and there was Lydia looking over Alvie's shoulder, eyeing her curiously.

"Your hands were moving," Alvie informed her. He smiled up at her. "It was like you were washing them under a faucet, but you looked like you were sleeping."

"Sleeping," Rose said. "Yes, sleeping." She yawned and stretched her arms daintily over her head, feigning a drowsiness she didn't feel at all.

Alvie straightened up and stood over her. Had the two of them just arrived home, or were they about to leave? "Nothing like a nap in the afternoon," he said jovially. And then he passed her, humming to himself, and went into the house. Lydia paused a moment and regarded Rose with an expression of distant concern before she followed him inside.

THE ODD THING, Rose began to feel, was the way her return to the present was always something of a let down, like waking from a pleasant dream in which she was again percolating with potential, a dream in which anything might yet happen. Her life these days seemed so drained of drama, so unvarying and dull, so empty of promise—as flavorless as the store-bought bread Lydia had lately been bringing home from the knew Skaggs they'd put up on Kolar Street.

And then, as the weeks passed, a balance seemed to tip— perhaps because Rose, herself, had begun to lean in the direction of memory. Recollection overtook awareness. The past outran the present. Rose slipped into a montage of cross-faded scenes: again and again she visited certain moments, the echoes of which never seemed to fade—the phone call that her small fortune of blue-chip stock had vanished, as feared, in the Crash; the night she burst into the hospital room to find Alvie, his left leg hoisted with pulleys and wires, slap-happy with morphine and his brother nowhere to be found; the bleak December morning she reached down and found Baby Doris's cheek cold as a lichen-crusted tombstone.

Again and yet again Rose found herself back in their rambling house in Temple City, and she was lying late in bed that April Saturday, cupping one hand under her belly. She'd lied to her mother, claiming it was influenza, but Rose knew better, and she knew she wouldn't be able to hide her condition long. This, she sensed, was the morning she would tell them. There was no need for medical tests to confirm what she already understood—though she knew her father would press the tests upon her for his own selfish certitude. And there was no need for her to confess who had done this— though she knew her father would disown her for her silence. It was *her* life, after all—and so were the three lives winking awake now in her womb. She lingered lazily under the blankets, sensing, even then, that this was the last moment of something and she had better take pleasure in it before she let it go. She rose, pulled back the curtains to the morning and stood watching the birds dart from tree to tree and the clouds in their scudding journey east. Rose then turned from the window, chose carefully which clothes she would wear, and moved without hurry down the stairs to find her mother.

The face of one of her grown boys loomed before her now, but she was in no hurry to swim all the way up to the surface to hear what it was he was telling her—she'd rather just float languidly yet a while, let the current take her where it would.

AND NOW IT is a Monday, a cold spring fog of a morning in 1924. Rose is on her way to donate her signature lemon pie to the Episcopal Ladies' Altar Guild Bake Sale. Leaving nothing to chance, she baked three pies the night before—just so she could choose the best as her offering. And the pie is indeed a marvel; the cumulus egg whites are piled up in a perfect caramelized symmetry.

But, still, that familiar flicker of disdain crosses the chairwoman's face when she recognizes Rose through the window in the church's basement door and sees the twin mounds of two bastard babies in the pram. Rose reflexively lowers her bare left hand below the level of the pram's push bar.

The Guild already has more goods than it can possibly sell, Rose is curtly informed (though the notice appeared for the first time in yesterday's church bulletin). And aren't those two handsome, strapping boys in that pram of hers.

And now Rose is pushing the pram towards home again, the rebuffed pie riding atop the fleece blanket under which her boys sleep, their faces crumpled against the chill. A dense meringue of fog has settled over the valley during the night, seeping east over the hills from the Pacific. It will burn off before long, Rose knows, and Richland will once again be drenched in sunlight. But, for the moment, the telephone poles she passes dissolve at half their height, and the houses on the far side of the street are bleached to invisibility, except for an occasional bleary porch light.

Rose arrives in front of her own house—which does not yet feel like home—and, without pause or deliberation, she passes it. She walks on to where Grove Street ends, and then she turns onto Telegraph Road. Soon she is passing the newest tract of homes, finished last summer and mostly still empty. There is no traffic on the street.

Rose presses on past the last ghostly building into the hazy orange groves, which run for miles in every direction. Soon she is pushing the pram along the hardpan shoulder of a farm road. The round heads of the groves are barely visible on either side of her as she makes her way deeper among them—deeper into the unfathomable fog. She presses on, the babies sleeping snugly in front of her, the heavy mist a cool veil against her face.

Rose has no idea where she is going, but she resolves to keep walking as long as her legs will carry her. And, in an act of willful solipsism, she imagines the world of everything she has ever known—every misstep she has taken, every slight she has felt, every twinge of regret—behind her now, fading to white.

CHAPTER SEVEN
NUMBER FORTY-TWO
1947

ALVIE DROVE the length of the palm-lined drive to the gravel parking lot at the end, which was nearly empty at this hour. He set the brake, turned the engine off, and leaned over the steering wheel to look up at the main building. Brookside Sanatorium, lit generously in the morning slant of light, looked like it might have once been the home of a packinghouse magnate. It was a convoluted Victorian mansion, three broad stories, with dormer windows in the sloping roof, and a shaded wrap-around porch crowned with lacy fretwork spandrels. It was picturesque, Alvie had to admit—just the way Lydia had described it.

Alvie got out of the car and hobbled around to the passenger side to help Rose out. He pulled her door open, and she gathered up her purse and looked up at him with that empty-eyed smile fixed on her face—the one she used to mask her mystification. She allowed Alvie to take her arm and help her to her feet. When she stood, Alvie was surprised, yet again, by her smallness.

Lydia, who had ridden in the back seat, now stood in front of the car, looking up at the main building and tugging down the back hem of her cardigan. Though it was only late September, a nip of autumn hung in the morning air, and a stiff breeze bounced the palm fronds up above them.

Rose stood beside the car fussing with her skirt and smoothing down her wind-tousled hair, while Alive surveyed the sanatorium grounds. An undulating tree-shaded lawn, mapped with box-edged pathways, spread out from the main house in all directions. The grounds encompassed a caretaker's cottage, a gazebo and, at the farthest edge, what looked to be a small pond. On all sides, orange groves pressed up against the distant iron fences.

"Isn't it lovely?" Lydia said, still looking up at the main building. The volume and brightness of her voice suggested she wasn't talking to Alvie. Alvie looked at his mother. She didn't seem to have noticed the house yet. Instead, she frowned down anxiously at a scattering of sycamore leaves that had blown against her shoes, as if concerned they might be some variety of crab.

"You can come home every weekend," Lydia pronounced loudly. She gathered her blowing hair and tucked it behind her ears. "But here you'll have friends to keep you company while we're all at work. Won't that be nice?"

Rose squinted at Lydia now, uncomprehendingly. She peered at the building in front of her and then looked up at Alvie. It was hard to know if she had any inkling what they were doing here—but then again she *had* seemed coiled and wary all morning, as if she'd sensed something afoot. She hadn't touched the eggs Lydia made for breakfast, and Alvie had found her sitting on the edge of her bed fully dressed to go out when he'd gone back to her room. Rose now slipped her hand up along Alvie's arm and gripped it above the elbow, as if she expected to be led somewhere, so Alvie took her across the lawn and up the path toward the big house.

A long wooden ramp angled up to the balustered porch next to the steep stone steps. A young black man—an orderly it seemed—eased a wheelchair down it as they approached. An old man sat in the chair under a plaid blanket, his head lolling to one side; half his face seemed tugged down in an asymmetrical grimace. The orderly smiled brightly and nodded to Alvie as he passed, as though the two of them had met, but the old man in the wheelchair took no notice. Alvie stepped between his mother and the resident in the wheelchair, worried she might spot him and gather some dark conception of this place—of her own bleak future, perhaps. He ushered her to the front steps and helped her climb them one by one, holding her elbow, his own bad ankle thrumming with pain. Lydia followed closely behind, chirping bland encouragements. *That's it. Just two more. Almost up.*

Inside Brookside's lofty main room, a half-dozen wingback chairs formed a semicircle around the big stone fireplace, though no fire was lit there. Each chair held a white-haired woman. Two were knitting. Another napped with an oversized *Reader's Digest* that seemed about to slip from her lap. One woman squinted eagerly at the empty wall to one side of the fireplace, as if waiting for the hand of God to write something. The three men in the room, also white haired, seemed to prefer the smaller circle of chairs around the old RCA Victor in the corner, which was not-quite-tuned to *Breakfast with the Bixbys*. Except for the orderly outside, Alvie hadn't seen any of Brookside's employees. He glanced at his watch. Shouldn't there be someone here to meet them?

"Let me go look," Lydia whispered. "I'll be right back." She disappeared through the archway at the far end of the room.

Alvie glanced at his mother, who still gripped his arm. Her hair was lush chestnut, only fading to gray in loose wisps at her temples. At fifty-four, she would easily be the home's youngest resident.

"Babe Ruth drove an Arrow," a gruff voice barked out suddenly. Alvie looked over at the old man who had spoken. He sat slumped in his chair next to the crackling radio, not ten feet away. Breadcrumbs dotted his chin and trailed down the front of his flannel shirt. His restless fingers seemed to be trying to undo his belt buckle, though the rest of him seemed unaware of that fact. Alvie glanced around to see whom the man might be addressing, but neither of the man's companions in the other chairs paid him any note; they seemed sunk in their own unfathomable ruminations. The old man caught Alvie watching him, and hiked himself straighter in his chair. "So did Emperor Hirohito," he told Alvie in a booming, quarrelsome voice, as if daring Alvie to contradict him.

Alvie's instinct was to pretend he hadn't heard and to drift away to safety, but his mother was there at his side, still holding his arm, anchoring him to the spot. Alvie flailed about for some suitable response to the old man, who, by the way he was leaning forward and eyeing Alvie angrily, seemed to be waiting for one. "I've always thought that," Alvie said in a tone of cheery subservience. "I was just saying the same thing the other day."

"That's just Mr. Karns," a bright, youthful voice said. Alvie turned to find a young woman in a blue nurse's uniform standing on Rose's other side. "Mr. Karns used to sell cars in town," the nurse said cheerily. She turned her attention to Rose, and her voice rang out more loudly. "And you must be Rose Farrell," she said. "We've been *so* looking forward to meeting you."

Back outside in the breezy September morning, Alvie felt the cold weight of the sky press down on him as he buttoned his overcoat. He'd spent his whole life under Rose's roof—first cared for by her, then caring for her—and now he'd just dropped her off, like some old steamer trunk, at a sanatorium full of strangers.

Lydia, still teary-eyed, linked her arm with his, and they walked down the stone steps and across the lawn to the parking lot. Alvie imagined Rose watching them from the window of her bare room, but he couldn't bring himself to turn and see if her bewildered face was framed in any of the upper windows; this whole throat-clumping situation was hard enough as it was.

But honestly, what else could Alvie have done? Rose needed to be cared for round the clock. In the last few months she had turned some kind of corner, and it was simply no longer safe to leave her alone. At times she still recognized her boys and could tell them apart—even when they were all seated at the dinner table, and she didn't have Alvie's limp to help her. But at other times she didn't seem to know them at all. She might call either of them *Mr. Weems*—a name Alvie had never heard before. At other times she'd know their names but seemed to think them still children. "You'll be late for school," she might call to them abruptly, at any time of the day or night. Or her voice would ring out suddenly from another room: "Time for bed, you two! And I won't hear any of your guff!"

Last Saturday morning, she had suddenly fixed Alvie with a gaze of dawning recognition from across the breakfast table. She beamed at him and set down her fork. "Why I used to have a son who looked just like you," she informed him brightly.

"That would be me, Ma," Frankie had said from behind *The Ledger.*

And then the next morning, Sunday, Alvie had come out of his bedroom in the morning and followed a strange autumnal scent into the kitchen, where he found a head of lettuce sweltering in the oven. If she'd set it any hotter than *warm*, who knows what might have happened?

Alvie opened the car door for Lydia, and she slid silently into the front seat where a wad of Rose's tissues were still wedged in a crack between the seats. Lydia sniffled and looked out the side window while Alvie drove back down the long drive. Once he pulled out onto the highway, he turned the radio on softly. "She'll be okay," he said at the windshield. "We can bring her home every weekend." Lydia didn't answer; she just kept staring out the window, so Alvie turned up the radio.

It was official, the news announcer told them: A Big-Apple World Series—New York versus Brooklyn.

ALVIE PULLED UP in the alley behind L&S Modern Appliances and got out, feeling frayed and unfocused—his mind lagging a beat or two behind his movements. He leaned in and got his lunch box and then pushed the car door closed. Lydia slid into the driver's seat and cranked the window down. "Aren't you forgetting something?" she asked. Alvie glanced into the back seat, expecting to find an overlooked coat or newspaper or thermos bottle, but Lydia leaned her upturned face out the window, and he realized he'd forgotten to kiss her. His dry lips brushed hers, and he straightened up to find her gazing at him with an expression he couldn't interpret.

"She'll be okay," Lydia told him.

Alvie did his best to smile at her, and then he turned to the steel delivery door and let himself in before she had put the car in gear. Alvie switched on the stockroom light and the banker's lamp on Mr. Levezzari's desk, and then he went through to the main store. The rows of fluorescent ceiling lights flickered on, and the showroom appeared in all its shabby brilliance: the tiers of bakelite radios, the shelves of sewing machines and blenders and percolators, the wall of hulking Frigidaires, the boxy aisle of washer-drier sets. Without looking, Alvie could feel the three televisions languishing on the chest-high shelf next to the stockroom doorway, and their presence felt like a rebuke.

The televisions had been Alvie's idea: it had taken him two steady weeks of pleading and cajoling, of reading aloud from *Radio Age* and wildly exaggerating sales projections, to convince Mr. Levezzari to order the three sets from the RCA catalogue—the 630 tabletop model, with the ten-inch screen. They arrived the last week of May, and Alvie vowed he'd sell them all by Independence Day. But when they arrived, Mr. Levezzari insisted they be put back here, next to the Kirby vacuum accessories, instead of rearranging the entire store so they'd be up near the front window where any sensible businessman would have put them. Then most of the summer had gone by, and none of the sets had sold—despite Alvie's leading his customers on the most circuitous route around the shop, so they would pass by the televisions on the way to the toasters.

Mr. Levezzari had no vision, no ability to imagine or speculate. He was more than willing to run out his few remaining years selling the same brands of refrigerators and washing machines and (god help us!) *radios*—when anyone could see that television was poised to revolutionize the way we lived. In a year or two, those clumsy console radios Mr. L insisted on keeping in the front window would be as archaic as a magic lantern show.

Without looking at the televisions, Alvie set about his morning inspection tour. He walked each aisle with a dust rag, polishing up chrome, repositioning plastic steaks and vegetables on refrigerator shelves, plugging in the tube tester and the lit display of Victron fans. When he was done, he looked up at the wall clock and felt deflated to find it was only 9:30; the store wouldn't open until ten. He drifted to the front glass doors and looked out on Ellis Street.

Across the way, a small knot of people stood waiting at the bus stop. What would it matter if he opened the doors early? Someone in line for the bus might trot across to pick up a box of batteries or an extension cord on the way downtown. He flipped the OPEN sign in the front window and unlocked the doors.

AFTER DINNER THAT night, Lydia went through the house and packed up knickknacks and novelties to cart out to Brookside the next day—anything that might help Rose pass the time in her new quarters or would brighten her austere room. She packed a selection of Dickens hardbacks, two decks of pinochle cards, an unopened jigsaw of Mount Rushmore, a pair of ceramic collies, a blue Wedgewood bowl, a Union Oil wall calendar—all of which she fit neatly into two cardboard boxes, which she lugged out to the trunk of her car.

When she left that evening for her apartment, she gave Alvie a quick hug on the front porch, kissed him briskly on the lips, and trotted across the lawn to her car, her every movement youthful and vivacious. From the porch steps, Alvie watched her drive the length of Grove Street. Only when her car disappeared around the corner, did it occur to him that she really needn't have gone. Who would have known if she had spent the night? Rose was gone, and Frankie had left for his own apartment not long after dinner. Lydia's car was so often parked at the curb, no one would think it odd to see it there. Alvie chewed on his lower lip and wondered if he should give Lydia a few minutes to get home and then dial her number and ask her to come back.

But, still looking down the empty street, he thought suddenly of Rose. He imagined her jittery first evening at Brookside, thought of her cowering in a wingback chair in that cavernous main room, restless hands twisting in her lap, eyes darting from one faintly menacing stranger to another. *Oh, god.* He guiltily pictured her being led up to her bare, echoing room and being left there alone. He imagined her lying wide eyed in the cheerless, creaking darkness. No, he couldn't call Lydia. Not tonight. It would feel like the worst kind of betrayal—a sordid exploitation of his mother's sad decline. He didn't yet want to plumb the dark and selfish benefits he'd reap from committing his mother to a home.

Alvie came in from the porch and pulled the door shut. He left the porch light on, switched off the hallway light, and waited a few seconds for his eyes to adapt to the darkness. How long had it been since he'd been alone in the house? Weeks? Months? Years, perhaps? It was hard to remember *any* time when there was not some other heart beating in these rooms. He moved through the house numbly, switching off lights, bolting doors, checking the knobs on the oven and stove—and he remembered, years ago, lying in bed, listening to his mother carry out this same lonely ritual. It seemed like he should *feel* something at this moment, but he wasn't sure exactly what. It was true: the last few months had been Alvie's favorite days in this house, and he should be heart-scalded to see them end so abruptly. With Rose and Lydia and Frankie around him every evening, he had finally felt part of a family— one more complete than he had ever thought possible. It was as if *he* had become the man this old house had always needed to feel whole. When he came in from the appliance store, it felt like he was arriving home to a human solar system that wheeled around him. *His* mother. *His* brother. *His* fiancé. And there was Alvie at the center, not in some cold outer orbit, where he'd always worried he would spend his life.

Even having Frankie around so much had somehow become agreeable—Alvie sitting at the head of the table, and his mother at the foot. And Lydia—lovely, headstrong Lydia!—setting out the pot roast and the corn and the bowl of steaming jacket potatoes and then taking her seat across from Frankie. The two of them, Frankie and Lydia, were finally starting to get along—though that would have been impossible to imagine just last spring. They seemed to have hammered out an unspoken truce. They addressed each other politely; Lydia no longer complained about those records Frankie was always putting on; Frankie paused in doorways to let Lydia pass through first. And for the last few weeks, Frankie had actually been helping her clear the table and do the dishes after dinner. Who would ever have pictured Frankie gently wiping a plate with a dishtowel and setting it back in the cupboard! Once or twice, Frankie had even donned one of Rose's old aprons, and Alvie, catching a glimpse of him as he passed the kitchen doorway, had to slip into the parlor to laugh.

The situation wasn't perfect, naturally; sometimes Alvie looked up from his dinner plate to find the air between Frankie and Lydia crackling with tension. And there was still a flash in Lydia's eye if Frankie arrived at the house unexpectedly on the weekend. But the two of them were civil to one another, and how could Alvie ask for more than that? But what would happen to all that now, with Rose out at Brookside?

FOR A WHILE Alvie lay awake on his bed, senses preternaturally pricked up: he heard every mouse scrabble in the attic, felt every wayward mattress lump, tasted the tang of the rosemary bush outside his open bedroom window. He rolled on his side and bunched the pillow around his ears.

When he heard clattering in the kitchen, he jolted awake, not sure he'd even been asleep. He rolled out of bed and shambled down the hallway barefoot. He'd wakened several times in recent weeks to find Rose in some bewildered act of housekeeping—buttering a potholder or sorting scissors and pens into the silverware tray. But the kitchen was dark and empty. Rose, of course, was gone. He flipped up the light switch and blinked back the sudden brilliance. The back door was closed, the deadbolt locked. Cool night air tousled the scalloped curtains above the sink. It took him a moment to notice one of the counter drawers pulled all the way open, Rose's steel measuring cups glimmering in the overhead light. He couldn't have missed that when he'd made his rounds. He felt the scalp-tightening chill of knowing his dead sister was in the room with him.

Alvie pushed the drawer closed, switched out the light, and limped back down the hall, rubbing the prickling at the back of his neck. The door to Rose's bedroom was half open, and he peeked inside like a trespasser. The room smelled of her: like cloves and talcum and those cherry cough drops she ate like candy. The light of the waxing moon glimmered through the neighbor's oak. It dappled her empty bed with luminous blue-white light and lent the polished dresser top a milky sheen. The room felt fusty and comfortable—as old-maidy as a wad of tissues tucked in a cardigan sleeve.

Feeling orphaned, he hobbled back to his empty bed.

ALVIE'S BAD ANKLE was pulsing like an air-raid siren by the time he mounted the third floor stairway. It was hard enough to climb steps in the best of circumstances, and the box he was lugging just made matters worse. He held it against his pounding chest, both arms aching, and wondered what was inside that could make it so heavy. Books, perhaps? An aquarium? Or had Lydia packed up all Frankie's jazz records to get the damn things out of the house?

At the top of the stairway he caught his breath and looked down the long third-floor hallway. There were too many doors, and, except for the small black numerals affixed above the lintel, they looked identical: white semi-gloss, equally spaced, wide enough to trundle a gurney through. How was his poor, befuddled mother supposed to find her room without someone to show her? Alvie hobbled along the corridor to number 205 and braced the box against the door while he strained to twist the handle. He managed to turn the knob and nudged the door open with his bad foot. Without waiting for Lydia, he pushed his way in, and set the box on the desk before his arms gave out. The walls of Rose's room were harsh white, and the air smelled of new paint. Alvie rubbed his lower back with both hands and went over to the window. A series of brass screws drilled in around the wooden frame made it impossible to open.

Lydia came in and set her own box on the floor on the far side of the bed. She straightened up and looked around appraisingly at the blindingly empty walls and the scuffed wooden floor. The headboard and foot of Rose's bed were gray tubular steel— like something from an army barrack, Alvie guessed—and the white blankets seemed unwelcomingly taut across the mattress.

Lydia pulled a blue comforter from the box on the floor and flung it out over the bed. With that one splash of color, the room seemed to change, to soften, to feel more convivial. She tugged out the wrinkles and then unrolled an oval braided rug across the cold, bare floor next to Rose's bed.

Alvie watched her adoringly. There was something about her expert domesticity that roused a thrilling—almost erotic—sense of anticipation. At home he'd sometimes watch her iron his work shirts, or he'd pause in the kitchen doorway while she set the table, and the sight of her quick, proficient movements made him ache with longing.

She moved Alvie's box from the desk to the bed—it seemed less cumbersome when she handled it—and pulled from it the carnival-glass vase Rose had kept on the parlor mantle. She fluffed a spray of cloth daisies that had been flattened by the ride and slipped them into it. "You could help," she said, without looking in Alvie's direction. She set the vase on Rose's new dresser and stepped back, head tilted, to inspect her arrangement.

Alvie went to the box and found a framed watercolor seascape. It took him a moment to place it: it had been hanging in the back hallway for years. He held it out at arm's length and peered around at the bare walls, as if this one small painting might transform the room if he could just find the right place for it.

"*Here*," Lydia said.

He turned to find her holding out a finishing nail and a small tack hammer.

"Over there," she said. "Next to the wardrobe."

AS ROSE'S ROOM brightened, so did Alvie's mood. His mother would be fine here. The place was no longer some cold, ascetic cloister; it was more a smart and frugal bedroom, where someone had lived comfortably for years. Rose's most cherished ornaments and baubles were here—her Waterford bell, her kissing figurines, her Roseville cornucopia. Her sand dollar collection was lined up along the windowsill. A row of her favorite books sat on her desk, buttressed by her brass globe bookends.

In the almost-empty box Alvie found a couple of photographs set in new pewter frames. One was a snapshot of Lydia and him—the one a passing stranger had snapped for them on the Huntington Beach pier the weekend they got engaged. The other was Frankie, in his dress uniform, in front of an American flag.

"Beside the bed, where she can see them," Lydia said. She was winding a clock over by the dresser.

Alvie set the photos on the bedside table. He tried a few different arrangements. "Are these the ones from home?" he asked. He nudged the photo of him and Lydia, so it partly obscured the one of Frankie. "Did you take these from the album?"

"No," Lydia said. "Frankie printed me another set."

Alvie picked up the photo of Frankie. His dress cap was tilted at a rakish angle. The olive fabric of his uniform seemed stiff and palpable. His brass buttons gleamed. "When did Frankie give these to you?" He set the photo back where it had been.

"I don't know," Lydia said vaguely. "Yesterday. The day before."

"But how could—?"

A clattering in the doorway interrupted Alvie's thought. The young black orderly from the other day was edging into the room with an iron birdcage and the question-mark stand it would hang from.

"What's this?" Lydia said.

Alvie jumped up from the bed and took his place between Lydia and the orderly. "There must be some mistake," he said. "You've got the wrong room."

"No mistake," a voice in the hallway said, and Frankie was there in the doorway. Cupped in both his hands was a small paper carton that looked like it should hold Chinese food. Something was scratching inside. "I got Ma a canary."

Lydia smiled. "How sweet," she said. She stepped around Alvie and bent, hands on knees, to look at the box in Frankie's hand, as if she might see through it to the bird inside.

"A canary?" Alvie said.

"It'll keep her company," Frankie said, "and it'll help her find her room." He gestured at the orderly who was now hanging the cage on its stand in the corner near the window. "It was Jiggs's idea."

Alvie glanced at the kid's name badge. It said *Luther Walker.* "We haven't been introduced," Alvie said.

The young black man turned and smiled at them all. A film of sweat seemed spread with a butter knife across his taut cheeks and his wide, dark forehead. One of his front teeth was a brighter shade of white than the others. He pushed the cage with a long finger and set it swaying on its stand. "Keep this right where it is," he told them in a sweet rumble of a voice. "Won't sing if he sees himself in the mirror."

Frankie went over to the cage, carrying the tiny box carefully upright, like an overfull teacup. "Jiggs plays sax," he said over his shoulder, as if someone might have been wondering.

Alvie's buoyancy had completely drained away by now. He caught himself glancing in the mirror, as if to make sure he were still visible. "But Ma can't take care of a bird," he protested. "She can't even—."

"Jiggs's going to feed it," Frankie said before Alvie could finish. He opened the little door in the front of the birdcage. "We got it all worked out. Ma won't have to lift a finger."

Lydia, grinning, stood on tiptoe behind Frankie, trying to look over his shoulder, down into the tiny box.

Frankie opened the carton's top a crack and peeked inside. "It sings like a man on fire." He reached into the box and quickly pulled out his fist and slipped it through the birdcage door. When Frankie let it go, the canary flitted around a few ecstatic seconds, and then it lit on the tiny dowel swing, which swayed all trembly under its minuscule weight. The bird was a mottled ginger—like a melted orange Creamsicle. Frankie latched the cage door. He crumpled the paper carton in his hands and turned to Lydia. "I named him after Charlie Parker," he told her, grinning. "He's called *Bird.*"

It seemed to be a joke—and Alvie was the only one in the room who didn't get it.

Lydia beamed at Frankie and seemed to rise up on her toes a little. "Real cute," she told him.

"BUT IT'S NEW YORK and Brooklyn," Lydia said from the driver's seat. "Why would anyone want to see that?"

"It's the *World Series,*" Alvie insisted. "It's *television.*" The idea had struck him out of the blue as they were leaving Brookside: the three RCA 630s set up in the front window of L&S—the first televised World Series game, out where the whole town could see it! It was the perfect marketing ploy, and it was completely free! How could it *not* draw attention to the wonder of this new technology?

"Maybe if the Aces were playing," Lydia said, frowning over the steering wheel at the post office truck idling in front of them at the stoplight. "But *New York?*"

Alvie bit his lip and tried to be patient. He'd never get her to understand. He looked out the side window at the cars parked along the curb outside the row of jewelry shops on Front Street. The light changed, and they started moving again.

"The Anaheim team folded years ago," Frankie chimed in from the back seat. He took a drag on his cigarette, then reached over and flicked ashes out his half-open window. "And they were California League. There aren't any major league teams in the west. *All* of them are back east."

"Well that just proves my point, doesn't it?" Lydia said, squinting back at Frankie in the rear-view mirror.

"The road," Alvie said. "Eyes on the road."

Lydia let out a peevish hiss and scowled out through the windshield again. She wasn't a bad driver—Alvie would be the first to admit that—but there was something about having her behind the wheel that had him on edge. Then again maybe it was the shrill, thumping pain in his ankle—which was why she was driving in the first place.

"All I'm saying is that a TV in the front window is bound to cause a stir," Alvie said. "It's free publicity." He glanced at Lydia. "Maybe you could give your girlfriend at *The Ledger* a call."

"I still don't see why anyone would care," Lydia said in that willful tone of hers. She tapped the brakes, accelerated into the traffic circle in the plaza, and veered off down Reasner Street towards home.

Alvie gripped the door handle. "People will care," he mumbled, sounding more petulant than he'd meant to. He looked out the side window again. A white-smocked man on a scaffold was lettering a new sign above a vacant shop window. Alvie twisted in his seat to look back over his shoulder at the empty shop as they passed. He tried to remember what had been in that storefront last month. That stationery store with the humidor in back? Or was it that pet shop with the mynah bird that spoke Spanish? Alvie thought of the canary they'd left singing in his mother's room, and he felt a tiny, unsettling flutter of something in his belly. He turned to face forward again and crossed his arms.

From the back seat, Frankie blew a column of smoke that grazed Alvie's cheek. "Why don't you tell her?" he said.

Lydia glanced in the rear view mirror again and then looked over at Alvie. "Tell me what?"

"Why people care about this World Series," Frankie said, his voice sounding somehow far away—like it was coming from the last row of a bus, and not just the back seat.

Alvie glanced back at him. He was slumped insolently against the center armrest, his knees propped on the back of Alvie's seat. Frankie took one last drag on his stub of a cigarette and flicked it out the window. Why did he have to tag along everywhere? Why couldn't he just get his own car, his own fiancée—his own damned life?

"What?" Lydia said. She signaled, checked her mirrors and turned down Grove Street. "What are you two talking about?"

Alvie sighed and turned on his seat to face Lydia. "This World Series might be a little controversial," he said, hoping his answer didn't sound evasive.

"Contro*ver*sial?" Lydia said. "*Base*ball?"

Alvie plucked at one of his shirt buttons. "The Dodgers are playing a colored first baseman," he said.

Other than her furrowed brow, Lydia's face remained blank, staring out through the windshield. It was like she was trying to make a connection and failing. "And?" she said.

"The Dodgers are playing Jackie Robinson," Frankie explained. He leaned forward now, his forearms on the seatback, his stubbly face intruding between them. "So suddenly everyone in this sorry-ass town is a Yankees fan."

Lydia sat straighter. "*Really?*" she said.

The muscles along Alvie's jaw tensed. This was so typical of Frankie. Everything with him had to be simplistic, inflammatory, so damned black and white. Frankie always formed some blustering half-baked opinion, and then he bullied everyone, cocksure of himself. Not Alvie. Alvie had a knack of seeing both sides at once, of finding a harmless middle ground in any controversy. He was the mediator, the faithful go-between.

Lydia pulled the car up into the drive, alongside the house, and turned off the ignition. But instead of handing Alvie the keys, she sort of sagged there in the front seat, hands in her lap, looking out the front window at the side gate. "People really care?" she said.

The back door opened, the car heaved higher on its suspension, and then the door swung shut again. Trust Frankie to stir things up and walk away.

"Well, what do you expect?" Alvie said to Lydia. "Naturally it's going to be controversial."

Lydia turned her head slowly, like doing so pained her somehow. "And you want to take *advantage* of this?"

Alvie felt like he was being accused of something vile— like war profiteering—and he felt the color rise in his cheeks. "Take advantage?" he said. "*No, no, no.*" He paused a moment to formulate his response, feeling like he'd been pushed out onto thin ice and needed to carefully weigh his choice of words. "I'm just trying to sell some televisions," he said deliberately. "I don't care which team wins."

The frosty blankness of Lydia's expression implied that this wasn't the correct answer.

"I don't necessarily agree with them," Alvie said, his words rushing in to fill the silent vacuum in the car. "But—come on—what do you *expect* to happen when black men and white men start playing together?"

A shadow behind them moved, and Alive glanced back to see Frankie head up the side steps to the kitchen door. Had he been lurking there behind them, eavesdropping the whole time?

"Lydia, you're making too much of this," Alvie said. "I'm just going to put a television in the front window of the store. That's all." He put a hand on her forearm. "It's just baseball."

Faint, tinny trumpet music started up inside the house. Frankie was at the gramophone again.

Without a word, Lydia held out the car keys to Alvie, and he took them, and then she got out of the car, and he followed her through the side door into the house. When they came out through the kitchen, the music from the record player was so loud it seemed to buzz in the hallway floorboards underfoot. "Frankie!" Alvie yelled. "Turn that damned thing down!"

Lydia strode back to the bathroom, so Alvie wandered, hands dug in pockets, to the parlor doorway, where Frankie stood in the middle of the floor listening to his music. "*Dammit, Frankie,*" Alvie shouted. He found himself rising up on tiptoe, as if to loft his words over the music. "Turn that racket down."

"You hear that trumpet?" Frankie shouted, as if Alvie could possibly miss music that was blaring so loud it rumbled in his chest. "That's Louis Armstrong."

Alvie winced and shook his head irritably. "That's very nice, Frankie," he shouted, "but would you *please* just...."

"*Wait,*" Frankie interrupted. "*Listen.*" He held a hand up, silencing Alvie. He just stood there with his eyes closed, and then he smiled suddenly. "*There. There.* Hear that trombone? That's Jack Teagarden."

"*Frankie!*"

"Brother," Frankie said, his eyes still squeezed shut, that exasperating smile splayed across his smug face. "*That's* what happens when black men and white men play together."

THE CLATTER OF typewriter keys paused, and Alvie looked up from his electronics catalog to see Lydia reading back over what she'd been writing. The house was quiet now that Frankie had finally left for his apartment. From his seat on the parlor sofa he watched her, and the image of her there at his mother's old writing desk made him smile. She looked like some madcap woman reporter from a Howard Hawks movie: cigarette between two slender fingers, her lively dark eyes moving back and forth over the page.

Alvie watched her take a brooding drag on her cigarette, and his mind did a sudden somersault—all unbidden, he saw her the way she must look to a man like Frankie: a dark perplexing beauty, full of sharp words and thrilling willful notions, a wisp of smoke leaking upward from her full forbidden lips. He saw in that moment that she might well be alluring, even to someone with no use for her fierce loyalty; her ability to organize; her good, manly common sense—all those things Alvie loved so deeply.

"Those photos," he said. "When did Frankie give them to you?" He watched her keenly for any sign of fluster—a quick furrow of the brow, a tug at the corners of her mouth, a glint of compunction in the eye—but she just continued reading impassively, as if Alvie hadn't spoken.

"Hon?" he said.

Lydia glanced up from the page. She reached over and stubbed out her cigarette on the saucer she was using as an ashtray. "Alvie, I'm trying to concentrate," she said. "Just let me finish this paragraph." She started typing again, frowning down at the words as they appeared on the page before her.

LYDIA WOULDN'T STAY. At ten o'clock she pulled the canvas cover over the old typewriter, snapped her purse shut and, saying something about errands she had to run in the morning and her general exhaustion, pulled open the front door.

She still seemed miffed at him, so Alvie accepted a brusque, perfunctory kiss, and, feeling powerless, he watched from the doorway as she backed out of the drive and rumbled away.

Back in the bathroom in his pajamas, Alvie studied himself in the mirror as he brushed his teeth. He spat out the toothpaste, and pulled himself to his full height to glower at his own reflection. From the comfortable vantage of retrospect, he thought of all he could have said and done in his own defense that day. He could have demanded that Frankie return the bird to wherever he'd found it. He could have insisted that Frankie be dropped off at his own apartment after they'd left Brookside so he and Lydia could have one evening alone. In the doorway just now, he could have pulled Lydia close and kissed her roughly, the way men did in movies.

At this last thought his image in the mirror slumped a little. Movie women always melted—but Lydia, let's face it, was not the melting sort. He bent over the sink and rinsed his mouth with a cupped handful of water from the faucet.

As he was about to pull the chain to turn off the overhead lamp, he noticed his mother's oval silver hairbrush on the counter's edge, and it struck him as odd. Hadn't he seen it last night on Rose's dresser when he looked in on her empty room? He picked it up by its cold, tarnished handle.

He turned it over. A long, tangled hair dangled from the yellow bristles. He tugged it loose and held it up in the yellow light between finger and thumb. This hair was much longer than Lydia's, and the color—how was it possible?—was the same coppery hue of his own. An electric current pulsed up his arm: he dropped the hair. He opened and closed his tingling fingers and watched the strand drift down through the air, looping and curling like a wisp of smoke as it fell towards the floor tiles. And then it vanished.

He dropped to his knees and scanned the floor tiles, but the hair was gone.

"THAT COLORED BOY is stealing from me," Rose informed them the next afternoon. She sat on the edge of her bed dressed absurdly in her best slate dress, wearing both a pillbox hat and her old string of pearls, as if she expected to be taken to a wedding or funeral. "Oh, yes. He steals," she said. "Every chance he gets."

Alvie looked at Frankie, who had turned from the window, and then at Lydia, who was slipping Rose's clean delicates into her dresser drawer.

Alvie scooted the reading chair a little closer to his mother. "He's stealing?" he said, his voice dropped near a whisper.

"He comes in when I'm not here," she said. "I've seen him."

"*Ma*," Frankie said. Then again, loud enough to get her to look in his direction: "*Ma-a!*"

Rose's head swiveled to look up at Frankie, and the smile that spread over her face suggested she'd forgotten he was in the room.

Frankie came over and knelt down in front of her. "He's feeding your bird, Ma," Frankie said. He gestured behind him in the direction of the corner cage, where the tiny bird was busy sharpening its beak against the dowel perch. "Jiggs comes in here to feed the bird and change the paper. He's not stealing." Frankie looked around the room in a pantomime of bafflement. "There's nothing here to steal."

Rose fingered the pearls on her necklace like a rosary. On any other woman, her furrowed brow would suggest she was mulling the idea over—but it was hard to know if Frankie's words were even sinking in. "He comes in when I'm not looking," she said primly.

Frankie took both her hands in his. "He's feeding your bird, Ma," he told her. "I asked him to."

For a moment Rose stared down at where Frankie's hands and her own were linked in her lap, and then her unfocused gaze drifted over to the window, and it was clear her mind had wandered away again.

Lydia closed the drawers of Rose's dresser and came to sit on the arm of Alvie's chair. She draped one arm across his shoulder, and stroked Rose's cheek with the back of her other hand. "Poor girl," she said.

Alvie regarded his mother's empty-eyed gaze. "You know, she could be right," he said.

Frankie shot an angry look at Alvie. He let go of his mother's hands and rose to his feet, brushing imaginary dust from the knees of his trousers. "I *know* Jiggs," Frankie said hotly. "He's a good kid."

"I'm not *saying* he stole anything," Alvie reasoned. "But maybe we owe it to the other residents to mention it to the manager. Maybe he could keep an eye out."

"Dammit, Alvie," Frankie said, in that superior tone of his. "You know what will happen if you say anything."

Lydia gently squeezed Alvie's shoulder. "He seems like such a nice boy," she said.

Alvie suppressed the odd, angry impulse to shrug Lydia's hand off his shoulder. "We don't know him from Adam," he told her. "And—frankly—the fact he knows my brother from some jazz bar doesn't help his case."

Frankie, who had been slouching against the dresser, straightened up suddenly, bristling with antagonism. "What the *hell* is that supposed to mean?"

Alvie rose higher in his chair. "You don't exactly spend your time with the Rotary Club."

Before Frankie could respond, Lydia was between them, standing with her back to Alvie. "He's *not* going to report it, Frankie," she said. "Don't get all worked up."

Alvie was struck momentarily speechless. What made *her* so sure of what he would and wouldn't do? And who had asked *her* to step in? He gripped the arms of the reading chair with both hands, but before he could formulate a suitable response to the situation, Lydia was steering Frankie to the door.

"I've got a box in the trunk," she told Frankie. "Come help me bring it up." Without even an apologetic glance in Alvie's direction, she led Frankie down the hall in the direction of the stairway.

Alvie looked at his mother. She was staring at the empty doorway and then she turned to look at Alvie. Her warm hand, light as a sparrow, perched on his knee. "Love birds," she told him. She glanced again in the direction of the doorway. "Those two are so sweet on each other." She smiled at him then, her narrowed eyes, glinting with mirth. She pressed her fingers to her lips as if to suppress a giggle.

Alvie felt frustration waver like the onset of a migraine behind his eyes. "*Ma*," he said, rubbing his forehead with one hand. "*I'm* Alvie."

Rose's gaze drifted up towards the ceiling and then meandered back to Alvie's face again. "They're sweet on each other," she said. And then: "Your sister thinks so, too. She's seen them kissing."

"Ma," Alvie said. "That was *Lydia*. She's not our sister."

Rose seemed affronted by this remark. She fixed Alvie with that look of wounded disappointment she'd always used to guilt him—and it made him squirm a little, even now. "Don't you think I know my own children?" she said.

Why—out of all her haphazard and senseless pronouncements—did this one catch at something in Alvie? "But, you don't *have* a daughter," he told her, bracing himself for something. "You have two boys."

Rose shook her head with an expression of great and weary patience. "*Doris*," she said, and she smiled ruefully at the name. "Don't tell *me* I don't know my own."

Alvie stood. He walked to the window, though he knew there was no view of the parking lot from this side of the building, just the old sycamore, its scarred and maculate boughs visible here and there among the browning leaves. He turned back to his mother. "Doris speaks to you?" he said, keeping his voice flat and steady. He thought of all the hints and gestures, the secret jokes and private signals that seemed to electrify the air between his brother and his fiancée when they were in the same room. "Doris has seen them? Frankie and Lydia?"

But Rose's mind had already wandered away again. She sat now gazing down at the veined backs of her hands, which rested atop her knees.

Alvie turned to the birdcage, where the canary, head turned quizzically to one side, studied him with a single beady, unblinking eye. He squeezed his hands into fists. "Let's go see Dr. Goldberg," Alvie told his mother, without turning to look at her. "Let's tell him about that boy who's been stealing."

ALVIE RINSED OUT the bowl he'd used to eat his can of baked beans—standing right here at the sink, dismally looking at his reflection in the kitchen window—and put it in the draining rack. Lydia couldn't stay angry forever. At least she'd never been able to hang onto a grudge in the past. He swept the scattered toast crumbs from the counter into the sink and rinsed them down.

Frankie was another matter. Frankie would hold onto this forever. He'd throw it in Alvie's face at every opportunity. Alvie had honestly never seen him so livid. If they hadn't been in Brookside's lobby, the whole situation would have come to blows, right there in front of their bewildered mother.

And then there had been the stormy silent ride home. Alvie was relieved to be dropped off first—though it would have made just as much sense, he could have pointed out, to swing past Frankie's apartment and then back up the other end of Grove Street. Alvie sheepishly got out of the passenger seat, and, as soon as the door was shut behind him, Lydia pulled abruptly away from the curb like a taxi driver, and took off down the street with Frankie still fuming in the backseat.

Alvie washed his hands and dried them on a dishtowel. How had *he* become the villain in this situation? Couldn't Lydia and Frankie understand how hard it was to navigate sometimes? What a burden it was to be the responsible one? Alvie wasn't like them. He couldn't just take one side of an issue and completely ignore the other possibility. Any controversy or quarrel or debate—like any baseball game—could go either way. He had acted with care, good sense, and a measure of caution. Would Dr. Goldberg really have fired the kid unless there had been other complaints?

He turned out the kitchen light and went into the parlor, where a few of Frankie's records were still leaning against the wall under the front window. He picked them up and flipped through them—a glossy full-cheeked face blowing into a trumpet; a white man in a black suit lounging on a piano bench; a black woman, mouth agape, screaming into a microphone—it was a world Alvie would never understand. He slipped the records into the orange crate with the others, picked a volume at random from Rose's bookcase, and slumped onto the sofa to kill the rest of the evening.

In the First Inning, Spec Shea walked Number 42, and the black man trotted over to first base. Alvie felt a hush descend on the small arc of viewers there on the sidewalk. He could hear the man next to him breathing heavily through his nose. On the television, the pitcher leaned in to squint at the catcher's signal, and Number 42 stepped off first base into that perilous no-man's-land of crushed brick, turned grainy gray on the television screen. Alvie watched the black man choose his spot a couple of yards from first base. He bent into a low crouch, coiled tightly, his hands floating up on either side of him, like he was expecting at any moment to take flight. He looked wary and watchful and rocked on the balls of his feet, ready to explode toward second base or dive back to the safety of first, teetering there on the brink.

I know that feeling, Alvie thought. It was that comfortless, edgy moment of being poised between uncertainties—that jangled interval of unblinking watchfulness, waiting for something to unfold, something over which you had no power.

The pitcher hurled the ball at the catcher, and Alvie clenched his fists as Number 42 rocketed toward second base.

CHAPTER EIGHT
FAT SADIE'S: PART I
1947-1954

FRANKIE SET OUT north after the incident, hitching rides along Highway One and sometimes paying bus fare when no one would stop or it looked like rain. He liked the looks of Half Moon Bay from the start—the way the town curved between the hills and water, how it looked in the afternoon slant of sunlight and then in the morning fog. So he stopped there, twenty miles south of San Francisco, even though he'd been planning on escaping all the way to Anchorage.

Frankie slept on the beach under a stilted lifeguard shed his first two nights in town, but then he picked up a job as the afternoon pinsetter at the bowling alley on Spruce Street and rented an austere and chilly room above an auto parts shop.

He lived frugally. He helped himself to a good heavy coat from the bowling alley's lost and found bin before anyone could claim it; that way he wouldn't have to pay to heat his room. He plucked unfinished cigarettes from the ashtrays on the scoring tables; he only took the ones marked with lipstick. He ate the shriveled franks that had revolved too long on the coffee shop's glistening rollers; they would otherwise have gone to waste.

The money Frankie had left each week after paying the rent, he took to the Pelican, a corner tavern conveniently placed at the exact midpoint of his walk home from the alley. What he didn't spend at the bar, he lost at the back tables—in hard-fought, bourbon-addled games of five-card draw. Frankie drank at the Pelican every night for a few weeks before he got into a tussle with one of the other patrons: the man had clearly bent the corners of all four aces in Frankie's own deck. Frankie had *watched* him do it. Frankie lunged across the table and knocked the offender over. It wasn't until he was straddling the man, ready to rain blows on his florid face, that he noticed the wheelchair, empty and capsized, beside them. Frankie was carried to the door and invited never to return.

Fat Sadie's, the only other bar in town, was all the way over on the north end of the bay, but what choice did Frankie have? The notion of spending every night alone in his room was just too dismal. What could a man like Frankie possibly do? Get a library card and take up reading?

That first night at Fat Sadie's, when Frankie slipped in off the boardwalk, Sadie was in the middle of one of her sets, growling and scatting her way through her own bawdy version of "Stairway to the Stars." Frankie sat down on the corner barstool nearest the door. He ordered a bottle of Falstaff. When it came, he paid for it, and took inventory of his wallet. He could afford two more, so he'd have to make them last. He swiveled around, leaned back against the bar and settled in to listen.

While she sang, Fat Sadie sashayed among the tables—which were widely spaced to accommodate her girth—dabbing herself with a pink hankie and striking poses she seemed to think might be alluring. Despite her great size, she moved with a certain lithe grace. She seemed supple as a Chinese acrobat, though she probably outweighed a whole troupe of them.

Her accompanist—he was maybe sixteen—hunched over the piano with an inert expression on his face. He was a lanky little runt with a sunburned nose and a cowlick. For some reason one of his white shirtsleeves was rolled up to the elbow, while the other was buttoned snugly around his wrist. He seemed much too young to be playing in a bar. As his fingers worked the keyboard, he lolled his head this way and that. His heavy-lidded, impassive gaze never seemed to settle on anything. The kid played well enough, though his jittery finger-work seemed somehow disconnected from the rest of him.

Frankie took a sip of beer, closed his eyes, and listened. It was an odd effect: if he couldn't *see* Sadie, she sounded petite and youthful—like Ella Fitzgerald in the Chick Webb years, or that blonde Andrew Sister. But when Frankie opened his eyes, there she was: a massive woman well into her sixties, all swaying bosom and haunches in her sleeveless blue dress. Her hair was dyed jet-black and cut in an absurd Betty Page. Her porcine face was pockmarked and glossy with sweat. Frankie closed his eyes again.

When Fat Sadie finished her set, she made her rounds at the tables, talking to the men and tucking their tips down her immense cleavage. The kid at the piano rolled down his one furled sleeve, buttoned it, and then slunk over to sit on the empty stool next to Frankie. The bartender poured the boy a glass of orange juice and slid it in front of him.

Frankie turned on his stool to face the bar. "She here every night?" he asked the kid.

The kid's gaze brushed over Frankie's face and then dropped to the glass of juice on the bar top. "You asking if Fat Sadie is a regular at Fat Sadie's?" the kid said in a querulous tenor.

Frankie, not sure if he was being mocked, squinted at the boy and then took a swig from his bottle. "So that's her?" he said. "That's Sadie?"

"That's her," the kid said. He shot a look at Frankie again—though the glance seemed directed at Frankie's hairline and not at his eyes.

Frankie emptied his bottle of Falstaff and wiped his mouth on his sleeve. "She's got a set of pipes on her," he said and then burped softly.

The kid chuckled. "Set of pipes," he repeated. He rotated the juice glass in front of him, scrutinizing it closely, like he was looking for the right approach. Finally, he lifted it, took a dainty sip and fell silent, still touching the glass to his lips.

Frankie, feeling rebuffed, swiveled around on his stool and leaned back against the bar again. The enormous woman was at the table nearest him now. She pressed her lips to the top of a blushing man's bald head, leaving a crimson pucker of lipstick, and then she strode in Frankie's direction. She dabbed at her bulbous throat with her hankie as she walked. When she got closer, Frankie could see just how much she'd been sweating. Her immense breasts, pressed together by her low-cut dress, looked like they were coated with bowling lane varnish.

"I don't believe I've had the pleasure," she said, offering Frankie a surprisingly petite hand. Frankie wasn't sure if she wanted it kissed or shaken, so he shook.

The kid on the next stool wagged a thumb in Frankie's direction. "This one wanted to know if you were a regular here," he said. "Wanted to know if Fat Sadie was a regular at Fat Sadie's." He laughed again, a kind of high-pitched squeal, and then flicked the rim of his juice glass with a fingernail, making it chime. "That's what this one wanted to know."

Only then did it dawn on Frankie that the kid was touched in the head. Frankie never would have guessed from the way he could play piano—and he felt thankful he hadn't picked a fight with the kid and got himself banned from the only other bar in walking distance.

"He's new, Jimbo," Sadie told the kid, who was now running one palm back and forth across the top of the bar like he was sweeping up grains of salt. "How would he have picked Fat Sadie out of this crowd?" Sadie swept out one hand with a kind of flourish, to take in the entire smoky room of men. The slack flesh that dangled from the underside of her arm quivered.

The kid rocked a little in his seat, humming tunelessly. He turned and fixed his eyes on a spot about six inches above Frankie's right shoulder, and then, like the correct answer to Sadie's question had just occurred to him, he turned to her grinning. "'Cause you're *fat*!" he said, and he let loose another squeaky laugh that writhed its way down through his whole wiry body.

Sadie gave the boy a playful cuff on the head. "I admit it, Jimmy," she said. "I ain't Rita Hayworth."

"No you ain't," the kid said. He shook his head, his eyes caught in an odd fluttery blinking. "You ain't Rita Hayworth."

Sadie turned from the kid and looked Frankie over, sizing him up. Her eyebrows were penciled in a little too high, which gave the impression that she found him surprising in some way. Despite her heavy makeup, Frankie could see a small smudge of moustache beaded with sweat. "It's nice to make your acquaintance, stranger," she told him.

"The name's Frankie."

"It's nice to make your acquaintance, *Frankie*," she said. She gave him another once over, and then bestowed a wink upon him before she turned and swayed her way down along the bar, greeting each of her admirers.

THE NEXT WEEK, on a rainy Friday, Jimmy the piano player got into a scuffle with a hulking Greek who had recently signed on to Mack Himmel's fishing fleet.

Frankie had no idea how the fracas got started, but when he looked up from his Falstaff, there the Greek was, a few stools down, bending Jimmy backwards over the bar. The Greek gripped the boy's throat with his left hand. His right hand, balled into a fist, bobbed around in the air behind him, like it was seeking the best trajectory for a single knockout blow. Frankie hesitated only an instant—a quick check for crutches or a wooden leg—but the Greek looked sound enough to hit with impunity.

Frankie grabbed his clunky umbrella (taken earlier that afternoon from the bowling alley lost and found) and slipped off his stool. He gripped the pointed end of the umbrella in both fists and stepped up behind the Greek. The heavy wooden handle circled in the air over his right shoulder like the thick end of a baseball bat, and then he swung at the horizontal crease where the Greek's burly neck met his skull. At contact, there was a dull splintering crack and a jolt that zinged up both Frankie's arms. Frankie watched as the huge Greek teetered and then slumped over on top of Jimmy.

The boy was now pinned on his back atop the bar, his skinny knees frantically churning the air. Frankie dropped the umbrella, grabbed the Greek by the back of his tooled-leather belt with both hands, and dragged him off the boy. The Greek collapsed in a weighty heap on top of Frankie's umbrella, knocking over a bar stool on the way down.

Frankie looked down at the man and poked him with the toe of his shoe—he was out cold but breathing wetly. When Frankie looked up again, everyone in the bar sat, stricken silent, staring at him. "What?" he said. He glanced around, just to make sure there was no seeing-eye dog he'd somehow overlooked. "What?"

None of the men answered. The only sounds now were the rain up in the rafters and Jimmy's whimpering from where he still lay sprawled on the bar. Frankie sighed. He bent, picked up the Greek's ankles, and glanced around again. It seemed clear no one was going to assist him. He looked at Jimmy. "Hey, Beethoven," he said. "Help me out here."

The kid stopped whining and looked at him, uncomprehending.

"I don't want to get all sweaty," Frankie told him. "I've got to wear this shirt again."

The kid stared blankly back at him.

"For God's sake," Frankie said. "Grab the other end, will ya?"

Jimmy started to whimper again, but he climbed down off the bar and slipped his long hands under the Greek's armpits.

"On three," Frankie told him. But when he counted to three, Jimmy could barely heft the Greek's shoulders off the ground. Frankie set his end down and looked around again at his silent audience. "Little help?" he said.

Sadie, from over by the stairway, called something to Bill the Bartender, and he came out from behind the bar, wiping his hands on his apron. Bill took the Greek's shoulders, and he and Frankie dragged the man in the direction of the door. "*Lift*," Frankie said. "The poor guy's ass is going to be full of splinters." Jimmy limped timorously ahead of them, whining and twisting his fingers. He pulled the door open for them.

When the Greek was safely deposited on the boardwalk outside, Frankie came back in and picked up his umbrella. It had an elbow crook in the middle now, and the wooden handle was split nearly in half. He tossed it disgustedly on the empty end of the bar. He took his seat and felt under each armpit. Sure enough, they were damp.

It took a moment, but people began to talk again, and soon there was the din of conversation that typically overtook the bar between Sadie's sets. In another moment, Jimmy came and sat beside Frankie, rubbing his throat and still whimpering. Frankie downed the last of his beer and pushed the empty bottle away. He wanted another, but Bill the Bartender was busy on the phone, explaining to the cops that there had been an accident: some drunk had taken a nasty spill on the boardwalk out front.

Frankie sighed and turned to Jimmy. "So what the hell was that about?" he said. "Why'd you pick a fight with a gorilla like him?"

Jimmy's throat looked swollen, and his Adam's apple had a smear of blood on it. His eyes were teary, so Frankie looked away. "You owe me an umbrella," Frankie said. And then Sadie was looking at him from the other side of the bar. He couldn't read the steely-eyed expression on her face, and her elevated eyebrows didn't help any.

"You some kind of bouncer?" she asked him.

He sensed he was about to get thrown out of another establishment, and wished he had got one last Falstaff before the long walk home in the rain. He turned the empty beer bottle in his hands on top of the bar. "Freelance," he told her. "It's just a hobby."

Sadie nodded noncommittally. "You ever think of turning pro?"

Frankie looked up from the empty bottle in his hands. He recognized her coolly neutral expression now: the look of a calculating businesswoman. "Is that a proposition?" he said.

A smile played across Sadie's lips. "It's only a job offer," she told him. "When I proposition you, you'll damn well know it."

Frankie set the empty bottle to one side and folded his hands on the burnished bar top. He returned Sadie's look levelly. "What does the gig pay?"

"Drinks," she said. "For now."

Frankie rubbed the stubble on his chin and tried to look like he was in a position to negotiate. "How *many* drinks?"

"Three a night," she said. "Five on Saturday."

It really wasn't much of a conundrum: Frankie would be here every night anyway, and he could either pay for his drinks or get them free. He shrugged. "Throw in an umbrella, and I'm your man," he said.

THEN, EARLY IN February, Bill the Bartender went out on his skiff one morning with his cousin Ernie and a bottle of Jim Beam. They just wanted to get a closer look at some passing gray whales, but the two of them were never seen again. That night Frankie was unceremoniously promoted from bouncer to bartender.

The next day, he rummaged through the lost and found cupboard at the bowling alley one last time—choosing a wristwatch and a tarnished cigarette case—and then quit his job as pinsetter.

FRANKIE'S NEW CAREER wasn't much of a challenge—Sadie's was mostly a beer and whiskey kind of place. Besides, all the regulars had witnessed Frankie's deft work with the umbrella, so no one complained if the service was slow. None of them wanted to see what he might accomplish, given the right motivation, with the Louisville Slugger tucked beneath the cash register.

"So what brought you up this way in the first place?" Sadie asked him as he was getting the bar ready on his second night. She was sitting on a barstool next to her strongbox, counting singles into the cash register drawer. "You running from the law or an angry husband?"

Frankie, as he rubbed down the beer taps with a rag, thought of Alvie, ashen and defeated, slumped in the driver's seat of Lydia's car outside Frankie's apartment. He remembered the gut-wrenching image of Lydia from behind, her clothes rumpled from their lovemaking, as she headed down the stairs in her red jacket to face her fiancé. "Something pretty close to that second one," Frankie said.

Sadie nodded. This was clearly no surprise to her, though her high-arched eyebrows might have suggested otherwise. "How did you meet her?" Sadie asked. "This wife in question?"

Frankie studied the damp rag he was holding. "She wasn't a wife," he said. "They were engaged."

Sadie smiled. She broke open a roll of quarters, and spilled them into the register drawer. "So, what was the problem?" she said. "Engaged isn't married."

Frankie wadded the rag into a ball and squeezed it a couple of times, watching the veins in his forearms pulse. "Let's just say there were complications," he said.

Something in the tone of Frankie's voice made Sadie take notice. She looked up from what she was doing and regarded him across the bar.

Her steady gaze made Frankie want to look away, but he'd long ago mastered that impulse at the poker table, and he kept his eyes trained on hers.

Sadie was the first to break the spell. She dropped her gaze to the cash drawer and lazily stirred the penny tray with one slender finger. "Don't tell me you were in love with her," she said.

AS FAR AS Frankie could see, Jimmy drank only orange juice; ate only grilled cheese sandwiches, pickles, and salt-water taffy. The sandwiches had to be served, piping hot, and cut diagonally, or he would have nothing to do with them. Sometimes, though he'd be groaning with hunger, Jimmy would examine the sandwich Frankie had set before him closely, find something indefinably askew with it, and push it away. Once a sandwich had been found wanting, it was impossible to convince the boy to eat it.

Jimmy had a knack of spinning silver dollars on the bar top and making them creep across his knuckles and back again like a magician. He'd sometimes hold one of the coins in his mouth while he played, until Sadie noticed his squeezed-shut lips and made him spit it out into her palm.

The boy loved flicking things with his middle finger to see what tone they would produce. He loved the sound of breaking glass and would nudge bottles off the edge of the bar if he thought he could get away with it. The tone of the back door buzzer enthralled him, and he would sometimes slip into the alley and ring it again and again until Frankie went out and dragged him back inside. Other sounds filled the boy with dread. A chair being dragged across the wooden floor made him flinch and clamp his palms over his ears. If the phone behind the bar rang, he'd whimper and sometimes bite the back of his hand if it wasn't answered quickly.

Every once in a great while, for a day or two, Jimmy would suddenly sink into himself. His eyes would go blank as poker chips, and he seemed unable to hear. Once he tumbled into one of those states, he became deaf to instructions or requests. If led to the piano, though, he would usually sit down and play. On those nights, Sadie would just have to sing whatever song came up next on his incomprehensible jukebox cycle. Sometimes he played the same tune two or three times running before he slipped whatever invisible groove he was caught in and launched into something new. One Thursday night he played *Moonlight Sonata* through twice, perfectly. With nothing to sing, Sadie had just pulled up a stool at the bar and listened with the rest of her confounded customers.

Until he snapped out of his trance, Jimmy couldn't eat. He'd crawl into the wedge of space between the piano and the bottom end of the staircase to sleep—if he slept at all. But eventually Frankie would come to the bar in the morning and find the door unlocked and Jimmy gone. And then the boy would show up again in the afternoon, back to his usual gangly self, humming and blinking and thumping at ashtrays with his fingernail.

ONE BALMY SATURDAY night, when Frankie had been tending the bar a few months, a truckload of sailors showed up on a weekend pass from the Hunters Point shipyard. Maybe it was all those starchy seamen huddled around their tables, but Sadie was in rare form. She'd just finished a highly eroticized version of "Ain't Misbehavin'," and stood with one hand on Jimmy's shoulder, catching her breath.

"*Frankie*," she called out without warning, once the applause had tapered off.

Frankie looked up, his chrome pouring spout poised over an ice-filled glass. Sadie had never spoken to him before during one of her performances. The whole place was silent.

"What do you think of all these fine young men in uniform?" she asked him. It seemed like a straight man set-up—like she was playing Bud Abbot to Frankie's Lou Costello—but Frankie didn't know the punch line. Caught up short, he looked out at the expectant faces at the three tables packed with sailors. A couple of sunburned ensigns twisted around in their chairs to look at him. No one spoke. Frankie ransacked his mind for some sort of rejoinder. He hoisted the bourbon bottle in the air in Sadie's direction. "Something tells me you'll have trouble walking tomorrow," he said.

The sailors' table erupted. They cheered and hooted and pumped fists in the air, while Sadie grinned at Frankie from the piano. When the laughter subsided, she hefted her huge bosom with both hands. "Anchors aweigh," she growled and made her penciled eyebrows dance at the sailors.

After that, Sadie subsumed Frankie into her act as a sort of comic relief. She might, at any point in the evening, lob a query over to her sidekick at the bar, and he would have to bat it back to her as best he could. The more they did it, the better Frankie got at delivering the punch line. His timing improved, and sometimes he'd hit one out of the park.

"Why can't I ever seem to get this place organized?" Sadie might demand of him as she mopped perspiration from her throat and hunted around on the piano top for sheet music.

"Because you're always so fucking busy," Frankie would answer, and he'd wait the prefect beat before he added, under his breath, "Or vice versa."

THROUGH THE NEXT three years, Frankie's life fell into a stable and satisfying routine. For the first time since he'd been discharged from the army, his days had a shape to them.

He woke around ten and arrived at the bar by eleven. While the floorboards above his head groaned under the weight of Sadie's morning toilet, Frankie made breakfast at the stove in the back room. He cooked up bacon, then fried bread and onions in the fat. Once he and Sadie had eaten together, he swept up, replenished the bottles, broke up ice in the freezer, changed out spent kegs. Around three in the afternoon he walked to the market. When he got back, Jimmy would be sitting on the steps outside, hugging his bony knees, waiting to be let in. Frankie would make another meal for Sadie and himself, grill up a sandwich for Jimmy, and at six they'd open.

And then for several hours, the bar was alive with song and laughter and voices. Every night, no matter how busy the drinkers kept him, there was always a moment or two when one of Sadie's songs hooked into Frankie. He'd be twisting a spout into a bottle of Black and White or making change at the register when that glorious voice of hers would unexpectedly set him abuzz—the same way it might suddenly resonate among the stemmed glasses hanging in their rack. Those were moments of grace, for Frankie. They were what he lived for.

After closing, Frankie would upend all the stools and chairs while Sadie counted out the register. He'd walk back to his room around two in the morning, going a bit out of his way to take the steps down to the beach because he liked to hear the waves and the clanging of buoys out in the darkness, and he liked the way the beacon from the Point Montara lighthouse raked across the foggy horizon.

He also loved thinking he was the last person awake in town.

In fact, Frankie had never been so wholly and consistently happy in his life.

ONE BRIGHT AUGUST morning, after days of coaxing and cajoling her, Frankie borrowed an old convertible and drove Sadie up to Fisherman's Wharf with the roof down. She'd been looking worn and doleful lately, and Frankie thought the air and sunshine might do her good.

Jimmy tagged along. As Frankie drove, the boy swayed back and forth in the rearview mirror, sometimes lifting his hands up above his head to catch the wind. Sadie seemed nervous to be wedged into the front seat—who knew how long it had been since she'd ridden in a car? She kept bracing an arm against the dashboard, as though Frankie might at any moment plunge them into oncoming traffic. Her hips crowded the gearshift and made it difficult for Frankie to drive. But north of Pacifica she started to relax, and soon she was singing along with the radio, and that made Frankie glad to be alive.

The two of them ordered the Neptune plate at the Kettle of Fish, a restaurant stilted out over the lapping San Francisco Bay. Jimmy ate the sliced pickles from both their plates and kept licking the saltshaker until Sadie scolded him and set it out of reach. Happy and full at the end of the meal, Frankie wiped his plate clean with the last of the bread rolls, but when the dishes were spirited away by their waitress, it was hard to know whether Sadie had actually eaten anything or just rearranged the food on her plate while she talked.

After lunch, the three of them took a walk along the pier, and Frankie was suddenly stricken with sadness. There was something tragic about seeing Sadie out of her element. Here in the city, she was just a nameless, enormous woman in a scarlet dress, carrying a ridiculous parasol. Her ruined face, starkly lit by unfamiliar sunlight, belied her dyed-black hair, and the planks they strode on seemed to moan under her weight. Frankie could feel the elbowing and eye rolling their passing stirred among the other people on the pier. None of these strangers knew Sadie—to them she was just an absurd fat woman, in the company of a retard who kept barking at the sea lions. Frankie clenched his fists. He wanted to grab the gawkers by the collar, to yell at their smug faces, to ask them who the hell they thought they were.

When they got near the end of the pier, Jimmy loped ahead of them to scatter the seagulls perched along the farthest rail. By the time they caught up to him, Sadie had slowed almost to a stop. Frankie stood with her at the end of the pier while she caught her breath. Jimmy busied himself with prying splinters from the wooden railing and dropping them, spinning, down into the water. Sadie smiled at Frankie and then pressed a hand over her sweat-slick bosom and looked across the choppy water at Alcatraz.

Frankie squinted out at the squat grey buildings hunkered on the rock in the middle of the glimmering bay. He smiled ruefully at Sadie. "Think of all the felons out there," he said, feeling that for once he could be her straight man. "A thousand hardened men all packed in together."

Sadie smiled slyly, knowing a set-up when she heard one. The wind pressed her red dress against the mounds of her body and stirred her black bangs. She shaded her eyes with one dainty hand and smiled out over the water. Her heavy rouge had gathered in clumps along the lines of her face. "Let me at 'em," she said, and Frankie thought his heart might break.

A week later, it dawned on Frankie that she was dying.

CHAPTER NINE
FIFTY HAPPY YEARS
1949

LYDIA WAS STILL SITTING at the parlor's drop-leaf secretary when Alvie woke. He blinked at the hissing television, their new top-of-the-line RCA console—a much-too-generous wedding gift from Mr. Levezzari. Alvie pushed himself up to a sitting position and yawned. His mouth felt pasty. The last thing he remembered was watching *Mary Kay and Johnny*, so he must have been asleep at least a couple of hours.

Alvie rolled his head around to work out the kinks in his neck and then paused to watch Lydia. She chewed her lower lip and read over what she'd just written. She frowned, jotted something at the bottom of the card, and then slipped it into the little blue envelope. She sealed it, licked a stamp and pressed it to one corner, then dropped it into the shoebox at her feet with the others. She opened and closed her writing hand, as if it were cramping up, and then flipped a page in their black leather address book.

Alvie yawned again and stretched his legs out under the coffee table. He bent up his bad ankle as far as it would go—it always stiffened up when he slept. "What time is it?" he croaked.

Lydia didn't look up from her work. She just opened the next blank card and frowned. "What did Flo and Eddie give us, anyway?" she asked. "Was it that salad thing or one of the crock pots?"

"How would *I* know?" Alvie said. "What time is it?"

"They're *your* friends," Lydia told him. She picked up her wristwatch, which lay on the desktop next to the address book. "Just after midnight."

"They're *our* friends," Alvie corrected her. For a woman who worked with words all day, she seemed to be having a difficult time adjusting to the plural pronoun of married life. Alvie rose, testing his ankle for pain, and went over to the television. He switched it off and then took a step back to watch the blizzard of static on the screen collapse down to a cigarette ember before it vanished. He hobbled over and stood behind Lydia. He set his hands on her shoulders and could feel the straps of her bra beneath her blouse. "Coming to bed?"

"Soon," Lydia said. "I've got a few more of these, and then some bills to pay." She bit her lower lip again. "Salt and pepper shakers?"

"Salt and pepper?" Alvie said. His thinking was still bleary, but even wide-awake he often found it difficult to keep up with Lydia's pivots of reasoning.

"From Flo and Eddie," she said, a pinch of impatience in her voice. "Why can't I remember what they gave us?"

Alvie looked over her shoulder at the blank card in front of her. "You're a writer," he said. "Can't you just make it vague?"

Lydia glanced up over her shoulder at him with one eyebrow raised, and then she looked back down at the card. "'Dear Flo and Eddie,'" she announced in that mocking tone she so readily slipped into when she was with her friends from

The Ledger. "'Thank you *so* much for the generous *ob*ject. Alvie uses it every time he does that thing it's made for. He says it works much better than the old one.' Yeah, *that'll* work."

Feeling a little rebuffed, Alvie bent and kissed her on the parting of her hair, and turned away. But then she stood, took both his hands in hers and kissed him full on the mouth. "Night," she told him, squeezing his fingers. "I won't be long." She sat again and scooted her chair closer to the secretary.

After a beat, Alvie ambled over to the sofa, his surprised lips still tingling with her kiss. He picked up his penny loafers, and limped down the hallway to his mother's old bedroom, which Lydia had fixed up as their own.

ALVIE LEFT THE lamp on Lydia's nightstand lit for her. He rolled onto his side facing the window and pulled the covers over him. The walls of the room were blue now—*cerulean*, Lydia called it—and Rose's old four-poster bed was painted a glossy white. The sagging canopy was gone, and so were the outdated olive curtains, along with their pleated valence. Rose's art-deco vanity with its oval mirror had been pushed across the hall into Alvie's and Frankie's old room—the *guest room* now—and an angular chest of drawers stood in its place, topped with a row of slender ceramic cats and backed with a plain mirror. The room—with its Chenille bedspread; its electric clock; and its steel-edged, Formica-topped nightstands—looked as sleek and modern now, as one of the window displays at Breuner's.

In the weeks leading up to the wedding, Lydia, in her paint-spattered smock, had made the room her own—*their* own. Alvie wasn't sure what he thought of the transformation, and the idea that she might set about modernizing the house's other rooms, one-by-one, made him uneasy. Wouldn't it begin to feel like someone *else's* house, not the one he'd always known?

Doris seemed to find the changes even more disconcerting than Alvie—though he could never, of course, mention that fact to Lydia. From the first day of redecorating, Doris had made her displeasure known. When the air was still pungent with paint fumes, a crack appeared in the exact center of the new full-length mirror, and over the next week it inched wider and wider until it disappeared into the lacquered wooden frame on either side. The diagonal row of matching picture frames Lydia had hung above the headboard, and planned to fill with wedding photos, was forever being nudged askew. One afternoon, when Alvie pulled the closet door open, a whole tribe of moths spewed out—despite the wardrobe's cedar floor—and set about battering themselves on the window and lampshades. He had opened the window and fled the room, and when he peeked in again an hour later they had vanished.

But after a week or two, Doris seemed to acquiesce. In fact, when they returned from their honeymoon she seemed to have moved across the hall into the guest room, which was now crowded with the old familiar furniture. In that seldom-used space, she could retire unmolested, muttering and rummaging about, for days at a stretch.

Doris, it seemed to Alvie, gradually warmed to the idea of a new feminine presence in the house. She seemed fascinated with each new womanly accoutrement. Lipstick tubes and tampons went missing. Bobby pins clattered in the garbage disposal. Alvie might enter the bedroom and smell a spritz of My Sin just squeezed from the atomizer on the dresser. Lydia's carefully laid out jewelry might be found stirred up—the earrings scattered, the wristwatch crystal smudged, the gold chains punctuated with tiny knots.

Alvie found it difficult to sleep on nights like this, when Lydia was absent from the bed, and he was alone with the rumor of his sister. Every footstep and murmur, every faucet hiss and cupboard creak, plucked Alvie from his drowse and sent a shiver through him. So, not long after one, when he felt Lydia's weight on the mattress beside him and she switched off the bedside lamp, he pressed himself into her aura of fleshly heat and sank into a deep, dream-cluttered sleep.

THE NEXT MORNING, before dawn, Alvie stood at the cracked mirror in the bedroom doing up his tie. Water began to fizzle in the house's plumbing, and he knew Lydia had just stepped into the shower. He imagined her lithe, familiar body streaming with water; the fogged mirror; the pebbled glass window above the commode, still dark at this hour. He smiled at his reflection. He loved these moments. This feeling of aloof and heedless intimacy—knowing that his wife was naked just a room away, and that he could enter that room if he wished, or that he could, instead, go about his morning with casual disregard.

He smoothed down his tie, pulled his blazer on, and appraised himself one last time in the cracked mirror. On his way down the hall, he paused at the bathroom door, through which he could hear the sensuous splatter and squeak of Lydia's shower. On impulse, he tried the knob, but found it locked. Still holding the knob, he pressed his forehead to the door. "I'm leaving," he called inside. "See you tonight." There was no answer.

In the kitchen, he filled his thermos with the coffee left over from their breakfast. But as he passed the dark parlor on his way to the front door, he heard a distinct tap from inside the room, as if someone had rapped smartly on the coffee table with a knuckle. Alvie stopped and looked behind him down the hallway. A sliver of light illuminated the hardwood floor at the base of the bathroom door. Lydia was still in the shower.

His heart thumping, he stepped to the parlor doorway, gripping the thermos in front of him with both hands, as if it might serve as a weapon. He peered into the dark room. The blocky, old-fashioned furniture was backlit by what little streetlamp light filtered through the drawn curtains. Their colorless, looming outlines endowed each bookcase and lampshade with a sinister tone. The faintly luminous television screen glowered in the corner. Nothing stirred.

Alvie was about to turn and leave, when a soft creak made him freeze again and clutch his thermos tighter. Was it his imagination or had Lydia's chair been bumped, to an almost imperceptible degree, in the direction of the secretary's open leaf? "Are you there?" Alvie whispered into the sentient air. He waited, his heart thudding. "What do you want?" he said. He held his breath and listened with his whole body. The room was mute.

Alvie reached around and switched on the floor lamp, and the parlor blossomed into color. He frowned into the sudden brightness. Everything was as they had left it the night before. Rose's crocheted Afghan and the throw pillows on the sofa were still arranged as though he had just now risen to switch off the hissing television. His *Radio-Electronics* magazine was still splayed face down on the coffee table. Lydia's shoebox of thank you cards and bills waited on the secretary's open leaf. Alvie went to the chair and nudged it with his thermos to hear what sound it might make. It tipped up a little on its forelegs but didn't budge and made no sound.

The hiss in the house's plumbing dropped an octave and then fell silent. Alvie glanced back at the dark hallway. The shower curtain jingled faintly. What would Lydia, with her hard-edged mind, have said if she'd witnessed him whispering into an empty room just now? Feeling sheepish, Alvie looked down at the shoebox of neatly stacked envelopes. The post office was just a block and a half down Ellis Street from L&S. He could duck in before he opened the store and save Lydia a trip. Feeling both foolish and generous, he tucked his thermos under one arm, lifted the shoebox, and hobbled out to Rose's old Chevy, before Lydia could open the bathroom door.

ALVIE LEFT THE Chevy in the post office parking lot and strode the last few blocks along Ellis Street, frowning down at the sidewalk. He was flushed with adrenaline, and he felt none of the pain this kind of walking usually produced his ankle. He paid no notice to the few early morning pedestrians who nodded to him or touched a hat brim as they passed.

His hand shook as he slipped the key into the alley door of L&S. He pressed the door shut behind him, twisted its dead bolt back into place, and then slumped against it. He took a few ragged breaths and drifted to Mr. Levezzari's desk. He switched on the banker's lamp.

He dropped into the rolling desk chair and pulled the envelope from the outer pocket of his blazer to study it once again. With bloodless fingers, he held it under the green glass lamp and tilted it to catch the light.

It was addressed in Lydia's hand—the precise and legible printing of a copyeditor—on a heavy card-stock envelope she'd no doubt brought home from *The Ledger*. He squeezed the plump envelope and again felt the spongy give of whatever she'd sealed inside. She must have gotten Frankie's address from one of the letters that sometimes showed up in Rose's room at Brookside—brief, innocuous notes jotted on feminine lavender stationery, all about the weather and some bar he worked in and making bland inquiries about Rose's health. But Rose was far beyond reading now, and probably wouldn't even recognize the name *Frankie* if one of the nurses bothered to read the letters to her.

Alvie tilted the lamp up and held the envelope to it, but the heavy paper was opaque. He turned it over, scrutinized the sealed flap, and then looked at the front again. The top left corner bore no return address, and he wondered what that meant. Was she trying to mail it to Frankie anonymously? Or was she more afraid it might be returned to the house if he had already moved on? The envelope felt heavy, bulky in his hands—as dense and impenetrable as the bathroom door she had locked against him.

FOR MORE THAN an hour after opening the store, Alvie busied himself behind the counter, sharpening pencils and straightening the rack of warranty forms. When there was nothing left to tidy up, he flipped distractedly through the stack of new fall catalogues, his thoughts churning and tumbling like clothes in a frontloading washer. If only the phone beside him would ring with a question about a Westinghouse warranty, or a customer would wander in off the Ellis Street to ask which brand of light bulb offered the longer lasting filament—anything that might get his mind off the still-sealed envelope that hung, naggingly, in the pocket of his blazer back in Mr. Levezzari's office.

He turned a page in the Admiral catalogue and found a picture of a man and woman snuggling on a living room sofa in front of a Big Sixteen—with its magic-mirror screen, AM/FM radio, and triple-play phonograph. The man wore slippers. An unlit pipe jutted jauntily from between his teeth. The brunette beside him clung to his arm. Both smiled at the television as though it represented the culmination of their every hope and dream.

Alvie and Lydia rarely sat together on the sofa; he loved watching television, but all those sitcoms and talent shows and Philco Playhouse dramas made no inroads with Lydia. She preferred to spend her evenings at her portable Smith Corona, clattering away at who-knew-what story or article or editorial for the paper. Only the televised news broadcasts would sometimes draw her in, and she'd sit next to him a few fleeting moments before she wandered away again.

This whole new phase of life, Alvie had come to realize, was unmapped territory. He'd never been privy to a real marriage growing up. He'd never glimpsed parental standoffs as he walked past the kitchen doorway, never overheard the late-night murmur of harsh words through the wall or the squeak of bedsprings. He'd never witnessed the cycles of giving and withholding. Marriage was, he thought, like some new and incomprehensible gadget, covered with buttons and gauges and winking lights, delivered to him without a manual—and he was just doing his best to figure it out, a little at a time, through trial and error, hoping against hope he wouldn't break the damn thing.

He flipped over the last page of the Admiral catalogue and then slipped it under the counter. The new General Electric catalogue was at the top of his stack now. The cover showed a glamorous blonde in a polka-dot apron, blissfully brandishing a spatula in the center of her exhaustively-appointed GE kitchen. Alvie picked the catalogue up and squinted down at the cover. The table was set with a full meal—turkey and potatoes and vegetables. A half-iced cake was posed on the counter, next to her gleaming countertop mixer. The woman looked about to burst into song, swept away in an ecstasy of ownership. It was true that Lydia cooked well and kept the house reasonably clean—Alvie had no complaints there—but her work was proficient and joyless; her domestic toil didn't feel like an offering of love; it provided Alvie no solace.

What could be in the damn envelope? Alvie tossed the catalogue on the countertop and turned his back on it to look out through the window on Ellis Street. The steel grate was still pulled across the alcove of the dark tailor shop across the way, and the angle of morning sunlight only reached the top apartment windows. L&S was always the first store on the block to open, though it rarely saw much business before ten.

Across the street, a woman appeared in an upper window and pulled the curtains shut, and Alvie felt it like a gesture of reproach. Why couldn't he just trust Lydia? Why didn't he just drop the envelope through the slot with all the others and forget about it? It had been almost two years since Frankie fled town—nearly two years since that morning Alvie had climbed the flight of stairs above the butcher shop and stood before Frankie's apartment door, fists clenched, feeling the dark and sickening gravity of suspicion hardening into certitude. The smell of fried onions was in the air that morning. The muffled sound of jazz and the clatter of wooden coat hangers came from inside Frankie's apartment. And then her laugh. And the door pulled open. And Lydia buttoning up her red coat.

A furniture truck rumbled past L&S, and the bell above the door jingled faintly like something half-remembered. Alvie turned back to the register. How had he arrived at this spot? How had he and Lydia come to this juncture after all they'd been through? Was it his fault? Wasn't trust an essential ingredient of love? Everything Alvie thought he knew about marriage had been gleaned from the radio sitcoms he'd listened to as a kid, or from the screwball romances he'd seen while he paced the aisles of The Palace—or, now, from the television programs he fell asleep watching each night. Nick and Nora.

Burns and Allen. Ozzie and Harriet. Could he *really* have expected the story of Alvie and Lydia to be so glib and effortless? Sure, the two of them had their moments of easy banter and heady romance and comical mishaps—but he hadn't foreseen the countless small grudges, the silent meals, the quick flares of temper, the crossed arms, the turning away.

KENNY SLOSS, THE fluty-voiced sales clerk finally showed up about a quarter after twelve to relieve Alvie for his lunch break. Having left his thermos of coffee in the Chevy back at the post office, and having no appetite anyway, Alvie went back to Mr. Levezzari's office with every intention of filing all the week's warranties, so the old man wouldn't have to do it himself when he came in that afternoon.

But as soon as he pushed open the Employees Only door, the envelope that poked from his hanging blazer's pocket seemed spotlighted, conspicuous as a struck gong. By now, he knew, Lydia would have gathered that he'd taken her box of envelopes: that fact could neither be ignored nor undone. Alvie plucked the envelope from the coat rack and carried it over to the desk, holding it out in front of him with both hands like it were some sacred reliquary. He could, he supposed, *pretend* he hadn't noticed it; he could act as if he'd dumped the whole box of envelopes into the mail slot without sorting through them and therefore hadn't seen this particular one addressed to his brother. He could even go to the post office *now* and send it on its way. He pictured that moment: sliding the envelope through the slot and releasing it into the dark inner workings of the postal system, like any other debt paid as promised. He imagined the small weight of it slipping from his fingers, and with it, perhaps, the immeasurable weight he now felt pressing down on his shoulders. The idea attracted him: he could avoid any confrontation, but it was a ruse he knew he could never pull off. And now, sitting in Mr. Levezzari's chair with the envelope centered on the desk blotter before him, he knew he was incapable of doing it anyway. This distrust he felt was rooted too deeply in him.

God. Damn. That. Frankie. He picked up the envelope again and leaned forward with his elbows on Mr. Levezzari's desk. She had betrayed him with his own brother, but he had forgiven her; he had married her, and all of that was supposed to be in the past. And yet it clearly wasn't, and here in front of his face was the proof: written with his wife's own hand, the glue on the flap moistened with her tongue. He had absolved her. He had vowed to trust her. But if he were to open her envelope now, which of them would be the betrayer and which the betrayed? He set the envelope on the blotter again and leaned back in Mr. Levezzari's chair. Out in the store, he heard a baseball broadcast flare up, and he knew Kenny had tuned in a White Sox game, thinking Alvie had left the building to get something to eat at the Woolworth lunch counter. On any other day, Alvie would have gone out to reprimand the boy, but today there didn't seem much point in enforcing the store's more niggling policies.

Alvie leaned forward in the chair again. He caressed the oak handle of the desk's top drawer with his fingertips, feeling the waxy coating of polish there, and then he pulled the drawer slowly open. There, between a carton of Rolled Gold cigarettes and a magnifying glass was the souvenir paperknife Mr. Levezzari had brought back with him from Venice. Feeling something close to fear, Alvie set the knife on the desk and pushed the drawer shut. He, licked his lips, steeled himself and picked up Lydia's envelope. He slipped the knifepoint under the envelope flap and slit it open.

Under Mr. Levezzari's banker's lamp he unfolded the three-column announcement clipped from *The Ledger*. He gazed down at the familiar photograph, feeling both deep relief and dawning remorse. The candid photo—taken by one of *The Ledger's* lensmen—showed Lydia and Alvie coming down the steps of Grand Avenue Methodist to a thunder of clapping hands and a flurry of thrown rice.

Even in the gray and white halftone, Lydia looked luminous. Her smile was broad and unguarded, almost unflattering. Alvie pulled the desk lamp closer and held the clipping under it. There he was: a step or two behind her, looking ill at ease in his black suit. In the photo he held his hand out to one side to keep his balance—steps were always hard to negotiate on his bad ankle—but with that fretful expression on his face, he looked like he might be warding off some approaching peril hidden just outside the photo's border.

Alvie stared down at the clipping and tried to remember that moment from a few weeks ago—the exact instant of the camera flash. But all he could reliably recall was that he'd wanted nothing more than to get to the bottom of the steps and escape all the clatter and hubbub in Mr. Levezzari's borrowed Lincoln, which was idling at the curb.

Alvie set down the clipping and picked up the envelope to see if there was anything else in it, but it was empty, and he felt suddenly emptied of something himself, though he could not have guessed what.

He wadded up the envelope and dropped it in the wastepaper basket under Mr. Levezzari's desk. And then, like it were a map to somewhere he hoped to travel to, he gently refolded the clipping, making sure he replicated the creases Lydia had made in it. He switched off the desk lamp and dropped the clipping into the wastepaper basket as well.

TWENTY MINUTES BEFORE the end of Alvie's shift, Mr. Levezzari sent him on an errand—though Kenny Sloss was behind the counter with, apparently, nothing better to do than pick nickels out of the register tray, using pencils as chopsticks. The jewelry store Alvie was sent to—Alton's—was the shop where Lydia and he had bought their rings last June, and, after trudging three blocks on his throbbing ankle, Alvie felt a little put out when neither the male clerk nor the girl at the register seemed to remember him.

"I'm here to pick something up for Mr. Levezzari," Alvie told the clerk. "Some kind of gift."

The clerk flipped through a paper folder of carbon copies, tugging one earlobe as he did. "Yes," he said. He pulled a carbon from the folder. "Just one moment, sir." The clerk squatted down beneath the far end of the counter and seemed to be pulling out drawers. Finally he straightened up with a black, velvet-covered jewelry box. He opened the box as he came back along the counter and then set it in front of Alvie along with the carbon copy. He crossed his arms.

Alvie looked down at the open box. It held an ornate gold pendant on a chain. The thing glimmered extravagantly against the black velvet, under the shop's glaring lights. "It's very nice," Alvie said, in case that's what the clerk was waiting for. "But Mr. Levezzari said it's supposed to be wrapped."

"Yes, yes," the clerk said with the put-upon air of someone asked to explain the obvious. "But I need you to sign off on the engraving." Alvie understood now what was expected of him. He turned the pendant over.

FOR MY ANNALEIS
IN CELEBRATION OF
FIFTY

HAPPY YEARS

Was it true? Was the old man coming up on his fiftieth anniversary? Alvie immediately understood why he'd been chosen for this intimate errand, but his sense of relief was quickly followed by a rush of apprehension. Should he be planning a surprise celebration at the store? Was he supposed to take out an ad in *The Ledger*? Would he be expected to give the old man a gift?

The clerk slid the carbon copy closer to the box. At the bottom of the form, Alvie recognized Mr. Levezzari's cramped printing, rising at a lopsided slant across the empty space. He checked the engraved words against what Mr. Levezzari had written, taking special care with *Annaleis*.

AS ALVIE APPROACHED the traffic circle in the Plaza that afternoon after work, he thought of turning down Glass Street, heading out past the high school to Brookside to visit his mother. He could stop by the Rexall on the way and pick her up a box or two of Luden's. It would be an unexpected treat for her to see him—though, considering how far gone she was these days, he wondered if *expected* or *unexpected* were concepts that could be applied to her anymore.

He came to a stop at the circle's entrance and waited for a break in traffic. Really what good would a visit to his mother do either of them? Wasn't it a purely selfish whim? In the privacy of her room, Alvie sometimes unburdened himself to Rose, as if her affliction were the screen of a confessional pulled shut between them. And Rose would sit—sometimes on her bed, sometimes in her wheelchair—working her lips soundlessly or plucking at the weave of her cardigan, her vacant eyes wandering the room. He couldn't explain, even to himself, why he did it.

Seeing an opening, he gunned the engine, arced around the traffic circle, and kept heading north on Fuller. He would go home to his empty house—but what then? He imagined himself sitting on the edge of the guest-room bunk, whispering aloud, as he sometimes still did, to the ghost of his sister. Wasn't she the one who led him to the envelope in the first place? Didn't she have some stake in this family's history? He thought of all the words he had whispered over the years in one or another empty room, staring at a bookend or a drawer pull or the leg of a table, hoping she was listening—and all the hours he had spent waiting for an answer that never came. How was it any better than talking to Rose?

He pulled to a stop at a yellow light on the corner of Grove and mindlessly tracked the progress of a woman with a double pram crossing the street in front of him. A boy on a bicycle pulled up next to him and stopped. It was ironic now that he thought about it: he had a mother—a body nearly emptied of intelligence; and he had a sister—an intelligence deprived of a body. These were his confidants.

Only in Lydia did he have a whole person—mind and body—to confide in and trust. But he knew now that he could do neither. What was wrong with him? How had he allowed himself to become so isolated from human contact, from *intimacy*? The very word—with all its sensual overtones—gave him a small shiver of discomfort.

The driver behind him tapped her horn, and Alvie glanced up at the green light. He let up the clutch and waved an apology at the rear-view mirror. As he drove along Fuller Street, he thought of the inscription on Mrs. Levezzari's gold pendant. *Fifty happy years?* If anyone seemed to exist in near-total marital misery, it was Mr. Levezzari. The old man's face twisted into a grimace any time he was called to the front counter phone, since it was likely to be his wife. Every June he seemed to shed ten years and grow two inches when Mrs. Levezzari went to stay with her sister in Saint Louis. Alvie had once watched the two of them consume an entire three-course meal at The Pepper Mill without exchanging a single word or glance. Yet how many people in history had ever reached their golden anniversary still in love? Did it *ever* really happen?

Fifty Happy Years.

Were love and trust and forgiveness just the words you said, and not anything you felt? Maybe it was like a baseball umpire, where the pronouncing of the words—*strike three!*— actually *made* the thing true, regardless of what path the ball actually took on its way to the catcher's mitt. And, now that he thought about it, wasn't that pretty much the same thing with marriage? *I now pronounce you man and wife.* Didn't the mere saying of the words make the thing itself true? And was all of that really any different than pronouncing the words *I forgive you? I trust you? I love you?* Or inscribing your happiness in gold?

WHEN HE TURNED onto Grove Street, Lydia's car was already parked at the curb. She wasn't due home for another hour at the earliest. He pulled into the drive and let the Chevy idle a few seconds before he switched off the engine. He grabbed his still-full Thermos from the passenger seat, and got out of the car. When he pushed open the front door, he found Lydia standing in the shadows at the far end of the hallway. He closed the door behind him and turned back to look at her. For a moment the two of them stood regarding each other silently.

"Did you open it?" she asked.

For a few silent seconds, Alvie reviewed his options. "No," he finally told her, feeling he could manage this one small lie.

"It was just the article from the paper," she said. "It was our wedding story. I didn't even write a note on it."

Alvie nodded.

Lydia took a few steps closer to him, and she was side-lit now by the light from the kitchen doorway, and it was clear she'd been crying. "I just wanted him to know," she said. "He's your brother. He should know." Her arms were linked in front of her, two fingers squeezed in the opposite fist. She seemed about to cry again. "I just wanted him to know we'd gotten over it," she said. She took another hesitant step in his direction and shook her head forlornly. And then she did begin to cry. "I wanted him to know *I* was over it," she sobbed. "It was a stupid, stupid thing to do." She raised her face to look at him, and her cheeks were wet. "Can you forgive me?" She seemed then to lose the power of speech and just watched him with that shattered, exposed expression he saw so rarely on her face.

Alvie waited a beat. His hands, for some reason, began to shake again. "I trust you," he said. "I forgive you," he said. He said, "I love you."

CHAPTER TEN
FAT SADIE'S: PART II
1947-1954

THAT LAST NIGHT Frankie helped Sadie up the staircase—after only her second set—he did his best to wedge his way between her and the stairway wall. When they got to the top they were both exhausted. Inside her room, Frankie leaned on the oaken footboard to catch his breath, while Sadie lowered herself onto the sagging mattress.

"Maybe I could clear out the back room downstairs," Frankie said, still breathing hard. "We could make *that* your bedroom, and you wouldn't have to take the stairs." He looked around Sadie's boudoir with its fringed red lampshades and its lace-covered side table. He sized up the plump leather easy chair and the vanity with its clutter of silver framed photos and jars of makeup. He was pretty sure most of it would fit in the room downstairs. "We could fix it up nice," he said. "Paint it any color you like."

When he looked back at Sadie, her expression suggested he was being impossibly naïve. She tugged up the front of her scoop-necked dress and shook her head with weary acquiescence. "I'm done climbing the goddamn stairs," she said.

Frankie nodded. "I don't know why we didn't do it weeks ago," he told her. He propped himself on the footboard of Sadie's bed with both hands and surveyed the room again. "I'll get Cap and Henry to help me," he said. "One day to paint. One day to move your stuff." He looked at her bookcase and her big oak wardrobe. Would it really all fit? "We'll move you back up here when you're feeling better," he said.

Sadie sat on the edge of her mattress waiting for Frankie to finish. She had an air of hard worn patience—the threadbare look of a longsuffering mother regarding her recalcitrant child. "I'm staying up here, Frankie," she told him, still a little breathless from the climb. "I'm done."

A burble of laughter from below rumbled up through the floorboards under Frankie's shoes. No one was down in the bar keeping an eye on the beer taps or the cash register. No one was looking out for Jimmy. On some deep subterranean level, Frankie understood what Sadie was telling him, but it was an idea he was unwilling to exhume just yet. "Get some sleep, old girl," he told her brightly. "We'll see how you feel tomorrow."

With Sadie eyeing him somberly, he stepped back out the door and pulled it shut behind him. He jogged back down the dark stairway into all that drunken noise and commotion.

AFTER THAT NIGHT, when it was clear that Sadie had no plans to ever leave her room again, Frankie carried her meals up to her three times a day. He carried them down again an hour or so later, after she'd picked them apart with her fork.

He fetched her Georgette Heyer novels from the dime store and progressively heavier blankets from Kreskies. He kept her account ledger and paid the bills by forging her ornate signature on the checks with the lavender ink she always used.

When things at the bar kept Frankie too busy, he slept on a mat, rolled out on the floor between the tables, rather than walk back through town for a few fitful hours in his room.

Without Sadie in the bar, Jimmy looked lost. Most afternoons he'd sit in the neighborhood of the staircase—a faithful spaniel waiting for the jingle of keys at the door—but Sadie never came down. A few times, when the bar was in full swing, Frankie managed to coax Jimmy into playing piano, but the boy would only slog into a series of doleful tunes, all dirge-slow and in minor keys. A pall would descend on the tables, and conversation would peter to a stop. Then Frankie would have to lure Jimmy away from the piano again with a handful of saltwater taffy, and he would have to set up free drinks until the mood lifted and conversations started up again.

Frankie took to spending his afternoons at Sadie's bedside in the roomy overstuffed leather chair she used to read in. Always cold and prone to headaches now, she preferred the blind drawn and the windows closed, so the room was dim and airless. Each afternoon, for about a quarter of an hour, a slant of sunlight sliced between the window's edge and the blinds and lit up clouds of dust motes wheeling sluggishly in the air.

By the light of a shaded forty-watt bulb, Frankie would read to Sadie aloud anything cheerful he could find in the *Examiner:* stories about Dutch masterpieces found at junk sales, or German shepherds who walked from Saint Louis to Wichita to reunite with their missing families. He recited *Collier's*, and *Harper's*, and *The Saturday Evening Post* from cover to cover each month. He read her languorous romance novels about sheiks and schoolmarms, senators and seamstresses. When he went downstairs each afternoon, dry-mouthed and hoarse, to open the bar, he left the door to Sadie's room ajar, so she could hear all the voices and hubbub.

Over the weeks, Sadie's fat melted quickly away. She managed to sip water or cranberry juice through a straw, but, like a fussy infant, she would push away oatmeal or mashed potatoes or applesauce as soon as the spoon touched her lips. She mostly lay there, propped at a forty-degree angle with pillows, and filled the air with foul smells that Frankie pretended not to notice.

"I'm rotting inside," she interrupted Frankie one afternoon when he was reading aloud from a limp copy of *Reader's Digest* he'd stolen from the dentist's waiting room.

Frankie looked over the top of the magazine to see her staring up glassy eyed at the leak-stained ceiling.

"Goddamn it," she said in that dry-leaf rustle of a voice she'd taken on. "This is no way for a person to die."

Frankie considered ignoring her observation. He wasn't cut out for bedside heart-to-hearts. He flipped to the *Humor in Uniform* section to see if there was anything there that might lighten the mood, but then he closed the magazine and covered it on his lap with both hands. At some point they'd have to talk about it. It was pointless to pretend that this was just a temporary matter that would right itself with time. And who else did the poor woman have to talk to? "You had a good run, girl," Frankie said softly, embarrassed by the lameness of his words, even as he pronounced them.

Sadie nodded, though the effort seemed to pain her. "I did," she admitted. "Not many girls could run an operation like this."

Frankie set the *Reader's Digest* aside and reached out to give her thinning arm a clumsy stroke. He scrounged around for something else to say. "And you're leaving behind a lot of happy men," he said hopefully.

Sadie tucked her chin down and picked at the lint on her bedspread. The back of her hand was mapped with blue veins now, and the clunky rings she still liked to wear were loose and clattered together softly as she moved. "Not as happy as you might think," she said without looking in Frankie's direction.

WITHOUT SADIE'S VOICE or Jimmy at the piano, the bar quickly slipped into a stony and dismal silence. Sometimes even the smallest sounds—the jangle of ice in a glass, the scrape of coins across the varnished bar top—could be heard over the listless mumble of conversation.

Frankie tried bringing in a radio, but the hiss of Billie Holiday's voice, shrouded in all that white noise, was only a cheerless reminder of Sadie's dulcet, bell-like tones. And the one station Frankie could tune in reliably—a station, oddly, from way out in Caspar, Wyoming—signed off the air every night at nine o'clock, leaving them afloat on their silence.

When a Friday night rolled around, and half the tables stayed empty, Frankie got on the phone and chased down Willie Sloane. He found the old man playing in a colored bar near Union Station in LA.

Frankie made wild promises over the phone—Willie could move into Frankie's room above the auto parts store, and he, Frankie, would sleep on a cot in the bar's back room; Willie could keep all his own tips at the piano along with a split of Frankie's tips at the bar; Frankie would get the piano tuned by a professional from up in the city.

TWO DAYS LATER, Willie was sitting on his suitcase talking to the shoeshine boy in the shade of the bus station where Frankie had promised to meet him.

As Frankie approached on foot, he shaded his eyes from the sun and took a good look at Willie before the old man could notice him. Willie sat chewing a matchstick, his legs drawn up, his long black hands capping his bony knees, listening to the shoeshine boy who sat astride his box chatting and grinning. The years had not been kind to Willie. His white hair grew now only in wisps and patches around his bald central pate, and the deep creases on either side of his mouth had been crisscrossed with smaller lines. He looked stooped and skeletal beneath his oversized white shirt. When Willie finally saw Frankie coming, he stood and glared at Frankie out of his one good eye.

"Old fart like you shouldn't be sitting outside in this heat," Frankie said by way of greeting.

Willie glanced over his shoulder at the bus station. "Some places don't take to colored folk," he said.

Frankie shrugged. "It's not because you're colored," he said. "They just don't take to ugly folk."

A smile played across Willie's lips, and the matchstick he'd been chewing darted from one corner of his mouth to the other. "Why don't you head on in there, and we'll test that theory," he said. The old man then turned to the shoeshine boy, nodded a goodbye, and hefted his suitcase, which was apparently weightier than it looked. "Where's the car?" he grunted.

Frankie grinned. "Do I look like the kind of man who'd drive a car?"

WILLIE STOOD AT the foot of Sadie's bed. His face was downcast, and he kept his hands linked together in front of him, like an old man caught skinny-dipping.

"This is Willie Sloane," Frankie said. "He's going to play some piano downstairs—you know, until you're back on your feet."

Sadie turned her massive head and squinted in Willie's direction.

"Nice to meet you, ma'am," Willie said. He shifted his weight uneasily from one foot to the other and then looked to Frankie for help.

"Willie made his name playing stride," Frankie said. "He knew all the greats. Jellyroll. Waller. You name it."

Sadie regarded Willie with a queenly haughtiness. The effect was heightened by the fact that she had stopped drawing on her eyebrows, so her unaccompanied eyes gleamed wintry and fierce. When she spoke, her voice was stronger and more prudish than Frankie had expected. "Perhaps you could step outside, Mr. Stone," she pronounced. "Frankie and I need to discuss the situation."

Frankie looked at Sadie. Her proud face was blank as a drawn blind. "Willie, why don't you go on downstairs and take a look around," Frankie said. "We just need to iron out the details."

Willie nodded and stiffly took his leave. Frankie listened to the old man's footsteps recede down the stairs while Sadie eyed him coolly.

"Close the door," she told him.

Frankie went to the door and pushed it with one finger until it clicked shut, and then he took Willie's place at the foot of the bed.

"You brought a colored man into my bar," Sadie said. "You brought him into my *room*."

Frankie stood weighing Sadie's words. It was the illness, he reasoned. It wasn't Sadie talking. Not the real Sadie. Her sickness had taken root in everything bitter inside her. He dug his hands deep in his pockets and sighed.

"I don't know what you promised that man," Sadie said. "But I want you to send him away."

Frankie took his time coming back down the staircase, calculating his options with this hand he'd been dealt. When he got to the bottom, he found Willie leaning against the bar with his arms folded. The old man's hands seemed to be gripping his thin biceps through his shirt.

"I want bus fare," Willie said. "And I want a ride back to the station. I'll be damned if I'm lugging my suitcase again."

With cards like this, all Frankie could do was bluff. "What are you talking about?" he said jovially. He scratched the stubble on his chin with a thumbnail and gave Willie an easy smile.

"You know what I'm talking about," Willie said. "You might have closed the door, but I could probably tell you every word that woman said. I've heard that shit my whole life."

Frankie held both palms up in a *don't shoot* gesture. "What are you talking about?" he said again. "She just wants you to audition. She wants to hear you play."

Willie eyed him suspiciously.

Frankie went to the piano under the staircase. He moved a tray of sudsy glasses to a nearby table and pulled the bench out invitingly. "Come on over," Frankie said. "Show the old girl what you've got."

Willie gave Frankie a look of weighty and righteous skepticism—as if Frankie, having taken no cards at the draw, had turned over a royal flush once all bets were in.

"Just come play the damn piano," Frankie said, waving him over.

Willie sighed and dragged himself over to the piano. He tested a few high notes with one long middle finger and then scraped the bench closer to the keyboard.

"'Stormy Weather,'" Frankie said. "Play her some 'Stormy Weather.'"

Willie's long brown fingers splayed out across the keys, paused a beat, and then rolled down through a series of blue notes and struck a chord.

Frankie looked up at the ceiling. "Maybe a little louder," he said.

Willie closed his eyes and played. The old man had a feinting, artful way of lurking in the vicinity of the melody, but never quite cornering it, drifting towards it and away but never striking the actual notes of the song he'd got you singing in your head.

Frankie moved to the foot of the staircase and stood looking up.

After a single run-through of the melody, Willie stopped abruptly and sat back, arms folded. He glared dubiously at Frankie.

Frankie regarded him from the bottom of the stairs. "I asked for 'Stormy Weather,' not the 'Minute Waltz,'" he said. "Do 'After You've Gone.' And air it out a little this time."

Willie made a sour face and poised his hands over the keyboard again. He played ten or twelve bars before the melody began to take shape. The music was a palpable bright fog: It confided the outlines of solid worldly things, but spirited them away again once you'd caught a glimpse.

"Keep going," Frankie said. "Just play it out." He stepped up on the lowest stair now, where Willie couldn't see him and peered up the narrow passageway. He gripped the banister and waited, biting on his lower lip. He listened while Willie turned the corner into the bridge and then folded back into the melody line again. Still nothing. He rubbed the back of his neck.

And then, finally, it came. That beautiful, ruined voice drifted down to him.

After you've gone and left me crying

After you've gone there's no denying,
You'll feel blue, you'll feel sad,
You'll miss the bestest gal you've ever had.

Frankie leaned back around the stairway wall and nodded at Willie. "Don't stop," he mouthed. "Don't you dare stop." Frankie slipped halfway up the stairs and found the right step where Willie's piano and Sadie's voice were balanced. He sat there sideways to the incline, hugging his knees and smiling. He had now accomplished that one grand thing he'd never managed to do before: he'd made music.

IT WAS ABOUT a week later that Jimmy played the song.

The boy was fascinated by Willie. He liked to sit—ramrod straight and so still he seemed to want to turn invisible—on the piano bench next to the old man while he played. Jimmy would stare down at Willie's fingers like they were confiding secrets to him. When Willie wasn't playing, Jimmy would follow him around the bar. He'd pick a seat nearby and sidle his chair closer and closer until he could have rested his head on the old man's shoulder. Jimmy would snatch up anything Willie set down—a paperback novel, a pencil stub, his pocket watch—and he would sniff at it or stroke his cheek with it until Willie made him give it back. Once or twice the boy tried persistently to run his palm over Willie's bald head, until Willie had to swat his hand away and scold him for it.

The afternoon Jimmy played the song, Frankie was behind the bar trying to unclog a drain with a straightened coat hanger. One end of the hanger was twisted like a tiny corkscrew, so, with hands submerged in murky water, Frankie worked that end as deep as he could into the drain.

Willie sat at the piano, showing Jimmy some new techniques on the keyboard. "First you got your shout piano," the old man said. "You got your James P. Johnson and Willie the Lion Smith—old boys like them and me." His long fingers sprawled out on the keyboard, and he began to play. He ran through a few bars of "Autumn Leaves" in stride style, closing his eyes and pursing his lips like he might just whistle along. "It's just the next twist on ragtime," he told Jimmy with his eyes still closed. "Keep an eye on the left hand, son. See how the bass run goes?"

Frankie looked up from his work with the coat hanger to see Jimmy rocking back and forth on the piano bench now. Frankie could read in his pinched up shoulders that he was getting too wound up.

Willie, oblivious, continued playing with his eyes closed. "And then you come up through swing," he said, "and it opens up a little more like this." The melody Willie was playing changed tempo in mid-phrase—the syncopation eased and the music from both hands seemed to meld together now like a confluence of two currents.

Frankie bent the free end of the coat hanger into a crank and did his best to turn it like a bit-brace drill. By the time the sink finally drained, and Frankie was rinsing off his hands, Willie was still playing "Autumn Leaves," but in a frenetic hard bop style now. Jimmy's jazz history lesson seemed to be nearing its end—and not a moment too soon by the look of it: Jimmy still sat on the bench beside Willie, but he had knotted his fingers together in his lap, and his anxious gaze was skittering all over the empty room.

"Hey, Willie," Frankie called from behind the bar, drying his hands on a towel. "Maybe you could ease up on the kid. He looks a little worked up."

Willie stopped playing and opened his eyes. He looked at Jimmy and then over at Frankie. "Boy looks okay to me," he said. He turned to Jimmy and softened his tone. "We're just two piano players," he said. He rested a hand on Jimmy's shoulders. "We're about to hold us a rent party, aren't we, son?"

Frankie coiled the coat hanger and tossed it into the bar bin. "Just don't get him wound up," he told Willie. "He's had a rough few weeks."

"Boy's just fine," Willie said to Frankie, and then to Jimmy: "Let's show your mama over there what you learned in school today." Willie slid to the end of the bench and tugged at Jimmy's sleeve until the boy slid in front of middle-C.

Jimmy sat looking down at the keys with a forlorn expression. He began a high-pitched whining.

"Go on," Willie coaxed, nodding down at the keyboard. "You can do it, son."

Jimmy stared down apprehensively at his own trembling hands, and then he looked over at Frankie, like he was hoping to be rescued from something.

Frankie shook his head and cut the label on a bottle of Johnnie Walker with his thumbnail. Willie was on a fool's errand; he could hammer at the boy night and day about styles of play, and nothing would stick.

But then Jimmy began to play.

It was "Autumn Leaves" again—but it wasn't exactly. It was more like the negative space *around* the song. It was a hollow mold of crashing chords and rushing notes that somehow articulated the unsounded melody at its core. Frankie's scalp tightened. He set the whiskey bottle on the counter and just stood there, stricken brainless, watching the boy's hands tumble up and down the keys. Goose bumps swept up both arms and converged in the small hairs at the back of his neck. He leaned forward against the bar, feeling like he might lose his balance.

Jimmy was in a frenzy now. He careened up through the octaves and back down again. His eyes lit from behind with a panicky fire.

Frankie had the feeling his ability to listen was lagging behind the notes. He felt like he was being outdistanced by this music. All he could do was strain to keep up with the rush of notes and try to grasp their meaning before they were gone. And then suddenly the song was done.

In the abrupt silence it took Frankie a beat or two to get his bearings, like he had just stumbled into the dark bar from the bright sunlight outside. He leaned more heavily against the bar, feeling a dizzy sort of giddiness.

"Jesus-God what was that?" Willie said in a throaty voice. The old man was leaning away from the piano, like he thought it might catch fire. "Did you hear that?"

Frankie ransacked the area around the register for a pen. "Quick!" he said frantically. "Write it down! Write it down!"

"I don't read music," Willie said.

"Well then *remember* it," Frankie pleaded almost in a panic. "Play it back before you forget." It felt to Frankie like something of great consequence had been picked up by the tide and was being pulled out to sea, beyond reach.

Willie looked down at the keyboard, his face ashen. "I *can't*," he said. "It wasn't like anything I've ever heard. How am I supposed to remember *that*?"

Jimmy was biting the back of his hand now and making a noise like a dentist drill. Frankie had never seen the boy this worked up before. Willie put a soothing hand on his shoulder to ease his rocking. "Easy, son," he said.

"Get him to play it again," Frankie said. He came out from behind the bar and joined them at the piano. "Do it again, Jimmy," he said to the boy. And to Willie: "Pay attention this time."

Jimmy stared at the keyboard, his lip quivering and his eyes tearing up.

Willie gave Frankie a scolding look and then turned back at the boy. "Don't worry, son," he said. "It's all right now. Everything's okay." The boy slumped against his shoulder, and Willie held him there, patting his hair soothingly. While Jimmy wept into his shirt, Willie's gaze turned up to the ceiling, as if he might be thanking God, or as if some remnant of the song might still be reverberating in the rafters.

"YOU KNOW WHAT that song was?" Willie asked later that night as he was sweeping between the tables after the bar had closed down. "It was the future."

Frankie looked up from the bucket of soapy water he was using to sponge down the bar. He wiped his damp hand on a bar towel, took the cigarette from his mouth and balanced it on the bar's edge where it wouldn't scorch the wood. "The future?" Frankie said dubiously.

"The future," Willie told him, with a tone of finality that implied he had given it a great deal of thought. He tucked the broom handle under one arm. "I took that poor boy through the whole history of jazz, right up to this very day," Willie said. He tapped on a tabletop with an index finger to punctuate his claim. "And then he leapt ahead and played us the next big thing—something I was never supposed to hear in this lifetime."

Frankie grinned at the old man. "This is Jimmy we're talking about," he said. "The boy who comes to *us* to tie his shoelaces."

Willie nodded. "He showed us the future, Frankie," he said. "Got me feeling like Old Simeon holding the Christ child. That boy's a *savant*."

Frankie took another drag from his cigarette and balanced it on the bar's edge again. "If *savant* is French for dumbass," he said, "I'm inclined to agree."

Willie shook his head gravely. "That boy's got his problems," he admitted. "But he's got a whole lot of genius in him as well."

Frankie shook his head and smirked. "I mentioned the shoelaces, right?"

Willie narrowed his eyes at Frankie. It was clear he wasn't about to concede his point. "Don't mean a damn thing," the old man said. "Albert Einstein can't tie his shoelaces either."

Frankie rubbed the back of his neck. "*Einstein?*" he said. "*Is that true?*"

Willie slipped the broom from under his arm and poked at the floorboards with its bristles. "Probably not," he conceded. "But how do *you* explain that thing the boy played?"

Frankie shook his head. He picked up his cigarette and took another draw. There was nothing he could say. He had no answer. There was no plausible explanation for the song. Maybe it *was* the future, but it was gone now, and he'd just have to wait to catch up with it again.

After Willie left that night, Frankie locked the bar and walked down to the beach with a cigarette and stood on the sand looking out on the dark sea and sky. Jimmy's song had completely fled his head by now, and that left him with a melancholy sense of loss he couldn't really account for. It was just a song, he knew, but it felt like more than that. It was one of those rare fleeting moments of grace, when chemistry and chaos bring about something beautiful—and it saddened him that he'd never hear it again.

Frankie took a drag on his cigarette and looked over his shoulder at the lights of town. It was just another loss, Frankie knew: one more to add to all he had left behind in Richland, one that would soon be augmented with Sadie's passing. The clear sky above him was crowded with stars, and he stood there just yards from the edge of a continent, his cigarette glowing in the dark, trying to figure, by dead reckoning, the distance and direction home.

BY THANKSGIVING SADIE had lost more than a hundred and fifty pounds. The new, thinned version of her face took on the unexceptional look of any of the other women Frankie might cross paths with in town—the grandmother tugging a sticky child along Myrtle Street, the aging housewife tapping watermelons in the grocery store, the spinster librarian whose spectacles dangled around her neck on a silver chain. And then she was thinner still. The joints in her elbows and wrists bulged under her loose flesh, and the hollows and ridges of her skull began to show beneath her rice-paper skin.

"God, Frankie," Sadie said one afternoon when Frankie was reading her mail aloud to her. "My whole life, all I ever wanted was to be this weight."

Frankie crumpled up the Elk's Club flier he'd been reciting.

"I was a hundred and eighty pounds on my twelfth birthday," Sadie mused. "People said the cruelest things right to my face." She blinked up at the ceiling. "Just think what they were saying behind my back."

Frankie paused, squeezing the wadded flier in his hand and wondering what track to take with his response. "So you were big," Frankie said, trying to strike a tone of jovial dismissiveness. "We all have crosses to bear." He lobbed the wadded flier in the direction of the trashcan and missed badly. "It's not like it held you back any." Frankie tore open the envelope from the electric company, took out the bill and shook it open.

"It held me back," Sadie said softly.

Frankie squinted at the numbers on the bill. "So what did being fat ever keep you from doing?" he said. "You don't seem like a woman who let anything stand in her way."

Sadie's breath whistled through her now-aquiline nose before she spoke. "It's not an easy thing to admit," she said, and the tone of her voice made Frankie stop reading and look at her. "I've never told anyone this," she said. "It's humiliating, but it's weighing on me, and I want you to know."

Frankie slipped the electric bill back in its envelope and set it on the reading table. He leaned forward, hands folded in his lap. "What's weighing on you?" he said, and his voice sounded tinny and apprehensive in his own ears.

Sadie pressed her head back into her pillow and let her eyes wander the ceiling, like she might find among them the correct wording for her confession. "I trust you, Frankie," she said. "This place will be yours when I'm gone. It's all arranged."

"God, Sadie, you know I hate talking about that."

Sadie feebly waved one hand in the air between them to silence him. "All I'm saying is I trust you," she said. "You're the only one I've ever told this to." She fell silent again, still looking up at the ceiling with rheumy eyes.

"What?" Frankie said, an edge of exasperation in his voice now. "*What* are you telling me?"

With an old-maidy primness, Sadie pulled the blanket up to her chin and held it there with both hands. She closed her eyes. "I'm a virgin," she said softly.

Frankie sat back in his chair, feeling suddenly loosed from his mooring on choppy seas. For a moment he looked blankly at the opposite wall, studied, uncomprehendingly, the oval mirror and the Norman Rockwell calendar still turned to August. Then he turned his attention to the window. He frowned at the drawn blind, dimly lit from behind by the afternoon sun. Finally he looked at Sadie, who still stared up at the ceiling. "You sure?" he said.

Sadie nodded, the blanket still tucked under her chin. "Don't that beat damn all?" she said.

Frankie nodded slowly. Fat Sadie a virgin. It *did* beat damn all.

SADIE DIED TWO days before Christmas.

IT WAS A Tuesday in January when the call came that ended Frankie's exile. When the phone rang, he left his newspaper and breakfast in the back room and slipped behind the bar to answer it.

"Frankie?" the voice on the other end said. "Is this Frankie Farrell?"

Frankie knew the voice at once. "Lydia?"

"Don't talk," Lydia told him. "Just listen. And don't you dare try to start something."

Her familiar stern tone hit Frankie's bloodstream like a drug.

"One word out of you," she said, "and I swear I'll hang up."

Frankie gripped the phone with both hands and looked at the tiny rectangle of brightly lit frosted glass in the bar's door. It would have been hard for him to speak, even if he'd been granted permission.

"I'm not calling to talk to you," Lydia said.

Did he detect a flutter of emotion in her voice? He could hear her breathing on the other end of the line, but it was a moment before she spoke again.

"It's your mom, Frankie," she said. "*Oh, god.*"

A shadow passed the front door.

"She died, Frankie. I'm so sorry."

Frankie turned his back to the door and listened.

"Alvie sent you a letter, but I was afraid it wouldn't get there in time," she said. "The funeral is Friday. I just thought you should know. That's the only reason I called."

Frankie heard the click of the receiver, and, standing there in the morning gloom, he pictured the black phone in the house on Grove Street as she walked away from it.

After a moment, he set his own phone back in its cradle and stood leaning with both hands on the bar, waiting for his head to clear. Sadie was gone, and Rose now too. He felt a stinging in the eyes, a sudden chest-hollowing sadness. He closed his eyes and drew a few ragged breaths. In his head he could still hear Lydia's voice as it had sounded on the phone.

He could go back home now. That much was clear. He could return to Richland for his own mother's funeral—and no one could blame him for that.

Though the sun was barely up, and his mouth was still slick with the taste of bacon, he poured himself two fingers of scotch, and carried it around to the customer side of the bar. He sat up on one of the stools, rested his elbows on the bar top, and took a sip. Feeling the smoky taste on his tongue, he thought of the life he had been leading for the last seven years. It was a life of steady employment and unshirked responsibility. A life of bills paid and promises kept—the kind of life no one back home would ever have imagined for him.

It had also been a life of celibacy. Except, of course, for that one night a month ago—the night Sadie had made her confession. After the bar had closed that night, Frankie had sat at one of the dark tables drinking Tanqueray from the bottle and conjuring to mind Lydia's every essential gesture: the way she gathered her hair at the back of her neck before letting it fall again, how she ran a finger under her wristwatch band when she was thinking hard about something, the fussy and self-conscious way she buttoned up her blouse after their lovemaking.

And then Frankie had set the gin bottle aside, knowing he was ready. He had wiped his mouth and stood. And then he had climbed the stairs to Sadie's room, feeling the dark, sad gravity of affection. And he had sensed, even then, that he would forever more be navigating, by dead reckoning, the bleak and unlikely regions love would bring him to.

CHAPTER ELEVEN
LOCAL WOMAN PIGEONHOLES TURKEYS
1954

LYDIA CAME DOWN the broad steps of the medical building and leaned against the blue mailbox bolted to the pavement near the corner. Dizzy with dread, she looked both ways down the street. Seeing no one near enough to hear, she said the word she'd been repeating in her head the whole time Dr. Evans was confirming her condition: "Shit!" Having said it once, it seemed to bear repeating, so she did in a kind of furious chant while she hammered the top of the mailbox with the side of her fist. "*Shit! Shit! Shit! Shit! Shit!*"

She took a deep, unsteady breath, hissed it out, and looked around the sun-drenched street again to make sure she hadn't been heard. Across the avenue, out of earshot, a woman pushing a pram paused in the shade of the butcher shop awning to peer in the window at the ropes of sausage bunting.

A pram. *Shit!*

Lydia took a few more deep breaths and clamped a hand to her forehead. How could she have let this happen? She was much too sensible for this kind of thing. Her head swam with ill-conceived and quickly aborted schemes. She bit her lip and started walking down Glass Street and then stopped, turned, and walked the other way when she remembered she had parked her car in the opposite direction, half a block down Lewis Street outside the toy store.

Toys. *Shit!*

The world seemed to be crumbling beneath her feet these last few weeks, beginning with the morning phone call from the home that Rose had passed away in her sleep.

And then the funeral and Frankie.

Oh, god, Frankie! His name knotted her all up inside as she stumbled up the too-bright avenue in the direction of her Ford.

She hadn't wanted the whole thing to start up again. She honestly hadn't. Seeing Frankie had been the last thing on her mind the morning of Rose's funeral. She'd slipped out to the kitchen before the sun had properly risen. She'd put the kettle on, and ironed one of Alvie's white shirts. The notion that Frankie might actually show up at the service had been drowned out by all her other worries. She'd buffed Alvie's black shoes with a kitchen rag and laid out his best dark suit. When everything was ready, she woke Alvie from his fitful sleep, to get him up and feed him and lead him through all the traps and turns and sudden pangs of regret she knew were part and parcel of a parent's funeral.

But there Frankie was at the cemetery. Could she really have been so surprised to see him? She'd been the one who called him to tell him the news. If only she'd left it to Alvie and his meticulously-worded letter! If only she'd never picked up the hallway phone!

At the cemetery, Frankie stood on the far side of the grave, well apart from the small gathering, as if he had existed only on the periphery of Rose's life and did not want to intrude among her rightful mourners. Amid the black and charcoal suits, Frankie wore khaki slacks, an open-collared blue shirt, and a crumpled looking linen jacket. He stood pondering the ground, hands dug in his pockets, shifting his weight from foot to foot. A small niggling voice from some critical corner of Lydia's mind piped up with: *Who would dress like that for his own mother's funeral?* But that question was immediately answered by a still smaller voice from some deep part of her: *A man.*

When at last Frankie looked up at her, he raised his eyebrows by way of a sad greeting, coughed into his fist and let his gaze fall back to the ground. That one glance was all it took, really. Sure, this man looked exactly like her husband, but there was a world-weary sadness in his carriage that bespoke troubles Alvie couldn't imagine. The slope of his shoulders hinted at burdens Alvie never had to bear. This was a man who lived in the world she and Rose strove so hard to protect Alvie from.

Frankie had taken a room at the Wilmont Hotel for the week, so he disappeared after the burial, but he was at the house the next morning, wanting to pay his portion of the funeral expenses. And the next day, Alvie had to cover the late shift at the store and kept the car, and Lydia had bumped into Frankie at the grocery store on her walk home from work. The three sacks she'd bought were just too much for her to manage, so Frankie had volunteered to walk her home.

As they strolled, Frankie kept himself to the curb side, the side with passing traffic, and on the corner of Lemon and Laurel as they waited for the light, it struck her like an epiphany: in her marriage she had always felt the protector, never the protected.

They mounted the porch steps and Frankie paused in the shade holding sacks in each arm while Lydia stirred around in her purse for her keys. Lydia unlocked the door, pushed it open, and stepped inside. When Frankie leaned in to pass the grocery bags over the threshold, Lydia had turned her head and kissed him on the cheek.

That was all it took. There was no looking back. They stumbled into the front hallway and dumped the grocery bags on the entry table. Frankie kicked the door shut with his heel and they were in each other's arms.

And now here she was, wandering along Lewis Street in the dizzying sunlight, looking for her car—which she found parked behind a diaper service truck.

Diapers. *Shit!*

"WHERE *ARE* YOU?" Thelma wanted to know.

"I got a late start," Lydia sighed. Someone had scratched the shape of a heart on the phone booth glass, and she absently traced it with the fingertips of her free hand. The tight, closed space smelled of Brylcreem and cigarettes.

"I can hear traffic," Thelma said in that nasally voice of hers. "Are you in town?"

"Look, can you cover for me today?" she asked, ignoring Thelma's question. "I'll come in this afternoon to write my article—I swear. I just won't be at the meeting."

"Spencer isn't going to like that," Thelma said.

Lydia tapped the center of the transparent heart with her fingernail. "Spencer will get over it," she said.

"Did you get your assignment?"

"Yeah." Lydia ran her fingers back through her hair and tried to remember where she'd left her notes. "I've got it written down somewhere. A Chinese woman, right? She does something with turkeys?"

"She's *Japanese*," Thelma corrected her. "And she *sexes* them."

Lydia pinched the bridge of her nose and blinked three times rapidly. She couldn't have heard right, could she? Or did Thelma know something? SCANDAL AT *THE LEDGER*. "Say that again," Lydia said, careful not to sound alarmed.

"She *sexes* them," Thelma repeated. "The turkeys. You know—she tells the girls from the boys?"

Lydia drew a relieved breath. She felt like laughing but shook her head instead. "You mean there's some confusion on that point?"

"When they're chicks," Thelma said. "It's impossible to tell them apart when they first hatch."

"Well then how does this woman do it?"

"Some kind of *Zen* thing," Thelma said, with a kind of verbal shrug. "You have to be Japanese."

"You're joking."

"No," Thelma said. "No joke. They're raised to do it. It takes years to learn."

A woman walked by Lydia's phone booth dragging a sniffling boy by the hand. The boy's red face was contorted in an agony of self-pity. His upper lip was crusted with snot. *Shit!* Lydia turned her back and rested her forehead against the glass of the booth. "A Japanese woman who sorts chickens?" she sighed into the phone. "And I'm supposed to turn this into an article?" She pinched the bridge of her nose again. "Spencer's pissed at me, isn't he?"

"Whatever do you *mean*?" Thelma said, her voice all singsong with irony. "And she sorts *turkeys*, not *chickens*."

"*Turkeys*," Lydia said. She wasn't sure if that made the assignment better or more insulting. This had to be punishment for all the story meetings she'd missed. Why else would she have been singled out for this assignment? "Spence has *got* to be pissed at me."

"I don't think so," Thelma said, her tone suddenly deadpan. "I think he believes this story calls for your unique blend of perspicacity and wit."

Lydia sighed. She turned and pressed her back against the booth. "You're pissed at me too." She could see the heart scratched in the glass again now. It seemed to float in the air over the cars parked along Lewis Street.

"A little," Thelma said. "Do you realize how much work you've missed in the last month? And who do you think ends up picking up after you?"

"*I know, I know*," Lydia sighed. "I'm sorry." She rubbed her forehead with her free hand. She could feel a headache coming on. "Things are just complicated right now."

"And you keep disap*pear*ing every afternoon," Thelma said. "I'd be upset *too* if my mother-in-law died, but…." Thelma fell silent, and Lydia could picture her biting the end of her blue pencil, the way she did when she was turning something over in her head. "Who am I kidding?" Thelma said, her voice a whisper now. "I'd be de*light*ed. But you know what I mean. You need to get over it. Life goes on."

"I know, I know," Lydia said again. "Believe me: I know."

"It's the cycle of life," Thelma prattled on. "The way God made us. Listen: one person gets old and dies. But then another one's born…."

Lydia clapped a hand over the mouthpiece of the phone. "*Shit! Shit! Shit!*" she said.

LYDIA PULLED THE Ford up in the ragged shade of a palm tree. At the far end of the gravel drive, a long steel barn stretched, like a moored battle ship, between a water tower and an old ranch house nearly hidden by trees. She cut the engine and looked over the steering wheel at the corrugated steel roof of the barn. It was so hot it warped the air above it in the noon sun. In her rearview mirror, dust hung in the air over the long dirt road she'd just driven along. She twisted the mirror so she could check her lipstick and then twisted it back in place.

When she opened the car door, the stench of the place hit her like a fist to the belly. She pivoted quickly in her seat, leaned out the door and dumped a sudden puddle of stringy vomit on the hot ground. The surprise of it stole her breath away, and then the nausea was gone as quickly as it had come.

She spat on the ground and then looked through the windshield to see if anyone had seen her. She spat again— trying to rid her mouth of that acid taste—and then pulled the car door shut. God, how long would it be like this? LOCAL WOMAN PUKES TO DEATH. She started up the car and pulled ahead, searching her handbag with one blind hand for a handkerchief to wipe her lips.

She parked in the only other shady spot, next to the picket fence that demarcated the green ranch house garden from the straw-like weeds. The house's upper story was hidden by the dense lavender foliage of blooming jacarandas planted in a wide circle around it. Lydia extricated herself from the car, and rose unsteadily, testing the air with her nose, hoping the nausea wouldn't rush upon her again. She shut the car door and walked up the front path towards the house. The walkway was littered with sticky jacaranda blossoms, and she tried not to linger on their sour smell. She crossed the wide porch and rang the doorbell.

"Can I help you?" a female voice called out sternly from behind her.

Lydia turned to find a woman striding towards her from the direction of the barn—at least she *seemed* to be a woman. She filled out her flannel shirt and overalls amorphously, like a Christmas stocking stuffed with fruit. Her close-cropped hair and sunburned face didn't help matters any. As the woman drew closer, she tugged at the fingers of one dirty work glove with her teeth, and then she pulled off both gloves and stuffed them in her back pocket. She strode manfully up the path towards Lydia.

Lydia smiled brightly. "Is Mr. McQuaid here this morning?" she asked.

The woman stopped in front of Lydia and grinned. She scratched the side of her nose with a splintered fingernail. "He's buried out back," she said, nodding in that direction. "So I'm guessing he is. You got business with him?" The woman held out a hand, so Lydia gave it a quick shake. It was callused and strong.

"This is the McQuaid ranch, right?" Lydia asked.

"Sure is," the woman said. "Sister and I run the place since Pop died. Just the two of us out here."

"They told me to talk to the rancher," Lydia said, feeling flustered. "I just assumed...." She let the sentence trail off unfinished, and then, in the uncomfortable beat of silence that followed, she offered her hand, which the woman rancher studied a moment, bemused, and then shook again. "I'm here from *The Ledger*," Lydia said.

The woman nodded. "Figured that." Her voice then took on a more welcoming tone: "I was just having fun with you. People are always coming out here asking for the man of the house." The woman turned profile, half facing the long barn, like she was impatient to return to it. "You're here to see the sexer," she said. "Come on, I'll show her to you."

The woman turned and strode up the path, and Lydia scampered after her. "My name's Lydia," she called after the woman, jogging a little on the loose gravel to catch up to her. Viewed from the rear, the woman's broad buttocks seemed to strain the threadbare denim of her overalls, which were clearly designed with a man in mind.

"*Agnes*," the woman said, tossing the name back to Lydia without a glance, like an apple chucked over her shoulder.

Lydia scurried to come abreast of the woman. "So why exactly do you need this person?" she asked. It was only as she asked the question that it occurred to her that she'd left her pen and writing tablet in the glove box of the car—but it would have to stay there, she sensed. Agnes was unlikely to stop for her.

"If we know the chicks' sex, we can feed them at different rates and get the best growth out of them," Agnes said. "If we don't, we've got to keep them all together a couple of months until they start to show."

As they approached the poultry barn, the smell of the place grew more intense—a claustrophobic blend of feathers and birdshit, feed and tractor oil, all mingling in the sluggish air. Lydia's head swam. Determined to ward off another vomiting spell by force of will, she breathed through her mouth and focused her mind on the large whitewashed double doors that stood open on the near end of the barn.

Lydia followed Agnes through the broad doorway, and the concentrated stench made her stomach giddy. She pressed a hand to her lips and then moved it to her belly. As her eyes adjusted to the darkness, she could make out another shapeless woman, also in overalls, standing akimbo in a small pen of dun turkey chicks. The birds swarmed around her boots like a muddy tide.

"That's Sister," Agnes said.

The other woman nodded a gruff greeting and then bent to pluck some chicks from the crowd. She dropped them roughly into a large steel bucket.

"The sexer's over there," Agnes said.

Lydia looked along a corridor of pens and cages towards the middle of the long barn. A tiny Asian woman was positioned in a brilliant rectangle of sunlight that shone down through an open vent in the rafters. She stood working at a folding table. Lydia followed Agnes down the narrow central walkway. On either side, she could feel invisible birds rustling and watching from the darkness of their cages, like resentful felons.

When they stepped into the open area in the center of the barn, the turkey sexer took no notice. She chose a chick from a pallet box on the table, three quarters full of squirming birds. She poised the chick over a steel bucket and squeezed. Feces squirted into the bucket with the sound of an old-fashioned cuspidor. With a graceful roll of the wrist she turned the chick over, inscrutably regarded its nether regions and then gently placed it in one of the two boxes on the far side of the bucket.

Illuminated in her golden shaft of light, her head bent slightly, her every motion serene and ritual—the woman looked immersed in some sacerdotal work of faith. She seemed more saint than sexer, and Lydia found herself watching with a kind of breath-held awe. The woman's tiny hands lifted another and another and another bird and set them each down softly in its rightful place. She seemed oblivious to the heat and the smell of the place, to the women watching her, to the thick and dusty air they all breathed.

"What's she looking for?" Lydia found herself using the sotto voice she might reserve for a library—or perhaps a cathedral.

"If I knew," Agnes said. "I wouldn't have to pay *her*." Her voice, too, was a reverential whisper.

"How long have you been working with turkeys?"

"Sister and I grew up right here," Agnes said. "We took our first steps in this barn." She shook her head, and a faint smile played across her chapped lips. "We know everything there is to know about the little bastards," she said. "Everything but *this*." She nodded in the direction of the tiny woman.

"You have no idea how she does it?"

"It's one of life's mysteries."

Lydia watched the woman's gentle hands lift, and squeeze, and tilt, and place. "Is she always right?"

"Last season we found two toms in with the hens," Agnes said. "But who knows: maybe Sister and I mixed them up afterwards."

Lydia nodded. "And they're always Japanese?"

"Every one I've come across."

As Agnes spoke, Lydia felt a chick-like flutter in her own belly, and she found herself watching the Japanese woman closely, as if she suspected the sexer might have felt it too— might have paused in her work to glance up at Lydia; might have, in a serene smile or gesture, offered Lydia some sorely-needed answer. But the woman, her face still tilted down, just went about her cryptic work; it was clear she had no idea Lydia was there. "She from around here?" Lydia whispered.

"Down near Capistrano."

"She speak English?"

"Not so you could tell."

Lydia pressed both palms to her belly and squeezed her eyes shut. There was something about the sexer's imperturbable calm she wanted for herself. She needed, just for a moment, to lose her sense of place—to feel unmoored, immersed, floating somewhere safe and enclosed and far from this place. But all around her she could feel the flutter and rustle of life, so she opened her eyes again to the concrete floor; the steel girders; the hot, lethargic air; and the mannish woman beside her.

Lydia felt the sudden need to leave, to get in her car and drive back to the world she understood, regardless of what she had to face there.

"SPENCER'S BEEN LOOKING for you," Thelma said as soon as Lydia came through the office door. But then she set her blue pencil down and took a closer look at Lydia. "Say, what's the matter?" she said. "You look a little frazzled."

"Oh, god," Lydia said. "You don't want to know. Look: can you keep him out of my way for just an hour? I can't deal with him right now." UNHINGED REPORTER SLAYS MANAGING EDITOR.

"I'll *try*," Thelma said. "But I'm not making any promises." She frowned and regarded Lydia over her cat's-eye glasses. "You *sure* you're okay?"

"I'll live," Lydia said. "Is Lionel still out with the flu?"

Thelma nodded, still studying Lydia.

"I'm going to hide out in his office to write this up," Lydia said. "And then I've got to slip out and take care of some business."

"You're taking another afternoon?"

Lydia sighed. "Thelma, it's impo*rt*ant," she said. "I'll explain it all when the time is right, okay? Until that time, I really need Spencer off my back."

Lionel's office smelled pungently of varnish and Upman cigars. Feeling a little queasy, Lydia went to the windows and rolled them both up to get some air in the room. She dragged Lionel's wastepaper basket next to his rolling chair in case she needed it in a hurry. His roll-top desk was unlocked and she opened it. Inside, next to a neat stack of papers and a rhyming dictionary, sat his sacred and gleaming Remington typewriter. Everyone else at *The Ledger* had to make do with the same old Underwoods that had probably been in the office since before Lydia was born. Lydia looked down at the crescent of gleaming well-oiled typebars. How did the man keep it so clean?

She looked around at the rest of the desk. The New York World's Fair paperweight seemed perfectly centered atop his stack of papers. Each pigeonhole in the desk was neatly filled: index cards, tidy bundles of receipts, a box of ink ribbons, a row of evenly sharpened pencils. Lydia lifted the lid of his small humidor. It held three layers of identical cigars, each turned so the ring label faced up. In the far corner of the desk, a polished silver frame held a photo of a smiling woman holding a baby in a christening gown.

Shit!

Lydia laid the photo on its face and turned her attention back to the typewriter. She lifted the bail and rolled a fresh sheet of onionskin under the platen. She released the carriage, and straightened the page against the left edge. She rolled the page down and typed her byline across the top.

She shook a cigarette from the crumpled pack in her bag and lit it. Through the open window she could hear the rumble and hum of afternoon traffic circling the Plaza. If she wanted to get out of here, she'd have to get the story done in one quick draft. She took a drag on her cigarette and squinted through the smoke at the blank page. She needed a title. She balanced her cigarette on the edge of Lionel's humidor, leaned back in his chair and looked again at the contents of his roll top desk. She leaned forward suddenly and typed her four-word headline in all caps. It wasn't great, but it would do. She puffed once more on her cigarette and set it gently on the humidor again. She poised her fingers over *asdf jkl;* and then quickly typed each word as it came to her.

SHE LOOKED FOR him in Clancy's pool hall, then at The Hat, and then at Gibson's Lounge. Each time she came through the door, she got the lingering once-over from the men lined up at the bar; these weren't the kind of bars women entered unescorted. LOCAL WOMAN FOUND DEAD IN ALLEY.

She finally ended up driving out beyond the switchyard to The Barn. The muddy parking lot was empty, but the front door stood ajar, even though the sign on the door said the place wouldn't open until six. She parked, got out, went to the door and peeked inside. There Frankie stood, hunched over the jukebox. A solitary half-full glass of beer was parked at the end of the bar nearest him. She pushed the door open, letting in the sunlight.

Frankie turned and smiled when he saw who it was. "Can you believe it?" he said. He frowned down at the song list, his hands on either side of the jukebox like he was playing pinball. "This is supposed to be a jazz joint, but this thing's full of the *Penguins* and the *Cadillacs.*"

Lydia looked around the cavernous empty bar; there wasn't even a bartender on duty. "You break in?" she asked.

Frankie shrugged. "Charlie and I go way back," he said— as if she would have any idea who Charlie might be. Frankie finally looked at her squarely and did a sort of double take. He straightened up and turned from the jukebox. "You okay?" he asked.

"Okay?" Lydia said, pressing a hand to her belly. "No. Not really. Not really okay at all."

And so, sitting at a battered oak table in a grubby bar, she told Frankie everything. When she was finished, she watched him from across the table, her shoulders knotted.

Frankie sat staring down at the countless beer-glass rings that scarred the table's surface, like he might be counting them. He finally lifted his head and looked at her. "Come back with me," he said. "We can start over up there. Nobody will care."

"*What?*" Lydia said. It was the perfect Frankie solution to any problem: Just walk away. SUSPECT FLEES CRIME SCENE. "And raise our baby in some dive bar?" She gestured around herself at the scuffed wood paneling; the warping floorboards; the rack of worn pool cues; the whole dismal, shabby room.

Frankie glanced around too. He seemed to be looking for telling differences between this run-down bar and his own— and he seemed to come up empty. He looked back at Lydia and rubbed at the stubble on his chin. "Sadie's has a nice room upstairs," he offered. "We could fix it up."

"The room where that woman died?" Lydia said. "No thanks." She frowned and rubbed at a smudge on the tabletop with one finger. "Besides," she said. "I can't leave Alvie. How would he get along?"

"You'd *stay* with him?" Frankie said, like the idea wouldn't have entered his mind. "How are you going to explain—you know—your *condition?*"

She ran her finger back and forth along the wood grain of the table and bit her lower lip. "I don't have to go through with it," she said.

Those words, as she pronounced them, loosed something she'd been keeping tightly leashed. First her hand shook, then her shoulders, and then her whole body convulsed in one great rush of chest-emptying hopelessness. Sudden unbidden tears boiled down her face.

Frankie looked ashen. He stood, glanced around the empty bar, and moved to the chair on her left. He tried to put a comforting hand on her elbow, but she scooted her chair away from him. She wasn't sure why.

Frankie folded his hands on the tabletop. "Just tell me what you want," he said, his voice unraveling with helpless frustration. "Just tell me what to do."

"I don't *know* what I want, Frankie," she said. She turned her face away from him. "I don't know who I want. I don't want to have to choose." She stared at the tear-blurred row of beer taps that ran along one end of the bar. She took a deep breath and tried to pull herself together. "God, why did you have to come back?" she said.

She could feel Frankie fidgeting beside her, though she wasn't composed enough to turn and look in his direction. And then he sighed, pushed back his chair, and stood—and Lydia felt a forlorn surge of panic. What if he just strode out the door? What if he just hopped on the next train; headed back up north; left her to face this impossible mess alone?

But Frankie just crossed the creaking floor, ducked behind the bar, and came back out with a handful of white cocktail napkins. He returned and sat down in the same chair beside her. He set the stack of napkins on the table and then nudged them in front of her. As a gesture, it made her want to hug him—or perhaps to strangle him—she wasn't quite sure.

Still half turned away from him, she picked up a napkin and looked at it. The words *William & Pamela* were printed across one corner in a scrolling cursive typeface. A pair of bells hovered above the names. She didn't want to think about how so many wedding napkins had ended up here, unclaimed, in a squalid bar. She turned the napkin over, but on the verso a naked cartoon cupid floated in one corner, tugging back the string of his bow.

A chubby baby aflutter on tiny wings! The spiteful irony of the image caught her off guard. She shook her head and laughed sardonically, and then Frankie's hand was on her arm, and that made her start crying again. Oh, god, she was a basket case! What had gotten into her?

Frankie stroked her arm gently, and she pulled away from him again. He slumped back in his chair.

Lydia opened the napkin and blew her nose into it, and then she used another to dab at her eyes. God, she must look a fright! She glanced at her watch. She should be home already with dinner on the stove. The thought of the house on Grove Street was like a cold, sobering breeze. She wadded the napkins in her fist and drew a deep, self-possessed breath. "I need to tell Alvie," she said.

"You're going to *tell* him?" Frankie said. He leaned forward again. "But what if you decide to...." He let the sentence trail off unfinished.

Lydia turned to face him. The seven years he'd been gone had altered Frankie's features a little. As twins, he and Alvie were no longer perfectly identical: Frankie's face was a little more lined now, Alvie's a little plumper. Still, it felt strange to see her husband's mild features astir on Frankie's face. It was like that optical illusion they'd printed as filler in *The Ledger* a month ago: the drawing of the young woman that becomes an old crone when you turn it upside down. How could such identical faces house such incongruent personalities?

She fixed Frankie with a stare she hoped would convey cool courage and rectitude. "Alvie is my husband," she informed him.

OH, ALVIE! POOR, poor Alvie! She'd waited the whole anguished evening for a chance to tell him, but the time had never felt right. All through dinner he chattered happily about the new RCA models that would be coming into the shop soon and about how a full quarter of the American population had watched Elvis Presley on Milton Berle. The future was here, he told her, doodling in the air with a half-eaten chicken leg as he prattled on and on.

Then, after dinner, he fussed and adjusted the television set, getting it ready for *The Steve Allen Show*, but then he fell asleep on the sofa, his chin to his chest, before the first commercial break. Lydia had to nudge him awake once the television signed off and steer him, somnolently, to the bedroom.

While Alvie snored atop the bedspread (fully clothed but for the lack of shoes), Lydia regarded her wan face in the mirror above the bathroom sink. She tilted her head back a little to catch the light from the ceiling lamp. She ran her fingers along her jaw line and up her lean cheek. Wasn't she supposed to be *gaining* weight? She bent over the sink, leaning closer to her reflection. Her lips were chapped now, her eyes glassy and rimmed in red. She tugged at the loose flesh of her face. Her complexion looked as sallow and waxen as the buttered supermarket hen she'd slid into the oven a few hours ago. How had Alvie sat across the table from her all through dinner without stopping to ask her if anything was wrong?

THEN, THE NEXT morning, she had to rush from the breakfast table twice to vomit. Returning to the kitchen a second time, she found Alvie still yawning behind *The Ledger*. She took her seat again and tried not to dwell on the pungent smell of bacon that hung in the air. She scowled at the scalloped curtains in the window above the sink and then looked back at Alvie, still in his undershirt, oblivious to her. A sort of umbrage rose in her. "*Alvie*," she said sharply.

Alvie looked up from *The Ledger*, his face wide and bland as a slice of Wonder Bread.

Lydia reached over, tugged the newspaper from his fingers, folded it, and set it on the table next to the plate of toast. "I've got some bad news," she said, her voice cool and expressionless. She waited while Alvie finished chewing and swallowed.

"What news?" Alvie said. His unwashed face took on a look of bleary anxiety. "What's happened?"

Lydia fixed her gaze on him. She knew she was exploiting her mood to make the telling easier—but what difference did it make? She'd have to tell him anyway. Why not now? "I'm pregnant," she said.

For a long moment the cold, hard-edged words seemed to dangle in the air between them like a tin mobile. It took a beat or two, but then a giddy smile broke across Alvie's face. He seemed about to levitate out of his chair. "Really?" he said. "*Really?*"

Lydia sighed. She reached across the table and took his soft hand in both of hers. "Think about it, Alvie," she said. "Just stop a moment and think about it."

She watched Alvie's forehead crease, but the dopey smile never left his face. How could a grown man be so naïve? A headache wavered behind her eyes, and she made an effort to blink it away. "Alvie, *think* about it," she said, her voice weary and threadbare. "When was the last time *we* could have made a baby?"

"That night we went to The Palace with Bob and Irene," Alvie said, without hesitation. "That William Holden movie."

Lydia's mouth dropped open. She slumped back in her chair and pressed a palm to her brow. The kitchen floor seemed to list suddenly, and she clutched the edge of the table with her free hand. "Oh, my god," she said, her mouth suddenly dry. "We *did.*" It had been so quick and perfunctory—and she'd been more than a little tipsy from the gimlets Bob had fixed them all after the movie—but it all came back to her now. She felt like she was falling, and tightened her grip on the table's edge. "Oh. My. God."

Alvie frowned and sat suddenly straight in his chair, like someone had dropped an ice cube down the back of his undershirt. "*Wait*," he said, a harsh edge in his voice now. "When else *could* it have happened?"

Lydia felt her face burn. *Shit!* She shook her head helplessly. Her lips worked a few seconds before they could produce any words. "Oh, god, Alvie," she said. Her vision blurred with tears. "Oh, god, I'm sorry."

Alvie blinked at her across the table. "*Frankie?*" he said. "Didn't he leave right after the funeral?"

"Oh, god, Alvie," she said again. A deep, sour rush of remorse flooded the pit of her stomach. "Oh, Alvie, I'm so—." But before she could finish the sentence, she clamped a hand over her mouth and bolted from the table.

From where she knelt on the cold bathroom tile, her head swimming with guilt, she heard the front door slam and then the squeal of tires.

"NONSENSE," THELMA SAID. "You can stay with me as long as you need to."

Lydia turned and looked her over. "Shouldn't you check with Steve first?"

Thelma's hands rode atop the steering wheel, and she scowled over them at the Pontiac idling in front of them at the stoplight. "Honey, here's the truth," she said. "He's gone back to live with his mother. He left before *Memorial* Day."

"Oh, Thelma, I'm so…."

Thelma waved a hand dismissively, cutting Lydia off. "Forget it," she said. "Those two were *made* for each other. And I kind of like the quiet."

The light changed. Thelma put on her signal and turned down Kolar Drive. "I should have told you before," she said. "I just didn't want it to get around work that I was *avail*able." She shrugged and adjusted the sun visor. "You know—*men*."

Lydia *did* know. The office was full of men, from the fifteen year old copy boy—What was his name?—to Lionel, who had to be nearing eighty. All day, as she moved about the office, Lydia knew she was on their radar. She could feel their *awareness* of her, like a breath on the back of her neck. If she bent to pick up a dropped pencil or to pull open a file cabinet drawer, the clattering typewriters behind her lagged.

Thelma turned onto Grove Street, and Lydia slid lower in her seat. "If there's a car in the driveway, just keep going," she said.

Inside the house, feeling guilty as a thief, she threw some clothes into a cardboard suitcase and stood looking around the room with a hand on her forehead, knowing there had to be important things she was forgetting. Why should she feel so jittery? she wondered. This was *her* house. WOMAN BURGLES OWN RESIDENCE.

But as she looked around the bedroom now—the same room she has tossed and turned in just last night listening to Alvie's oblivious snoring—everything seemed bulky and alien. The mute shirts hanging in the closet, the coins scattered on Alvie's dresser, the vase of cloth daffodils on the nightstand, all seemed imbued with a strange new gravity—like the belongings of someone recently dead. As she clasped the suitcase shut, she heard Thelma's voice out front. She grabbed the suitcase, ran down the hallway, and, standing well back, looked out the parlor's front window.

Thelma stood at the bottom of the steps with her hands on her hips, blocking Frankie from coming up on the porch. "She doesn't want to see you," she was telling him. "Which one *are* you anyway?"

Lydia ripped open the front door. "Stay a*way* from me, Frankie," she hissed. "I don't want to talk to you."

"*Frankie*," Thelma said from the base of the porch steps. "So you're the other one."

Leaving the front door swinging wide, Lydia jogged down the steps, slipped behind Thelma and ran across the brittle grass to the car. She slid into the passenger seat, pulled the door shut, and sat hugging the suitcase in her lap.

Thelma had moved to the center of the lawn now. She backed towards the car, facing Frankie with one finger raised— like he was an unfamiliar dog on the loose.

Lydia turned and stared straight ahead through the windshield while Thelma got in and started up the engine. She could feel Frankie hovering beside her on the other side of the glass, but she would not turn to look at him. When they finally pulled away from the curb and sped down Grove Street, she pressed her hands to her temples and fought back the urge to cry.

"*Here's* what I don't get," Thelma announced, her eyes on the road. "Why *him?* It's not like he's any different than the one you've already got." She lit the turn signal and made a wide turn back onto Kolar Drive. "Now, that boy who comes in to fix the Underwoods?" she said. "*That* I could get behind."

Lydia stared out the side window and didn't answer. Thelma hadn't a clue. To her Frankie and Alvie were indistinguishable as turkey chicks, but the two of them were really worlds apart. Alvie? Well, Alvie was honest and good. He was the man you'd hand your keys to and trust to feed your cat. He was the man who would push aside the glass after half a beer. He was the man you hoped would find the wallet you left behind on the bus stop bench. Alvie was whoever everyone needed him to be—trusty friend, steadfast neighbor, employee of the month, citizen of the year. He plodded along, predictable as sunrise.

And Frankie? Frankie was *himself*—in every gesture, word and mood—regardless of what anyone else might need from him. He might leave you waiting for an hour or two outside the train station. That armful of calla lilies he gave you might have come from a church or mortuary. He might order a few rounds before he thought to check his empty wallet. But even his more egregious lapses in judgment made a certain endearing sense in the larger scheme of things. Frankie's life was one of those jazz records he always listened to—each dizzying improvised note arriving just in the nick of time.

Lydia could sense Frankie falling far behind her now, still out on the front lawn looking down Grove Street to where she'd disappeared around the corner. Oh, god, Frankie! That tilt of his head when he was really taking you in. That lazy dangle of the cigarette from his lips. That firm, assured touch of his hand on your bare skin. Oh, god, that sly, sidelong smile! How could anyone think those two were alike?

Thelma's apartment was two flights above the travel agency on Brewer Street. While Thelma, her left arm loaded down with page proofs, paused on the sidewalk to rummage around in her purse for her keys, Lydia studied the posters: gondolas gliding under Venetian bridges, palm-shaded Jamaican coves, crumbling Scottish castles, all fading to azure in the big front window.

Thelma held the street door open, and Lydia slowly climbed the dark stairwell, lugging her suitcase with both hands. She waited at the top for Thelma to unlock the apartment door. Thelma's place, which Lydia had never seen, was a cramped living room, a back kitchen and a little bedroom off to one side. Thelma strode through the living room into the kitchen, and Lydia lagged behind, not sure whether to follow.

"Come on back," Thelma called, over the sound of water running in the sink.

Lydia set her suitcase on the floor next to the loveseat, and followed Thelma.

The kitchen was, oddly, much larger than the living room. Though Thelma couldn't have been expecting company, the sink and dish rack were empty, the counter hard scrubbed, the ancient toaster gleaming. The worn pine table was not scattered with salt or breadcrumbs or abandoned dishes as it always was on Grove Street. All Thelma's table held was the neat stack of blue-line proofs she had just set there. Though it was far from elegant, Thelma's whole apartment showed a compulsive tidy order. The place looked—well it looked *copyedited*, Lydia thought. It looked *proofread*.

"Go on," Thelma said. "Sit down. Take a load off. I'm having tea if you want some."

"That would be nice," Lydia said. She pulled out a chair at the table and sat.

Thelma took some cups down from the cupboard and fetched a tiny jug of cream from the fridge. Lydia looked at the page proof on the table. Her article on the turkey sexer was, surprisingly, on the front page below the fold. LOCAL WOMAN PIGEONHOLES TURKEYS. Lydia tilted her head to read the lede. She'd been so distracted when she wrote it, she had no idea how much her copy had been edited. "Spencer put it on the front page?" she said.

Thelma, at the counter, was arranging cookies on a plate. "What's that?"

"My article on the turkey sexer," Lydia said. "It's on the front page."

"Spencer loved it," Thelma said. "Real human interest stuff." She brought the plate over and set it on the table at Lydia's elbow. Couldn't they have just eaten the cookies from the box? "'There's a charming mystery at the heart of it,'" Thelma said, mimicking Spencer's fusty, nasal tones. "His words exactly." Thelma paused with both hands on the back of one of the chairs. "It'll kill him if you leave the paper," she said. "You know that don't you?"

"Oh, *please*," Lydia said.

Thelma shook her head. "Big stories anyone can write," she said. "Only you could make the front page with a woman who stares at bird crotches."

Lydia laughed uncomfortably. "It's a calling," she said.

Thelma smiled down at Lydia, but there was an incongruous sadness in her eyes that made Lydia want to look away. "You sure you can give it up?" she said. "Just like that?"

Before Lydia could answer, the kettle on the stove whistled shrilly, and Thelma turned away.

"SO YOU GET to pick between the two of them," Thelma said, rinsing the teapot at the sink. She was clearly trying to buck Lydia up, making this sound like some wonderful adventure she was about to embark upon. "It's a great opportunity when you stop and think about it." She shook water from the teapot and set it, capsized, on the drying rack. "There isn't a paternity test in the world that could tell between those two," she said. "It's a total toss up. Fifty-fifty."

Lydia, still at the kitchen table, winced and looked down at the dark stain of tealeaves at the bottom of her tilted cup. "It's not really a toss up," she admitted. "If you're talking about their relative chances of being the father, it's more like twenty to one."

"*Twenty?*" Thelma turned from the sink. Her face took on an exaggerated expression of horror. She pressed a palm to her chest and did a choking sort of laugh. "You little tramp," she said. "No wonder you missed so many meetings."

Lydia offered a fretful, perplexed smile. "Oh, god, Thelma," she said. "I'm *horrible*."

IN THE STILL-DARK morning, Lydia lay curled on the sofa, pretending to be asleep the whole while Thelma showered and dressed and percolated coffee. Thelma finally slipped out the door, her arms loaded with page proofs and her purse dangling from the crook of her elbow. The door clicked shut, the lock turned, and Thelma jingled away down the stairs with her key ring in her teeth.

In the silence that followed, Lydia lolled on her back and contemplated an oval stain on the popcorn ceiling. She imagined *The Ledger* office, still locked up at this hour. She could smell the ink ribbons, the paste-up glue, the moldering newsprint. She could picture the planes of dust-swirled light slicing through the slatted blinds, the hulking maze of desks and typewriters, the mute black phones stale with cigarette smoke. Thelma would soon unlock the door and move among the desks, turning on lamps. In an hour the office would be filled with the ringing of phones and the ceaseless clatter of typing. The realization that she might never go back that office filled her with a raw jumble of release and regret.

Lydia pulled the loveseat's Afghan around her shoulders and gathered it at her throat. She stood and walked barefoot across the carpet to the polished tiles of the kitchen. Thelma had left a cup's worth of coffee cooling in the unplugged percolator. Lydia poured it into a mug and sipped it looking out the open kitchen window at the back alley and the red fire doors of the roller rink across the way. Though it was August, the smell of rain seemed to rise up from the dank brickwork.

She remembered walking to that same rink as a child and having to borrow a steel key from the man at the counter; her clamp-on skates were second-hand and came without one. She remembered how the light from the rink's high windows seemed to glide across the varnished floor as she skated in wobbly circles. She remembered the Friday night USO dances held there on the parquet and the clusters of Marines who smoked in the alley all afternoon while the band set up inside. She remembered the arsonist fire that charred the wooden façade—front page news her first week at *The Ledger*. She turned from the window, feeling unaccountably sad. She placed a hand on her belly. She wanted her unimaginable child to someday feel this same sense of place, this rootedness. Whatever else happened, whatever the consequences, she couldn't leave this town.

WHAT FOLLOWED WAS a day of sighs and waiting—though Lydia could not have said just what it was she was waiting for. It was a morning of closed curtains, and drawn blinds lit from behind. It was an afternoon of distant, muted voices rising up from the street below, and the slow creep of shadows across the kitchen tiles. For a while, someone, somewhere, practiced scales on a piano. For a while, laundry flapped restively on a clothesline hung across the alley. For while, a chiming ice cream truck followed its route through the neighboring streets. Lydia could not remember the last time she had lingered so long in a place this hushed, this insular.

The mantle clock chimed four o'clock and then settled down again to tock off each hollow second. Lying curled on the love seat now, Lydia grew aware of her own aching heartbeat. She held her breath and closed her eyes and felt her heart's gentle, persistent thump. It was as if that steady human rhythm at her core was also waiting for something—a counter-rhythm, perhaps—that tiny frantic murmur of a pulse that would soon accompany her own.

THELMA GOT HOME around seven, bearing that day's *Ledger* and a grocery sack of sausages, onions, tomatoes and bread. Lydia, rousing herself from her meditative torpor, took the sack from Thelma and made her sit down at the kitchen table; *she* would make dinner tonight—it was the least she could do. While Lydia cooked, Thelma browsed the *Redbook* she'd found down in her mailbox.

"Your husband came by the office today," Thelma said while Lydia was frying up the sausages. Her words had a studied off-handed tone, like she was trying hard to make the news sound inconsequential. "He was limping, so I knew it was Alvie."

Lydia bit her lip but didn't turn from the stove. "What did he say?"

"He never actually came inside," Thelma went on. "I could see him out in the hallway through the frosted glass in the door. He was just pacing—like he was trying to screw up his courage or something—but he never came in."

Lydia frowned down at the sizzle and pop of grease in the pan.

"And then he loitered around outside the front door for a while," Thelma said. "I could see him down there from the window by my desk." She licked a finger and flipped a magazine page with a practiced display of nonchalance. "I kind of felt sorry for him," she said. "So I went down to tell him you weren't even *in* the office, but he was gone before I got to the street."

Lydia's eyes stung suddenly—but there were onions in the pan after all. "Did he look angry?" she asked.

"For*lorn*," Thelma said, after a thoughtful beat. "Despondent. Piteous. Distressed." She chose each word carefully, like she was copyediting. "*Mel*ancholy," she said.

Lydia carefully rolled each sausage onto its palest side and hoped Thelma would soon run out of synonyms.

THE NEXT DAY, after Thelma left, Lydia found the newspaper into the living room with the turkey sexer's story in it. Would that really be the last thing she ever wrote for the *The Ledger*? PROMISING CAREER CUT SHORT. She sat on the love seat and read the story through. She folded the paper neatly and placed it on the side table. She pulled her feet up under her and sat stroking her belly.

She thought of the Japanese woman in the barn with that swarming puddle of turkey chicks. She could picture the woman perfectly, lit brilliantly in her shaft of light, deep in her mysterious, imperturbable work. For some reason the image made her throat ache. She wondered what it would be like to be so unerring, so free from hesitation, so perfectly equipped to choose—and then the notion hit her: perhaps she had got the story all wrong. What if this goddess of poultry were *assigning* the chicks their sex, and not just detecting it? What if her work was an astonishing act of creation and not mere discernment? What if she were involved in the most sacred and womanly occupation of all—making life? The notion was absurd, she knew. They were just birds, and she was just a woman—but the wild idea seemed to take root in her.

She stood and took her empty cup to the kitchen. She rinsed it and set it on the dish rack to dry. She went back to the living room, sat again on the loveseat and considered the newspaper spread out flat on the coffee table before her. LOCAL WOMAN CREATES LIFE. She thought of the sexer's shrewd and delicate hands, her lowered impassive face, her complete immersion in her work.

Lydia felt a heartening flutter in her stomach, and it occurred to her that she hadn't vomited since she'd arrived in Thelma's apartment two days ago. She tugged up her blouse and ran both palms over her bare stomach. When the truth arrived in her mind, it was like a six-column banner headline: The future for her unborn child, whatever it would be, was not something that would *happen*. It was something she, Lydia, would have to keep creating as she went along, in one long, astonishing, harrowing improvisation.

Thelma was right; this *was* a wonderful and improbable opportunity. Lydia *did* get to choose her baby's father—but her choice was not between Frankie's and Alvie's strengths and foibles. Her task was to choose which man could best keep up this exhausting work of creation she had embarked upon—which man would, every day, craft a future in which her child could live and love and flourish.

With that realization, an inscrutable ease overtook her. The choice was clear.

She smiled and stood and drifted over to the bright window. She drew back the gauzy inner curtains and looked out on the morning—on all that beautiful, human traffic on Brewer Street. A group of girls from Saint Killian's followed a nun in the direction of the library. A pair of old men sat sharing a bag of peppermints on the bus stop bench across the way. A man in a blue striped apron swept out the hardware store alcove. He paused a luxurious moment, leaning on his broom, and tilted his face up to the sun. A woman pushed a pram diagonally across the street to Lydia's side, and tilted the front wheels up to climb the curb.

As the woman with the pram passed him, a man sitting on the curb below Lydia's window tipped his gray fedora to her—and something minute but elemental in that small gesture made Lydia's heart thrill with recognition. She took a sharp breath and placed her hand over her heart.

She wrenched the window up and leaned out. "Frankie?" she said, her heart thudding.

Frankie doffed his hat and glanced up over his shoulder. He quickly stood and turned and held his fedora high so it shaded his eyes. He looked up at her smiling.

"What are you doing here?" she said.

Frankie looked at the travel agency two floors below her, as if it had just appeared there. He looked up at her again. "I was thinking I'd take a trip."

She grinned. "Oh, yeah?" she said. "Where to?"

He looked at the store again, as if trying to get a fix on the photos in the window. He tipped his head to one side and then turned his face up to her again, that wonderful slanted smile on his face. "Brazil," he said. "But right now I'd settle for a good cup of coffee."

Looking down at Frankie's miraculous presence, Lydia felt a kind of affirmation, a confirmation—by fate, or providence, or some impossibly sovereign Creator—that all would be well. "Really, Frankie," she said. "How did you find me?"

He slouched and rubbed the back of his neck with one hand. "That car your friend drove," he said. "I saw it outside *The Ledger* yesterday. I followed it."

It was that simple, Lydia thought—but somehow this mundane explanation of Frankie's arrival didn't diminish the heady current of magic she felt. "You were out here all night?"

Frankie shrugged. "You had to come out sometime," he said. He held his fedora at chest level now and worried the brim with both hands as he gazed up at her. "I thought maybe we could talk. You think you might be willing to come down and get that coffee?"

Lydia beamed down at him, knowing full well her answer, but enjoying the brief, delicious withholding of it.

Frankie just stood smiling up at her, his hat like a breastplate in front of him. He seemed oblivious to the pedestrians and cars that crept by all around him.

"I don't want to leave this town," Lydia said.

"Then I don't either."

"What about your bar?"

"Willie can run it."

She smiled down at him, at the passing traffic, at the whole vital and bustling street. "Wait right there," Lydia told him. "I'm coming down."

CHAPTER TWELVE
BIRTH IN THE FAMILY
1955

ON THE DAY Lydia's child was born, Alvie locked up L&S three hours early. He posted a hand-lettered cardboard sign on the inside of the glass door with black electrical tape:

CLOSED
BIRTH IN THE FAMILY

He backed his new Dodge Lancer out of the space behind the store, drove around the front of the building, and headed west on Ellis Street, out towards the edge of town in the direction of Santa Ana.

When he was a few blocks from the hospital, Alvie made a sudden U-turn on Westminster and headed back to the flower shop he'd just passed. He pulled up at the curb and got out. The shop was a narrow red-brick storefront wedged between a fabric store and an art supply shop—just a door and a window, under a blue and gold awning. When Alvie pulled the door open, a bell jingled above his head. He stepped out of the daylight into the perfumed darkness. His eyes were still adjusting to the dim light when the girl behind the counter, who couldn't have been more than sixteen, asked if she could help him.

Alvie balanced his weight on his good ankle and looked around at the damp glass-fronted cases. "It's for a new baby," he told her. "For the mother, I mean."

The girl beamed at him. "How exciting!" she said. "And how are you related?" She seemed so youthful, so bright eyed, so heartbreakingly eager to please.

Alvie smiled at her ruefully. "I suppose she's my sister-in-law," he said. "So I suppose the baby is my niece."

The girl laughed at his uncertain way of putting things. "Is there some question in the matter?" she asked, playfully.

Alvie regarded her a few long seconds as she stood on the far side of the counter, looking back at him expectantly. "You have no idea," he told her, and something in his tone stole the smile from her lips.

In Alvie's mind, there was, in fact, no question in the matter. He'd held onto the secret so many years now it seemed an integral part of him—like a thumbprint or a nervous tick. He'd kept it since that morning, so many years ago, when his mother had sent him to the Rexall for some aspirin, and he'd lingered, instead, in the hallway outside Doctor Wilkins' office. He'd pressed his ear to the closed door and held his breath, listening to their talk inside. He'd heard the doctor's words clearly, not fully comprehending them at the time—but filing them away in his mind with the hunch that they'd someday be of consequence.

Alvie asked the girl for a dozen white roses, guessing they'd convey no bitter or unintended message. He also knew that Lydia would like them. That's how he was with her: when he really tried, he knew just what would please her—but that was a far cry from knowing how to make her happy.

Alvie watched the shop girl hunt among the buds and gently tug them one by one from their steel bin. The day had finally arrived. The baby was born. A new era was dawning for them all.

HE DROVE AROUND for almost an hour that morning when Lydia had told him she was pregnant. Then, lacking the imagination to do anything else, he had simply gone to L&S and opened the store for business. He had rung up steam irons and shavers and a big Zenith console that day—he'd even helped load a chest freezer into the back of Tom Hartley's flatbed—without anyone asking him if something was wrong. And he remembered wondering, as he stood at the register with a solicitous smile, what the hell was wrong with him. What was it he lacked that would have allowed him to react in the visceral moment of things—the way Frankie would have done; the way any normal man would have done?

And that same evening, as he drove back to Grove Street, he had resolved to stand his ground, to fight for what was his. He would talk to Lydia when she got home; he would tell her Frankie's secret—that he, Alvie, had to be the father. But around midnight, when it seemed clear that she was spending the night elsewhere, Alvie finally thought to look in Lydia's dresser. Her hosiery drawer looked stirred up, and the drawer where she kept her under-things was nearly emptied. He went to the closet, pulled open the doors, and found it likewise depleted. He couldn't have named any one thing that had gone missing; he only knew there was much less of Lydia present than there should have been.

Feeling, himself, depleted, Alvie drifted across the hall to his boyhood bedroom and sat on the edge of the bottom bunk. "I don't know what to do," he spoke aloud. The emptiness of the room seemed to swallow his words. "I'm lost here." He surveyed the scuffed dresser, the shelf of adventure novels, the old humidor still full of Frankie's baseball cards, and all the other relics of his and Frankie's boyhood. After a moment, he stood and went to the closet. On the floor of it he found Frankie's half-full crate of LPs. He hefted the box and carried it down the hall into the parlor, savoring the pain that pulsed in his ankle. He set the crate on the floor and switched on the floor lamp.

Alvie kneeled and examined the first album's cover. A white trumpeter leaned out over the water on what appeared to be a yacht. He held his horn to his lips, blowing it out across the gray sea in the pose of an angel. Below him huddled an assortment of windblown black men and white men in dark glasses.

Alvie picked up the album, slid the record from its sleeve, and set it on the turntable. He pivoted the tone arm and dropped the stylus into the groove. Music stampeded from the speakers loud enough to wake the neighbors. Alvie grabbed at the volume knob and turned the music down to a reasonable level, his heart now racing.

For a minute or two, then, Alvie stared down at the spinning record and listened to the quiet, incomprehensible blaring. He could find no order in it; it was just a riot of instruments that put him on edge like the clatter of dishpans. He tried to concentrate on it—to hear in it what Frankie might hear—but the sounds seemed to leap blindly in every direction. It made no sense to him.

It was like when Lydia would try to show him something in one of the books she was reading—a story or a poem that had made an impression on her. And Alvie would plod through it, dutifully sounding out each syllable in his mind, but all those words would somehow fail to accumulate the same profound meaning for him. And he would pass the book back to her, nodding politely, and she would look at him like he'd let her down, yet again, in some small but meaningful way.

Alvie went to the bookcase now while Frankie's record continued to play. He tilted his head and ran his eye along her shelf of books—novels and stories and slender poetry collections. The authors' names on the spines were familiar to him, though he'd never actually made it through a single one of their books. *Faulkner. Dickinson. Wordsworth. Hemingway. Ashbless.* Their artistry was impenetrable. They might as well have written in Swahili.

And Alvie had to admit the same was true of Frankie and Lydia, themselves. The two of them had always seemed to babble to one another in a language that he, Alvie, couldn't begin to comprehend—and it wasn't just a language of words; it was spoken in glances and gestures, shrugs and smiles, throat clearings and touches on the elbow.

He went back to the record player and frowned down at it. He'd heard this part before; it was like the music had slipped into some kind of groove. He listened closely, trying to remember where he'd heard this melody, and then it dawned on him that a conversation was taking place in the music. A piano and some kind of trumpet—or was it a saxophone?—were swapping quick bursts of melody, drawing out the same phrase and folding it over on itself in different ways. And with this one observation Alvie felt like he'd stumbled across a kind of Rosetta Stone with which he might begin to decode some part of the world outside his own. For a good hour, Alvie kept lifting the needle and resetting it, listening to the same song over and over until its every movement felt familiar.

AT SOME POINT in the dark hours of morning, Alvie, lying in bed, discovered that Lydia's pillowcase smelled of her. It was a faint autumnal scent, like a wind-stirred orchard. He pressed the pillow to his face and breathed her in. Was this the smell of her shampoo—or her soap perhaps? Or maybe one of those pots of lotion she was always dipping into when she got ready for bed? He peered now through the darkness at the inert shapes of the bottles and jars strewn across her dresser top. Then again, maybe the scent was simply *her*—some alchemic reaction between her lithe body and her sharp, fierce will.

WHEN LYDIA'S ALARM rang at six, Alvie woke from an ankle-deep and dreamless sleep. He slouched out to the cold kitchen, made toast, and ate it dry. He didn't attempt to brew coffee; he knew, from experience, it would be undrinkable. Instead he boiled some water in the kettle and poured it over a bag of Lipton, but that was no substitute for the cup of strong coffee he usually found waiting for him when he shambled out of the bathroom each morning.

Back in the bedroom, he gazed listlessly into the mirror over Lydia's dresser while he did up his tie. Her pots of lotion and creams and all the other mysterious feminine accoutrements were now arranged in a tight oval in the center of the dresser top. They hadn't been laid out like that the night before, he felt sure. He picked up a jar of Dorothy Gray cold cream and set it back down again. He turned to face the empty room.

"Is this some kind of message?" he said. "Are you trying to tell me something?" It was insane, he knew, to be talking aloud to a sister who had died more than thirty years ago. Yet here he was. "Did you see her leave?" he said in a voice pitched loud, to traverse realms of being. "Do you know where she went?"

He turned in a slow circle, searching the room for any subtle sign of movement or response. The walls on every side stood vertical and mute.

"I don't understand," Alvie said, looking down at Lydia's clutter of jars and bottles. "I don't know what this means." With no idea what else to do, he began opening jar after jar—Tussy and Jergens, Mary King and Moonlight Mist—tilting each under his nose before he moved on to the next. But none of them confided Lydia's scent. He went then to the bathroom and twisted the metal cap off her jar of Lustre-Crème shampoo. He studied the grooves her fingers had left when she'd last scooped it out, and then he lifted the jar to his nose. It only smelled of soap.

He screwed the lid back on the jar and went out into the empty hallway, feeling, oddly, like Doris might be watching him from some angle up near the ceiling. "*Why?*" he called out to the vacant air. "Why are you *doing* this? What do you want from me?" His words boomed down the hallway and seemed to reverberate softly in the phone's bell. He walked to the phone and picked it up. He called Kenny Sloss, and told him to open the store without him this morning—he'd be in after lunch.

As he drove Lydia's Ford towards the center of town that morning, Alvie kneaded the steering wheel with both hands, and rehearsed in his mind the scene ahead: he'd stride into *The Ledger* offices and confront her at her desk. He didn't care who was there to see him. He'd make demands. He'd reveal what he knew about Frankie. He'd insist on whatever medical tests could confirm his brother's sterility. What could she possibly do then? What feasible claim could Frankie have on her? This time he had the upper hand, and, by God, he would use it. By the time he reached the Plaza, he had worked himself into a small, righteous fury.

He parked the car in one of the diagonal spaces on the circle, and, in a rush of adrenaline, he slammed the door so hard the old Ford rocked on its wheels. He strode along the curved sidewalk, feeling hard and resolute—a boxer set to enter the ring.

But as he headed through the street door and up the narrow staircase, he felt his angry resolve subside with each step he climbed. And then, standing in the second floor hallway, he smelled it. There was just a hint of it in the air at first: that leafy, nutty scent of Lydia's pillow.

Alvie looked at *The Ledger's* frosted glass door and pictured Lydia at her desk in the crowded newsroom on the far side of it. He imagined the abject expression her face would register when she saw him striding between the desks in her direction.

She tried to be tough, he knew. She liked to appear unassailable and always in control. But there was that quick flicker in her eyes when she was blindsided. And, when frightened, her flinty words were undercut by a voice that went thin and quivery as tinsel. He thought of the sleeplessness that often haunted her. How he'd sometimes wake when she slipped back into bed smelling of cigarettes, and he would know she'd been sitting on the kitchen steps agonizing over something she could never bring herself to tell him. She was so hard on herself, so unforgiving of her own small foibles.

Lydia's scent was stronger now—a swirl of walnut and tea leaves—impossible to deny. And then it was potent enough to make Alvie's head spin. He leaned his weight against the wall and kept his gaze fixed on the closed door he had been so set on bursting through with the whole heady momentum of his rage.

He thought of the dresser back home, still crowded with the balms and ointments she had left behind. And he wondered, nonsensically, what he should do with them if she never returned. Even if he got rid of them—along with her clothes and her books and every other thing she'd owned or loved or touched and left behind—he could never empty the house of her. She'd haunt those rooms, being everywhere and nowhere at once, like the absent sister who had led him to this moment. That pillow-scent was *her*; it was Lydia; it was intrinsic—something native and essential to her—and Alvie felt a sudden sweeping sense of loss.

He breathed the air deeply. That sad and beautiful human smell. That whiff of frailty and mortality and longing. Lydia had an agonizing choice to make, and in this moment Alvie knew he had the power to make that decision infinitely harder for her and its consequences more painful for everyone.

Or he could give her this: He could simply turn and descend the stairs. He could allow her to sort things out in her own flawed and human way.

Whatever she decided, he and Frankie and Lydia would find their way together; that much Alvie understood. The three of them were bound by blood and history. Their future, whatever it held, was something they'd go through together. It would be like a song they all played—some raveling blend of overlapping melodies—a clashing and harmonizing of individualites, which would somehow blend into a complex and poignant whole.

When he got back down to the Ford, the scent of her still lingered, like smoke, in the folds of his shirt.

* * *

ALVIE DROVE THE last three blocks to Santa Ana General with the dewy roses—which the girl had wrapped for him in a cone of pink paper—on the seat beside him. Their perfume hung in the air around him like a sad memory.

In the parking lot, Alvie turned off the ignition and sat there in his Dodge. He held the roses in the crook of his arm, their damp, sweet scent rising, and looked up at the top windows of the hospital, steeling himself.

He'd give himself this moment—just a few more seconds—to prepare for the role he'd committed to. Lydia loved him, he guessed, in some fundamental but restricted sense. She had made her choice, and he had promised her—without her knowing—that he would live with it. He looked down at the dozen white roses. Each bud was a beaded swirl of astonishing beauty.

When he was good and ready, he would go inside and ride the elevator up. He would stop at the nurses' station and ask for directions. And then, smiling gamely, he would push open the door to Lydia's room and find his daughter—her scrunched crimson face; her swirl of red hair; that curious, apple-shaped birthmark on one collar bone—in the arms of the woman he loved.

Acknowledgements

A heartfelt thanks for all those who slogged through many versions of this story and offered help, insight and patience, most notably:

Jim Blaylock; Erin Arendse; Revy, Ryan, Hedgie, Janette and Steve Buchanan; Melody Versoza; Katie Caffrey; Shelley Garcia; Kat Tompkin; my intrepid fellow Chapman workshop students, including Kevin, Nidzara, Morgan, Jamie and Rebecca; Brian Kehlenbach; and the great, late Tara Riesner.

More books from
Harvard Square Editions: